UNDER THE

From the Editor's Introduction:

"In a very real sense, I regard myself not as the 'inventor' of Darkover, but its discoverer. If others wish to play in my fantasy world, who am I to slam its gates and in churlish voice demand that they build their own? If they are capable of it, they will do so someday. Meanwhile, if they wish to write of Darkover, they will.

"All the selfish exclusiveness of the Conan Doyle estate has not stopped lovers of Sherlock Holmes from writing their own stories and secretly sharing them. Why should I deny myself the pleasure of seeing these young writers learning to do their thing by, for a little while, doing *my* thing with me?

"Or, look at it this way. When I was a little kid, I was a great lover of 'pretend' games, but after I was nine or ten, I could never get anyone to play them *with* me. My friends grew up and got tired of them; I never did. And now I have a lot of fans, and friends, who will come into my magic garden and play the old 'pretend games' with me.

"Far, far away, somewhere in the middle of the Galaxy, and about four thousand years from now, there is a world with a great red sun and four moons. Won't you come and play with me there?"

—MARION ZIMMER BRADLEY

THE AGES OF DARKOVER

by MARION ZIMMER BRADLEY

The Novels:

The Founding:
  DARKOVER LANDFALL

The Ages of Chaos:
  STORMQUEEN!
  HAWKMISTRESS

The Hundred Kingdoms:
  TWO TO CONQUER

The Renunciates (Free Amazons):
  THE SHATTERED CHAIN
  THENDARA HOUSE
  CITY OF SORCERY

Against the Terrans—the First Age (Recontact):
  THE SPELL SWORD
  THE FORBIDDEN TOWER

Against the Terrans—the Second Age (After the Comyn):
  THE HERITAGE OF HASTUR
  SHARRA'S EXILE

The Anthologies,

with the Friends of Darkover:

  THE KEEPER'S PRICE
  SWORD OF CHAOS
  FREE AMAZONS OF DARKOVER
  THE OTHER SIDE OF THE MIRROR

THE
KEEPER'S PRICE
AND OTHER STORIES

by
Marion Zimmer Bradley
and the
FRIENDS OF DARKOVER

Edited by
Marion Zimmer Bradley

DAW BOOKS, INC.
DONALD A. WOLLHEIM, PUBLISHER

1633 Broadway
New York, N.Y. 10019

FIRST PRINTING, FEBRUARY 1980

6 7 8 9

PRINTED IN THE U.S.A.

TABLE OF CONTENTS

DEDICATION

To Andre Norton
who inspired us all
this book is affectionately dedicated
by the Friends of Darkover

Introduction

A WORD FROM THE
CREATOR OF DARKOVER

One of the many misconceptions suffered by young writers trying to break into print is this: to think of the editor as a harsh, cruel, unfeeling and judgmental individual who gets sadistic jollies out of rejecting manuscripts with impersonal printed slips, insists that his writers must have a "big name" before he will condescend to read anything they submit to him, and in general tries to put every obstacle possible in the path of the would-be young writer.

There are many things wrong with this picture of the professional editor, the main one being that it simply isn't so. As an editor myself, over a period of years, and also from working with many editors—including the editor of DAW Books, Donald A. Wollheim—I can say that most editors have kept their own personal sense of wonder about good science fiction, and that they spend much of their professional lives in search of a good new writer. Because no matter how many fine writers an editor may have in his (or her) "stable" of published authors, it's never possible to rely on "names" alone. Authors die. They get sick and miss deadlines. They go off for a year to Europe, Africa, Khatmandu or Trappist monasteries. They have babies or decide to spend the next three years researching the Great American novel. For whatever cause, this leaves the editor with nothing to publish; and when he doesn't publish, he doesn't make any money.

And so the editor spends a good deal of time leaving no stone unturned in the search to find and encourage new writers. And one of the stones turned by Don Wollheim was *Starstone*, the magazine of apocryphal Darkover fiction by the Friends of Darkover. I have always encouraged young writers to write in my world; I think it's fun. Besides, how else can I get to read Darkover stories without going to the trouble of writing them?

Don knew that I made a habit of publishing, in *Starstone*, various short bits of Darkover fiction which I considered too short, or too fragmentary, to develop into novels. He spoke to me once about doing an anthology of short Darkover fiction and when I told him there simply weren't enough of these short stories to make up a paperback, he suggested that I might include the best of the short stories written by the Friends of Darkover, some of whom showed tremendous talent.

Another misconception about professional editors in the science fiction and fantasy field is that they have a prejudice against women authors. This is another misconception, so exasperating that I have been known to call any woman who repeats it to me a liar to her face. One young woman who sank to the level of vanity publishing, excused herself by saying to me (to me!), "Well, I had no choice. Everybody knows that women can't get published in fantasy or science fiction." And this, believe it or not, in the days of Ursula le Guin and Anne McCaffrey winning Nebulas and Hugos!

Well, even back when ninety per cent of science fiction *readers* were men, there were a great many women who never made any secret of their sex, writing and editing science fiction. *Weird Tales* was ably edited for many years by Dorothy McIlwraith, *Famous Fantastic Mysteries* (one of the best pulps) by Mary Gnaedinger, and *Amazing Stories*, for a long time, by Cele Goldsmith. Leigh Brackett, Catherine L. Moore, Wilmar Shiras and Judith Merrill—not to mention myself—were all writing long before the current explosion of feminism, back in the thirties, forties, and fifties. Nor did the supposedly all-male readership of the science fiction magazines complain about any of them.

And nowadays, Don Wollheim has been heard to remark in private conversation that two out of three of the best new writers turn out to be female!

However, it was not with my intention that this anthology turned out to be a collection of fiction by women.

I have become a little unpopular in feminist circles by my persistent refusal to be typed as a "woman writer" or to collaborate in telling my grievances against the publishing world which is supposedly in male-dominated hands or to identify with the extremes of feminism. Though I regard myself as the descendant, as far as writing goes, of Catherine Moore and Leigh Brackett, I owe almost as much to Ted Sturgeon and E.C. Tubb and Rider Haggard, and Darkover itself was influ-

enced enormously by the worlds of A. Merritt, and Austin
Tappen Wright's *Islandia*. I am old enough—just—to remember the struggle woman writers and poets had to get rid of
the labels of "authoress" and "poetess." Authors and poets
have no gender; my adolescent daughter, just beginning her
career as an actor, is equally scathing about attempts to call
her an "actress." (What she should say to "actperson" I dare
not even surmise, but that's neither here nor there. . . .)

I resolutely refuse to countenance apartheid, even when it
is camouflaged and rationalized as "women's space."

Yet, ironically, this is an anthology composed entirely of
fiction by women. I had hoped at least that my brother Paul
Zimmer (who supplied some of the best scenes in *Spell
Sword*) or my son, David Bradley, who is editor of a small
semi-professional fantasy magazine, would see fit to con-
tribute to this anthology; but both were busy on their own
projects.

And then I remembered that with one rather dubious exception, most of the amateur Star Trek Fiction (that done for
the sheer love of it, for the amateur press, and most of it
much better, in my humble opinion, than the commercial
stuff turned out by Alan Dean Foster or the late James
Blish) was also written by women. And this gave me a hint
of why the phenomenon of Darkover fiction is, by and large,
a feminine phenomenon.

Women, I think, are not encouraged, in our society, to
create their own fantasy worlds. Society has long had a
vested interest in limiting the imagination of women, into that
role which society has decreed for them; nurturers, mothers,
teachers. Less than a hundred years ago, it was still a bitterly
debated question whether education for women could serve
any purpose other than to create, in women, a longing for
careers which, in the course of nature, must be denied to
them. Only a woman who wished to renounce her "female
vocation" as wife and mother, and become one of the unde-
sirable career-woman stereotypes, (the hag, the ball-breaker,
the old maid, or at best the sexless and self-denying nun,)
could have any kind of independent career.

And, although novel-reading was long decried as a shock-
ing vice, especially for women, when women were allowed to
read at all, a special category of fiction grew up especially for
women; the romantic and domestic novel. In these stories,
women were shown by precept and example that the happy
ending for every woman was to find Mister Right, marry

him, and forget all her other aspirations and daydreams. Even the books where women had interesting careers—*Sue Barton, Student Nurse*, is a classic from my own childhood—the happy ending for Sue was to find a romance with a nice young doctor, and marry him. Whereupon I quipped that she might as well have saved herself the trouble of emptying all those bedpans.

Science fiction, of course, was not considered to be suitable reading for women. Boys were given adventure books; girls were given romantic stories about other girls who filled in the time with mildly amusing trivial adventures until they met the right man. Perhaps the most positive thing that can be said about these "girls books" was that the more intelligent and aggressive girls did not like them very much.

I, for instance, was bored to tears by them. So was Leigh Brackett, who pioneered space-adventure fiction by women. Leigh has been accused of "writing like a man, and a man steeped in macho at that," but this was an act of rebellion for her generation, taking some courage; many women earning a living by their pen would have written trite romances and love stories, while Leigh wrote, as she told me once, "the kind of thing I liked to read myself." Women played little part in these books because, in the books of Leigh's childhood, and mine a few years later, women rarely did anything interesting; and neither Leigh nor I myself was interested in providing some dumb daughter-to-a-mad-scientist for the hero to rescue and marry later on. Leigh said once, "If I had a woman in a story, she was *doing* something, not worrying about the price of eggs and who's in love with whom."

But Leigh and I were the exceptions, the driven ones. We *had* to write, and we weren't going to write romantic claptrap, either. For every one like me, and Leigh, and C.L. Moore, and Juanita Coulson, there were dozens of women who learned to do what their parents said, conceal their own daydreams and read the books proper to their gender and station in life.

Then, to a whole generation of girls, *Star Trek* on television opened up the world of science fiction. And they had a new world to write about.

Boys who wanted to write usually made up their own worlds, often beginning with a set of toy soldiers, or cutouts, or space cadets. Girls were not encouraged to do it. I did it; but I lived on a farm, isolated from teenage group pressures, and no doubt I was what a psychologist would have called "inadequately socialized." Which is a polite way of saying that I somehow escaped the peer-pressure brainwashing which tells a girl that her main "developmental tasks" are concerned with dancing, dating, cosmetics, and similar teenage mating rituals. (Not long ago, reading about some popular female rock star whose downhill descent into drugs and alcoholism, and eventual death, was sentimentalized as having begun with an adolescence when she "wasn't even invited to the junior prom," I stared in amazement, wondering why anyone would have *wanted* to go to the damn prom unless parents or peers were badgering them into it.) My own teens were cheerful and unbothered by boyfriends or worry about the lack of "dates"; my own adolescent crises (and I had many) were the failures to get a part in school operettas and solo parts in choral concerts!—I had a good, but not outstanding, singing voice—and the insistence by teachers and school psychologists that I should write less, dance more, and try to make friends among girls who seemed to have no interest in anything except dances, hairdos and the kind of movies I called "romantic slop." I spent my adolescence reading, memorizing opera scores, and writing incredibly bad novels, at first in imitation of Walter Scott and Bulwer-Lytton, later, when I discovered science-fiction, in imitation of Henry Kuttner and A. Merritt. To do this I invented my own fantasy world, which eventually became Darkover. And when I began selling, and was asked if I had any trouble, as a woman, breaking into a "man's field," my reaction was scornful.

"Heck, no. I never met an editor who cared whether I was male or female or a chimpanzee who had learned how to type, as long as I told a good story."

Only very recently have I begun to realize that, in truth, I had simply managed to evade, by a combination of luck, indifference and tough-mindedness, a brainwashing which ninety per cent of women undergo. I had always believed that my fellow women could have avoided it too—"they can't brainwash you if you're not listening,"—but now I am not so sure.

For my experience was not universal. Not until women saw *Star Trek* did they start identifying themselves, just as young children did, with the heroes and heroines of that universe. They were too old to put on Vulcan ears and *Enterprise* T-shirts and play at being Spock, Kirk, Uhura and their friends, so they wrote stories about them. And, in a wave of amateur fiction completely unlike any phenomenon in science fiction history, these stories somehow got themselves published in amateur magazines. There were *hundreds* of them; or let me amend that; there were *thousands,* though I have only read a few hundred.

And when they were sated with *Star Trek,* many of them turned to Darkover. I don't agree with Jacqueline Lichtenberg that "Darkover is just an advanced version of *Star Trek* for grownups." I was never that much of a *Star Trek* fan, and not till after I knew Jacqueline did I ever learn much about the phenomenon of *Star Trek* fandom. Jacqueline, driven like myself, one of those who created her own fantasy world in her teens and transmuted it into a professional series as an adult, used *Star Trek* fandom, calculatedly, (as I used the fanzines built around the old pulp fiction) as a way of learning her craft and getting her early writings in print; she wrote a whole series of *Star Trek* novels. Then, having found her feet and perfected her craft, she began to speak in her own voice and build her own characters, and has now published two novels, and sold three others, in her own world.

And so I am pleased and honored that many talented young women are now using the Darkover universe as a stepping stone to finding their own voices in writing. True, a great deal of what is written in Darkover amateur fiction is not very good. Much of the amateur music which was written for the poems and songs in Tolkien's *Lord of the Rings* was not very good, either. But in giving a talk once about Tolkien's verse, I said (long before Darkover was a known series at all) that the most astonishing thing to me about Tolkien's verse was that it could get so many, many people to writing music! Almost everybody, it seemed to me, who had ever thought of writing music felt compelled to put some of Tolkien's verses to an original musical setting.

And so I am awed and humble at the notion that the very concept of Darkover could encourage so many young women, previously inarticulate, to try their voices at creating new characters and new situations in Darkover. In the jargon of feminism, one could say Darkover gave them a "safe space in which to try creativity." Surrounded by a world ready-made for them, they could concentrate on character and incident, and not need to make up a whole world of their own.

And some of these women, having tried their wings in the thin air of Darkover, have gone on to write other things. Others have used Darkover, and are still using it, to explore the dimensions of their own world view, at the same time perfecting their craft and technique.

And so this anthology, partly in recognition of their talents, and partly in recognition of my debt to them.

Because most of these women have chosen to write short stories. Now, I never thought of myself as a short story writer. My early short stories are not very good. I have always felt more at ease with the longer pieces, novels and novelettes.

But it is easier to tell somebody else how to do something than it is to do it yourself. (Them as can, does; them as can't, teaches.) And, by reading the Darkover short stories written by my young fans, and sometimes criticizing them and trying to explain just what is wrong with them, I have somehow learned to write short stories myself and been encouraged to try my hand at this best and subtlest of fictional forms. The four stories in this volume are, I think, among the best of my short stories, and they were written because, after seeing the kind of mistakes I could recognize in other people's stories, I could learn to avoid them in my own writing. So that I have learned as much from my fans as I hope they have learned from me about the art of writing.

Some critics have been disturbed about the possibility that I might exploit my dying fans, or steal their ideas, or use their work in my future novels. No, except that everything I read somehow finds its way into my subconscious, there to undergo the sea-change which alters raw ideas into fiction. But this is just as likely to happen with a story by Roger Zelazny—or Daphne du Maurier—or Agatha Christie—or Pearl S. Buck.

Of course I get ideas from my young fans, just as I *give* them ideas. But as for stealing their ideas—I have *quite* enough ideas of my own. If their ideas find lodgment in my head, it is in the same way that I "got the idea" for my novel *Planet Savers* by reading a classic study of a multiple personality, as an assignment in my psychology class; or that I might get an idea from *National Geographic* or *Scientific American*, which are the magazines in which I browse when temporarily short of inspiration. Leigh Brackett's *The Starmen of Llyrdis* was one of my favorite books; it is based on the idea that only one race of men can travel the stars, while others are limited to the world where they were born. I read this story, loved it, and then one night was cogitating, and thought, "Yes—suppose one race had the monopoly on space travel, and kept all others on their planets because the earth-bound could not endure space travel due to physical limitations, as in Leigh's book—but suppose the one race who could endure space travel, were lying about it, to keep their monopoly?" That was how my novel *The Colors of Space* was born. It's nothing like Leigh's *The Starmen*. Nor is *The Bloody Sun* anything like Ted Sturgeon's *Baby Is Three*, although I began with Sturgeon's idea of a human gestalt of intimately linked telepaths.

This is why I don't mind other writers writing about Darkover, and at the same time, I have no wish and no need to exploit their ideas. If I ever do make use of a fan's writing, it will be so altered and transmuted by its trip through my own personal dream-space that even the inventor would never recognize her idea, so alien it would be when I got through with it!

Nor do I feel threatened by stories not consistent with my personal vision of Darkover. To me, all Darkover stories written by anyone else are presumed to be in a parallel world to "my" Darkover; or *one* of the parallel universes, which can be very close to my own Darkover, or very different, just as the young writer wishes.

Because, in a very real sense, I regard myself not as the "inventor" of Darkover, but its discoverer. If others wish to play in my fantasy world, who am I to slam its gates and in churlish voice demand that they build their own? If they are capable of it, they will do so someday. Meanwhile, if they wish to write of Darkover, they will. All the selfish exclusiveness of the Conan Doyle estate (which went so far as to demand that the late Ellery Queen anthology, *The Misadventures of Sherlock Holmes*, a very fine volume of Holmes pastiches, be withdrawn from sale and never reprinted, thus denying Holmes lovers a wonderful reading experience) has not stopped lovers of Sherlock from writing their own stories and secretly sharing them. Why should I deny myself the pleasure of seeing these young writers learning to do their thing by, for a little while, doing *my* thing with me?

Or, look at it this way. When I was a little kid, I was a great lover of "pretend" games, but after I was nine or ten, I could never get anyone to play them *with* me. My friends grew up and got tired of them; I never did. And now I have a lot of fans, and friends, who will come into my magic garden and play the old "pretend games" with me.

Far, far away somewhere in the middle of the Galaxy, and about four thousand years from now, there is a world with a great red sun and four moons. Won't you come and play with me there?

Marion Zimmer Bradley

Diana Paxson, in addition to being one of the sisters mentioned in the introduction, is *literally* a sister; she is married to my brother Don, who writes under the name of Jon de Cles. Her story comes first in this collection, not by virtue of nepotism, but because it is, chronologically, the earliest in recorded Darkovan history, coming only a few generations after *Darkover Landfall.*

Like many of the writers in this collection—in fact, typically of the women in this anthology—Diana juggles housekeeping, young children, a full-time paid job, and a serious artistic career. She has illustrated children's books (and consented to do the map for the hardcover edition of the Darkover books), was instrumental in the founding of the medievalist Society for Creative Anachronism, and has sold short stories to *Isaac Asimov's Science Fiction Magazine* and such anthologies as *Millennial Women* and *Swords Against Darkness*. In addition she is writing a fine tetralogy for children, still seeking a publisher (I keep reminding her that Madeleine L'Engle's history-making *A Wrinkle in Time* was rejected by several publishers before going on to win the Newberry Prize, and *The Earthstone* is in my estimation, at least as good a children's book).

With all she has on her hands, I'm specially touched and honored that a new writer of Diana's stature would come into my world to write "Vai Dom."

Diana's work seems, to me, to dovetail with Darkover, for Diana works for the Office of Education,* devising curricula for Native American children. To help Navajo and Hopi children cope with the problems of a technological society capable of walking on the moon, and still not lose touch with their own special heritage, seems to me very much akin to the problems facing Darkover in the conflict against the Empire.

In this story Diana addresses herself to the

* Far West Laboratory for Educational Research and Development.

17

problem of how a colony founded by citizens of
a technological, democratic society so quickly became, on Darkover, medieval and feudal.

VAI DOM

by Diana L. Paxson

*Although the political history of Darkover has
become much more accessible to scholarly inves-
tigation in recent years, there are some questions
which will probably remain unanswered. To the
historian, one of the most frustrating of these
must be the nature of the process by which
people whose political background was character-
ized by representative government, centralized
authority, and a merit-based administrative hier-
archy evolved the loose federation of feudal states
which dominate the planet today.*

John Wilkes Reade
Darkover—Problems and Premises

Silently the funeral guests raised their pewter mugs to the
empty chair at the head of the long table, drained them, and
set them down. Darriel di Asturien swallowed the last of his
mead, fighting the sourness in his stomach and the distraction
of the visions that flickered behind his eyes. He tensed as his
sister Kierestelli began to refill the mugs. He was the eldest
child. In a moment he must begin the toasts to his father's
memory. He could not give way to the old sickness now!

There would be many pledges made tonight, draining the
mead casks as if the storeroom held dozens more. But perhaps it was a fair exchange. Where the casks had lain, Darriel's father rested now, held incorrupt by the cold. They
would bury him when spring came. If spring came. . . .

Darriel covered his eyes, trying to visualize springtime, to see the slopes leading up to the plateau azure with flowers. But his mind betrayed him with the heady scent of *kireseth*; colors swirled before him, blue changing to the crimson stain of his father's blood upon the snow.

They were calling him. Somehow Darriel stood. He heard himself saying the words he had made a litany to harness his thoughts during the dark nights since his father died:

"To Dawyd di Asturien, who believed that the plain beside this river was worth cherishing. He gave his life for it, and I name him as he named the river—*Valeron*." His voice was shaking as he finished.

His half-brother Loryn got to his feet. "I drink to my foster father, who, when the councilmen of Dellerey ordered us back to the town after the Ya-men's first attack, would not leave the rich fields he had made. We will not betray his dream."

There was a growl of agreement from Beltran as the third di Asturien brother rose to drink to the memory of a father who had been sometimes hasty, but never unfair.

The rough-planed floorboards creaked as old Gabriel Ross stood to give his toast. "To Dawyd, a worthy grandson of the man who founded Dellerey only seventy years ago." Gabriel had come with Dawyd to settle the plain at the rivermouth and built a farm a half-day's journey upriver from theirs.

Darriel felt the coldness in his belly thaw as he drank again and again. Thirty-eight human beings now lived beside the Valeron, and they had all come to Dawyd di Asturien's funeral feast. A child's fussing stilled as its mother put it to the breast. Darriel's gaze wandered across the unfinished frieze of wall plaques whose carving had been Dawyd's winter task, focused on the strong faces around him, reddened by the light of the lavish fire as if it were day. Firelight glimmered on the carved heads of stag ponies wreathed in leaves and flowers; flashed on the knife that rested on hooks above the hearth.

That knife was the most precious heirloom of the di Asturiens. Its metal was supposed to have come from the hull of the star-ship that had brought their ancestors to Darkover almost a century earlier. Certainly the smiths at New Skye had not the art to forge such metal today.

Darriel's visions were dulling now, *gratia Dios!* They were an inheritance too. But like his red hair, the power of past and future to overwhelm present perception came from his

mother's side of the family. She had been a descendant of
Elorie Lovat, whom legend called the chieri's child.

Darriel looked back at his guests, stiffened as Robard Macrae pushed back his bench. In the eternity it took the young
man to stand, hesitating as if he sought for words, the weight
of vision crushed Darriel again:

*Robard, shaking his fair hair back from his face as he de-
fended Darriel from the taunts of his brothers, his sixteenth
summer, when the sickness came almost every day . . .*

*Robard, refusing just as stubbornly while Darriel's father
begged him to bring his family to stay with them at El Haleine until winter ended and the danger of attack by the Ya-
men was past . . .*

*Dawyd di Asturien, sinking beneath the Ya-men's clubs
and beaks while his sons were too overwhelmed by their
numbers to go to his aid. So many——there had been too many
for only four men. The creatures had withdrawn when
darkness fell. Then the blizzard came, and when it was over
the Ya-men were gone into whatever fastness hunger had
driven them from before. But it was too late then . . .*

*Robard's steady eyes meeting Darriel's above a campfire
. . . his father's frozen snarl when they had found him at last
beneath a tangle of emaciated Ya-man bodies and draggled
plumes . . .*

"No!" Darriel cried aloud. "Your hypocrisies shall not dishonor my father's memory. If you had joined us here as my
father bade you, we could have held them with no loss, and
Dawyd di Asturien would not have died!"

Robard's hand went up as if to ward off Darriel's words.
"A man must judge his own duty or he is no man—I thought
my family safer where it was."

The confusion of vision was burned away by the red glow
of the mead, the red glow of the fire, the crimson flicker of
the knife poised above the hearth. Darriel looked at Robard,
and saw a Ya-man's plumes instead of the other's bright hair.

The bench crashed behind him as he sprang to his feet. He
made his way down the table. The guests' murmurs stilled as
he halted, staring at Robard across the table's width.

Robard's sister laid a hand on his arm. Gently he removed
it, pushed her and her small son behind him. Still without
taking his eyes from Darriel, he came around the end of the
table. Wordless, the two young men settled into an identical
stance, feet apart, knees bent, arms poised with open hands.

They had done this so many times before. But not like this . . .

Anticipation tingled along Darriel's spine, tautened the muscles of neck and arms. But he was aware only of his growing lust to smash the beaked face he saw. He heard a moan, and did not know it came from his own throat. His tension built, broke. He leaped for his foe.

Their hands groped for purchase on each other's bodies; feet scraped as Darriel sought for more leverage. A gust of snow hissed against the oiled skins stretched across the windows. The combatants swayed, breathing in harsh gasps, then stilled, strength straining against strength so equally that their aliveness was revealed only in the ripple of muscle, the pulse of a vein.

The ripping of Robard's shoulder seam split the silence, loosened Darriel's grip. Robard twisted, hooking his opponent's knee. Off-balance, Darriel thrust suddenly and the two men crashed to the floor, thrashing furiously as instinct drove Darriel's fingers toward Robard's throat.

The men had made a circle around the combatants, their faces intent.

"Young fools!" muttered Gabriel.

"But Darriel spoke truth . . ." Beltran di Asturien replied.

Again the locked figures twisted, rolling over and over on the planked floor. Robard, in command of both his body and his wits, maneuvered their struggles toward the raised stone platform of the hearth. The two bodies heaved; there was a sound like a cracking stick. Robard jerked free of Darriel's embrace.

Darriel felt agony flame in his right arm and realized dimly that trying to use it would bring more pain. But his enemy was getting away! He scrambled to his feet. His brother Loryn started toward him. The movement distracted him; he turned a little and glimpsed the red glitter of the knife above the hearth. A single smooth movement brought him to it, and it into his hand.

The stillness throbbed in his ears as he stalked toward his foe. Robard edged away, watching him with a desperate pity.

Darriel paused.

A gray faintness was warring with the fire in his mind. He lifted the knife, began to weave a pattern with it to confuse his opponent's gaze, but as he moved pain lanced his other arm. He looked at Robard and saw now the face of the Ya-man, now that of his friend. And as he wavered, Loryn seized him suddenly from behind.

He staggered. Gabriel Ross gripped his wrist with all the gnarled strength of his sixty years. Darriel felt his fingers weaken, whimpered as the knife was torn from his grasp. People were all around him now, filling the space between him and his enemy.

His enemy . . .

Darriel's eyes focused on Robard's pale face.

"Traitor! Traitor! Were you fathered by the whole council of Dellerey?" he whispered, struggling against his pain. "Run while you can—next time I will not stay my hand."

Robard straightened. "I'll not call you bastard, but true son to a tyrant crazed by pride. Mad or sane, Darriel di Asturien, there will be death between us before you see me again."

Robard's face seemed to dim. Darriel heard him call his young brother Rickard, gather the rest of his family. Then the mist thickened around him and he fell.

Darriel woke to the sound of running water; the steady drip-drip of icicles, the trickle of snow melting from the eaves. He lay without moving, savoring the softness of the down mattress, the warmth of woolen blankets and the coverlet that Kierestelli had woven of strips from the pelts of rabbithorn. He felt a breath of air on his face from an open window—cool but not chill, and pure as if the air had been made new. His mind was blessedly clear.

His father was gone. He had drawn steel on his friend.

But the impact of those memories was blunted by images of anxious faces, the sound of great winds rushing, and his dream. Or had they been only dreams? Behind his eyelids he could see them still—massive walls of stone and palisaded logs surrounding El Haleine, and starving Ya-men dashing themselves against them in vain.

Darriel heard a muffled oath and a rustle of cloth. His eyes opened on the bronze-brown sheen of his sister's bent head, backlighted by the rosy light of noon.

"Kierestelli?"

She straightened, holding the needle she had dropped, and thrust it firmly into the torn shirt in her lap.

"Did I wake you? How do you feel?"

"Well, but tired. How long did I sleep?"

"Sleep! For two weeks you were raving. You have been *sleeping* since yesterday afternoon."

Now he noticed the bruised skin beneath her eyes, how her soft lips had thinned. "I'm sorry . . ."

She sighed. "We thought we were going to lose you, too. It was the sickness, wasn't it?"

He nodded. Of all his mother's children, only Kierestelli had shared the shattering of that agony when reality seemed to slip away, and then only for a little while. It made a special bond between them, and since that time she sometimes seemed to know his thoughts without need for speech, and he hers.

"At the feast it was the sickness speaking, not you," she went on. "Robard knows how it is with you—couldn't you . . ." Her voice faltered.

Robard, oh my friend! For a moment Darriel closed his eyes. Then, "Maybe, if it had been a private fight. But the whole valley heard my words, and his. He insulted father as well—do you think that Loryn and Beltran would let me forgive that? Men would scorn either of us if we sought forgiveness now." He smiled bitterly.

She shook her head, knowing the futility of saying more.

"Kierestelli, while I was ill, I . . . dreamed," he said then.

Her eyes grew suddenly intent. "Like your dream about the forest fire two summers ago, or the one before mother died?"

He nodded. "We must fortify this place. The Ya-men will come again—not this year, or maybe the next, but they *will* come."

"Of course—in the summer, when the Ghost Wind blows," she replied. "But they are intoxicated then, and easily frightened by our fires."

"No, in wintertime."

"This winter was a freak! The weather should have broken over a month ago. The Ya-men were starving . . ."

"Yes, and they will starve again, and attack again. I don't know if there's some cycle, or if the climate will keep getting worse, but haven't you noticed the weather growing colder, even since you were a child?"

She stared at him, pulling her shawl closer around her.

"This was the first really bad winter we've had," he went on, "but first snowfall has been earlier every year. If we plan ahead I think we can still get the crops in. But the Ya-men don't raise food . . ." He struggled to raise himself against the pillows, ignoring the twinge from his splinted arm. "*Breda,* now *I* am responsible for El Haleine! Help me convince Loryn and Beltran that we must be ready when the Ya-men come again!"

Her eyes were like a forest pool. They mirrored uncertainty, apprehension, desperation, as the intensity of his vision reached her. Then her mouth firmed in the same lines as his own.

She nodded.

The di Asturiens worked grimly through that summer and the next, ignoring the scoffing of the neighbors, stinting food and sleep to get the walls built and the crops in as well. Darriel went to Dellerey once during that time, finding two men who would work for him in exchange for land and a widow to help Kierestelli keep them all fed and clothed.

He heard that Robard Macrae had been to the town too, and brought back a girl named Alyssa Allart to be his bride. But the di Asturiens were not invited to the wedding feast. Later he heard that she had borne Robard a copper-haired daughter, Margalys, but he sent no gift.

The walls of El Haleine rose steadily—four feet of hewn stone surmounted by a ten-foot palisade. They embraced the hall built by Dawyd di Asturien twenty years earlier, its weathered timbers gray beside the new logs, then curved around the barn, the sheds, the well. The men were just hanging the heavy gate, braced and barred beneath its arch of stone, when the first storm of the third winter came.

Darriel swallowed the last of his stew and listened to the whistling of the wind. There was usually a wind blowing here at the river's mouth, which was why Dawyd had named the place El Haleine. But as always when he noticed that wind, Darriel remembered that *aleine* meant a man's force, his courage, as well, and thought of his father.

He felt the edge of hunger still, but he did not ask for more. Kierestelli knew how many nuts were in each basket in the storeroom, how many tubers in the cellars, how many frozen joints of meat hanging in the smokehouse, and she had calculated to the ounce how much they could use at every meal if the supplies were going to last until spring. By early autumn the coats of the stag-ponies had been as heavy as dire-wolves's pelts. This one of Darriel's predictions had been correct, at least—the winter would be long.

His brother Beltran was carving a trencher, the shavings falling away beneath his knife in delicate curls. Loryn's dark head was bent over a saddle that needed repairs. After a moment's examination, he straightened and began to rummage in the scrap-leather bag. Rafael Carvalho sat dozing in an armchair by the fire. The other man from Dellerey had already gone to bed.

Darriel thought of the unfinished boot in his workroom, but made no move to fetch it. His head ached, and though he wore a knitted vest beneath his wool shirt, and a sheepskin jerkin over it, he felt cold. If only the wind would not howl so!

He stilled, sensing something different about the sound of the storm. Clumsily he sought to send his awareness outward to probe that disturbing note. He heard a shrill, keening cry. No human throat could have made it, but surely it was more than just a wind!

He stood transfixed by the stab of fear in his gut, and by a bitter, brilliant joy. Kierestelli, coming from the kitchen with a dishcloth still in her hand, stopped and stared at him, and Loryn and Beltran followed her gaze.

There was another cry, unmistakable, as for a moment the wind failed.

"The Ya-men . . ." breathed Kierestelli. Beltran stood, the trencher clattering to the floor.

The sound released Darriel from his trance. He shouted to his brothers, to the other men. Swiftly they shrugged into jackets and cloaks, checked the knives at their belts, snatched bows and quivers and their heavy bronze-headed spears. A cold blast of air swept the hall as they tumbled through the door. Then they heard it slam behind them as they sought their posts on the platforms behind the walls.

Darriel raised one arm to shield his eyes from the bitter swirl of snow. The logs beside him trembled at an invisible blow. He bent to the notch in the palisade, peered through it and made out a dark shape leaping below. Shadow from shadow, the Ya-man's nine-foot height seemed to extend toward him. Darriel wondered if even fourteen-foot walls would keep them out.

For weapons, the savages had only rude clubs, but they were unhumanly strong, and desperate for the food and warmth they knew to be inside. The walls shuddered repeatedly as the Ya-men tried to beat them down. Darriel nocked another arrow, leaned over the top of the palisade, and loosed it. There was a howl of pain and one of the figures disappeared.

The wind was lessening. Was he deluded, or had the fury of the attackers weakened as well? Darriel wondered how long the attack had gone on. He and the others waited, their limbs growing stiff as they peered through the snow, while the world around them grew still.

When they came back inside at last, the candles told them that they had been gone for less than an hour.

"No Ya-man knows enough to strike in triple-time," said Loryn. The knock had sounded scarcely louder than the popping of the fire in the pre-dawn stillness. The men tautened, waiting for it to come again.

Tap . . . tap . . . tap . . . The intervals were longer this time. Darriel was already on his feet. The others followed him as he dashed for the door.

A single small figure lay collapsed against the gate. Swiftly they bore him into the hall.

"It's Martin Delangelo from Macrae's place," Kierestelli whispered, recognizing the man even though his face was glassy with frostbite and bloodied from a gash in his skull. Rafael started to unclasp his jerkin while Beltran struggled with his boots.

Darriel bent over him as Martin began to stir.

"The Ya-men . . ." he breathed, shuddering uncontrollably.

"We know," said Kierestelli. "Drink this now, you have to get warm." She held a mug of mulled wine to his lips. He tried to sip, spluttered, his head fell back.

"They came two hours ago—a big band. . . ." He gasped, drank again. "More desperate than ever. They beat down the door to our Hall. . . ." His eyes focused on Darriel, dilating with pain as the warmth of the room began to penetrate his frozen limbs.

"They breached the Hall!" he repeated. "They struck young Rickard down while Master Robard was getting the rest of us into the cellars. We left Rickard there behind us, dead on the floor of his own home . . . I hope he is dead! *Ah, Dios!* I hope he is out of his agony now!" Martin's head rolled helplessly.

Lifting dazed eyes, Darriel saw Kierestelli's face grow white and remembered he had once sensed some feeling between her and Robard's young brother.

"Robard pushed me out through a ventilation shaft. . . ." The words tumbled frantically from Martin's lips. "He told me to find you, Master Darriel—he begs you to come! They cannot hold the door forever, and they have no warmth or water there. The baby . . . was ill even before those devils came. . . ." The old man shuddered once, then fainted away.

Beltran's laughter broke their appalled silence. "He *begs* you to come, Dari—did you hear that? Our father's blood is paid for now!"

"Are we merchants, to trade in lives?" Darriel whispered. "The price was too high!"

"Rafael, heat water—Martin is cold as ice—if we do not warm him through at once he will die. . . ." Kierestelli's voice was desperately even. Darriel sat back, letting her take charge. His brother's words, Robard's words, made a litany in his brain.

There will be a death between us before ever I see you again. . . . Darriel felt something shift in his mind and groaned, groping for support against the hearth. There was an agony in his shoulder; he knew that Robard had been wounded there, though Martin had not said so, perhaps had not even known. It would be like Robard to hide his own pain. Argument babbled around him. Darriel leaned back, powerless to prevent the torrent of awareness. Images mingled in his mind.

As if the past three years had never been, he felt Robard's anguish as he refused what Dawyd di Asturien had asked. Then, inexplicably, Darriel was watching himself, his red hair gone gray, fighting back-to-back with Robard against a dozen ragged men. . . .

But the present! What was happening now?

He saw Robard dimly through the shadow of the cellar, and beyond him the huddled shapes of his mother and sister, his brother-in-law and their son, and a pretty woman who must be Alyssa. But Robard's arms were around his child. Far worse than the pain of his wound was Robard's despair as he listened to the Ya-men's howling. The baby whimpered fearfully and turned her face against her father's chest.

A backlash of grief swept the vision away. Darriel opened his eyes.

"Robard asked," he answered Beltran, "and I will go to him."

"What?"

"We are going to Macrae's."

"You are mad! Who will defend El Haleine?" exclaimed Loryn.

"Why should we?" asked Beltran. "He would not come when we asked him!"

"Robard Macrae did what he thought was his duty," replied Darriel. "He did not know that Father would die. We do know what will happen if we do not go to his aid. If two of you come with me, the others can hold El Haleine. The Ya-men have learned not to dash themselves against our walls—but even if they do try, they will not get in."

Beltran stared at him. They all stared at him. But no one gainsaid him when he began to put on his gear. A half hour later Darriel rode out with Beltran and Rafael, leaving the walls of El Haleine behind.

They urged the stag-ponies along the narrow path through the woods, under a sky more blue than lavender in the early light. The hour of travel between Robard's home and El Haleine had never seemed so long. But the trees thinned at last. Beyond them they could see the gleam of the Valeron, white fields sweeping away to the shadowed cliffs that divided lowlands from plateau, and the Hall.

Ya-men were running in and out of the building, carrying food, draping themselves in the blue curtains with their woven border of garnet-flowers. Above their high-pitched giggling the di Asturiens heard the dull thonk of wood being pounded, then splintering as a board gave way.

Darriel spoke low-voiced to the others; swiftly they tied the stag-ponies among the trees and crept closer, readying their bows.

The strings sang once, again, and again. The giggling changed to whistles of anguish as the Ya-men fell. Others dashed from inside the Hall, howling. One of them realized where the arrows were coming from and sprang toward the trees.

Beltran stepped out to meet him, jabbing upwards with his spear. Darriel moved to flank him, shot at close range as another savage swung at Beltran with a cone-fir branch to which needles still clung. The arrow transfixed the creature's scrawny chest. It paused, the hideous features turned momentarily comical by surprise. Then its face changed and it fell.

The remaining Ya-men were rushing them now. Darriel could smell their acrid odor even in the cold. He dropped the bow and snatched up his spear. Step by step he moved forward, with Beltran and Rafael beside him and a little behind.

"This for my father!" he hissed, bracing himself as a pale

form leaped toward him. He felt the shock as the bronze spearhead met alien flesh; set his teeth, and drove it in.

There was a cry to his left. He turned, felt something brush his shoulder, and whirled to catch another of the Ya-men before it could get its cudgel up to strike at him again. Beltran was down. Darriel straddled him, trying to face in every direction at once.

Momentarily he sensed the Ya-men's fury, their pain, their fear, and was shocked to feel in himself pity for the necessity that had driven them here. He had grown up knowing them as insubstantial flickers among the trees, aggressive only when the Ghost Wind blew, and then possessed by a maniac hilarity.

We are the intruders here, he thought, *but we did not bring the long cold. Darkover masters us all. . . .*

There were only three of the Ya-men left, facing them uncertainly over the still shapes of their fellows, and the purple stains on the snow.

Darriel felt Beltran stir below him and glanced down. His brother was pale, but trying to smile. Darriel stepped aside, one eye still on the Ya-men, and helped Beltran to his feet.

"Are you hurt?"

"Some cracked ribs, I think, but I'll do . . . Let's finish this job!"

Darriel nodded. Slowly the three began to advance once more. There was a startled hissing from their foes, then one of them gave a long, mournful cry that raised the hairs on Darriel's neck. Clubs were shaken at the humans, then dropped in the snow. As swiftly as if they had been ghosts indeed the Ya-men turned and flitted away across the white fields.

The men did not follow them.

"Margalys would have died," repeated Robard. "They would have *eaten* her!"

"They are gone—it's over now," said Darriel anxiously. "Let Alyssa tend your shoulder, and try to rest." He pushed the other man back down on the bed. The rest of the family were busy around them, replacing furniture, building up the fire. Rickard's body had been taken away.

"I couldn't protect them, Darriel—I couldn't take care of my own. . . ."

Darriel stared down at his friend, knowing that this was the thing that would not let him rest, and finding no answer to his agony. When they were boys, Robard had protected *him*.

Margalys was crying fitfully. Alyssa bent over the cradle, crooning a song that had no words. After a little the baby's sobs became hiccups, then died away.

"Listen to me, Dari—" Robard spoke again. His gaze was intense beneath knitted brows. "You were right about the Ya-men, and about the weather. To save my family I had to ask your help. I think it may be that way again . . ."

"No!" whispered Darriel, not knowing yet what he denied.

"I understand about the 'madness' that burdens you—none better—" Robard smiled bitterly. "But don't you see that we need such madness now? It is a gift—cherish it, master it, *use* it! I will follow where you lead. . . ."

Uncomprehending, Darriel looked at him, seeing his own face mirrored in Robard's gray eyes.

"Don't you believe me? Why should you—we are both proud men. I will swear it to you, Darriel di Asturien." Robard's smile grew rueful. "Indeed I must, lest I forget what I have learned today."

"An oath of obedience?" said Darriel, horror thinning his voice. "We came here from Dellerey because the council wanted to order our lives. How can I command you, Robard—you are my friend!"

"There's no time to vote when the Ya-men are breaking down your door," said Robard. "My duty to the family requires this of me. Your duty to those who live in this place your father found requires it of you."

Darriel looked desperately about him. Alyssa had the baby in her arms and was walking her up and down while Robard's mother bound Beltran's ribs. Robard's nephew had climbed onto Rafael's lap to look at his spear. Across the miles he could sense Kierestelli at El Haleine, watchful and anxious; and more faintly, the terror of the retreating Ya-men.

Darriel felt a cold touch on his palm and looked down. Robard had drawn his own home-forged knife and was laying its hilt in his hand.

"Darriel—take my blade, and my oath . . . please. . . ."

A chill ran from the knife up Darriel's arm to pierce his heart. He heard Robard's words echoed by a multitude of voices, saw the shining of the crude knife reflected by myriad blades. Without willing it, his hand drew out the di Asturien knife. He recognized the memory of the last time he had seen that blade in Robard's eyes. But the point was toward Darriel now.

Robard laid his hand on the hilt. "By the hand I lay on your blade, I pledge you my life."

Darriel's hand closed over that of his friend as if their lives were meeting through that touch, through that metal which had sped among the stars.

"Be my protection, then. . . ." His voice trembled. "And may this blade find my heart if I be not yours, and if I am not. . . ." *Domine* . . . childhood tales supplied the ancient word. "If I am not a worthy lord to you. I call to witness whatever gods have led us to this place!"

The blades lay mated in their hands. Incapable, for his very life, of saying more, Darriel took the knife that Robard had given him, slipped it awkwardly into the sheath at his side. Robard's fingers closed on the hilt of the di Asturien blade. He hesitated, then sheathed it in his turn.

"*Vai dom* . . ." he reapeated softly. He dropped back among the pillows, his face relaxing at last.

Darriel smoothed the matted hair back from Robard's brow, watched as the other man's eyelids closed, his breathing deepened, as if it were safe to sleep now.

Darriel was unnaturally conscious of the weight of the new blade at his side. He felt as if the world had steadied beneath him, but the emptiness at the heart of it that had grown during the three years when he and Robard had been foes was still there.

"Robard, Robard, what have you done?" he whispered. "If you knew truly what it is to see things as I do, you could not have called it a gift!" Was there anyone, anywhere, who could truly understand. Darriel sighed. "I did not want to be your lord, Robard, but your friend!"

On my desk in Berkeley rests a cheerful little sculpture—actually a ball with a charming chubby face, and the letters TUIT engraved on its bald dome. This was my introduction to Cynthia McQuillin, who was selling these and other delightful little creations at some convention or other. When I came to know the young lady better (and Cynthia is very young; in her early twenties, she may possibly be the youngest contributor to this anthology) I was moved to ask in the pages of *Starstone* "Is there anything this young woman can't do?" Later at that same convention I heard her sing and play the guitar; she claims to have composed over 450 songs; and while I am not a critic, she seems to be a facile melodist with a genuine lyric gift. She makes both "serious" sculptures and drawings and amusing ones like the "round tuit" on my desk. At present she tells me she is "working on a musical comedy with some friends . . . and collaborating on an illustrated children's book and a book of cartoons in which a publisher has expressed an interest." She sings in a sweet, rather husky mezzo-soprano, rather in the folk-song vein. She's active in Darkover fandom, the new Andre Norton "Witch World" fandom, and others. And she also, as "The Forest" will tell you, has a sensitive ear for the written word, and a feel for the creation of aliens.

She is also psychic, spent two years working as a research assistant for a parapsychologist, and has been a teaching assistant, and laboratory technician, in a local college for the science and ESP classes.

"The Forest" was one of the entries in our recent short story contest; and while it did not win a prize, or even place very high in the contest—the competition was keen, with several professional writers entering, and stories judged sternly by adherence to commercial fiction techniques—I was personally struck by the skill with which Cynthia handled aliens, and made my fearsome and dimly sketched Ya-men (from *The Winds of Darkover*) into believable characters. The standard fictional techniques can be learned without much trouble; the ability to tell a story and make the reader believe in it is something which must be inborn in a young writer. And this, I firmly believe, Cindy McQuillin has in full measure. I think, after reading "The Forest," the reader of this anthology will believe in it too.

The period of this story, though never made plain, is obviously very soon after the established colonization of Darkover in *Landfall,* and thus it follows "Vai Dom" in logical sequence.

THE FOREST

by Cynthia McQuillin

The sun was warm and high as Caselin crossed the meadow, a sack of the sweet high mountain berries swinging at her side. Thoughtfully the girl paused to watch a rabbithorn grazing a little way downslope. She was fond of animals. A secret smile of pleasure warmed her as she dug her toes deep into the cool grass, and brushed a strand of dark hair from her eyes.

At length she laid aside her sack and gathered up her skirt of plaincloth so that it wouldn't rustle. Then she crept down toward the unsuspecting rabbithorn. As she came near it she sank lightly down on her knees and made a soft crooning sound. Startled, the beast looked up, and seeing her, would have fled, but she spoke to it softly. Stayed, as if by a spell, the timid creature stood poised for flight, its small heart pounding. Talking softly all the while, the child drew something from the pocket of her skirt. It was a sweet tuber, one favored by the horses and chervines as well as children. She held it out to the rabbithorn. Delicately the beastie sniffed the offering and then, as though deciding she was harmless, he relaxed and began to nibble the tidbit. Caselin giggled. The soft fur of the rodent's muzzle tickled her palm as he searched for more.

"All gone," she said with a gentle sigh, holding both hands open.

The rabbithorn looked somewhat disappointed, but allowed her to pet him before starting about his business again—to find food while the grazing was good.

The village youngster laughed in delight as she watched it go; then she got up and ran lightly back to where she had left her morning's gathering of berries.

Margali would be pleased with her, she knew, for she was more than fond of the berries, and Caselin had found a whole thicket of them. True, it was a good two hours walk upslope of the village, but the other children would be happy to have a day's freedom to wander the valleys and slopes gathering berries. Life was hard in Les Owen. But then, where was it not in the Hellers?

Caselin paused for a moment by a small stream to drink. The water was icy cold and numbed her tongue, but the sensation pleased her. Caselin was a happy child. Margali, the wise woman who had fostered her since her birth, was free enough with the girl and kind-hearted, and at ten Caselin was well loved by the villagers and children alike for her gentle spirit and loving temperament. If she was spoiled, she was not vindictive or cruel, and she returned favors done her in her own manner.

She looked thoughtfully at the silver sparkle of the stream, thinking how nice it would be to laze away the afternoon lying in the cool damp grass, watching the quick bright fish as they darted through the play of light and shadow. She sighed, remembering that Margali had sent her to look for herbs and flowers which were needed to replace her healing stock. They would be more than needed come winter, and it was a pleasant enough task to occupy an afternoon.

She had just loosed the other sack from her belt and stooped to pluck up a handful of feverwort from a shady place near the stream when she heard a sharply keening cry. It was faint, seeming to echo from deep in the forest on the edge of which the stream ran. Slowly she rose, listening intently for another cry, but she heard no such sound; rather, almost too soft to hear, came a pitiful mewling whine, as if some creature were in terrible pain.

She stood frozen in indecision. She had been warned repeatedly, as had all the children, that she must never enter the deep forest. There were dangers that lurked there in the forms of great carnivorous beasts, or worse, so that even the adults would not willingly venture into it. Living all of her life beneath its awesome shadow, Caselin had a great fear of the forest. Still she could not bear the sound of a creature in pain.

Finally resolve hardened in her small heart. She could not walk away from this creature's need for her own safety or fear; if she did she would never be the same person she had been, and she knew she would grow to hate the weak thing that she had become. Strange insight for a child of ten.

With a deep breath Caselin tucked the sack back into her belt. Leaving the berries where they lay, she gathered up her skirts to cross the stream and enter the forest. She moved lightly beneath the ancient trees, hardly daring to breathe lest she disturb the towering conifers, or whatever dangers lurked within their shadows. Every few feet she would stop and listen for the tormented sound that drew her ever on. At length she began to shiver; the trees, dark resinous pillars with blue-gray clustered boughs, cut off the warmth of the ruddy summer sun. Slowly and quietly Caselin pulled open the coarse sacking she had tucked into her belt and wrapped it about her as best she could, knotting it to leave her hands free.

She had come quite some way by then, and the sound was nearer now, though weaker, as though its source were near to the end of its strength. With determination many might have thought suited to one older, she pressed on, moving more quickly and with less caution. In the back of her mind grew the thought that she must not be caught in the forest by night. She could be of no use to the creature or herself in the dark, and that thought wakened her fear of the gloomy forest until it seemed to smother her. She began to run.

The underbrush grew thicker and more tangled, so that she had to force her way through it. The branches snatched at her hair and clothing until her once neatly plaited hair was all but undone, and her clothing disordered and soiled with resin stains and dirt. Still she pressed on, a sense of urgency welling up inside her.

At last she stopped, out of breath and near to despair. Surely she would have found what she sought by now, unless she had lost her direction. Wiping frustrated tears from her flushed and grimy cheeks, she sank down in the fragrant carpet of pine needles. *Perhaps*, she thought, *if I rest and then think very calmly I shall find my way*. It was what Margali had always told her to do, and she had a great respect for her foster mother's advice, so she sat back, pushed the hair out of her face, and thought.

It was a minute or two before Caselin realized that she could no longer hear the sound that had brought her so far. At first she panicked, but she quickly put this aside. *No,* she said sternly to herself. She would still find her way. *In all the time I have followed it, the sound has never changed direction. So,* she reasoned, *if I keep on in the same direction I will find it.* Calm once again, she got up and straightened her clothes and hair as best she could and started on. She didn't notice that the forest had grown noticeably darker.

When next she stopped to rest, she sat listening intently, sure that she must be near. She had gone more slowly this time, for fear in her haste she might overlook what she sought. Her patience was rewarded: there was a scrabbling sound and then the cry again, weaker, but clear enough to tell her that she was very near indeed. Blessing the goddess as she rose, she started on with renewed spirit, and relief. It was with a sense of triumph that Caselin pushed her way through the last barrier. Her joy was short-lived. She froze with terror.

At first she could only see the grotesque feathered figure, its eyes maddened with pain. Her heart pounded like that of the rabbithorn she had earlier coaxed, and all of her instincts told her to flee, but she couldn't move. When it didn't attack her, she relaxed ever so slightly and began to look more closely at the creature. It was indeed a Ya-man—but this one lacked the height of the demons that had attacked the village in savage rage with the coming of the ghost wind. No, this creature was only a little taller than she was herself, though savage looking and birdlike.

It made no move, only stood there eyeing her, so that finally Caselin came a step closer. With a small cry, the birdling thrashed about weakly and then was still.

Cautiously the girl drew nearer to discover that the creature had blundered into one of the snare traps that the woodsmen used to catch the animals whose pelts were their livelihood. Startled as the thing began its struggles with new ferocity, she stepped back. *Well, there's no choice.* She would have to free it or it would die. Summoning all of her courage, Caselin took a deep breath and stepped forward, placing one hand firmly on the creature's shoulder, so that it could not thrash around so while she examined the trap.

"Be still," she said, as evenly as she could, seeking to calm it with her voice as she would a wounded dog. "I do not seek to harm you." It looked steadily at her, its beak poised to strike—but it did not. Rather, a trembling ran through its fragile-seeming body.

Caselin shrank from the feel of the blood-matted feathers, but held firm as she examined the bulwark of wood and iron that held the creature pinned. It had never been meant to hold anything as large as the bird-man, and so had caught the creature in the door and frame-work as it snapped shut. The catch had jammed or the thing's struggles would have freed it eventually. Unfortunately it had been caught in a tangle of wood and wire which mercilessly constricted its chest and one shoulder, so that it was slowly smothering. Its struggles gave it momentary space for breath, but it was now too weak to fight.

Letting her hand slip from the Ya-man's shoulder, Caselin stooped down to examine the mechanism of the catch. The creature was now watching her without fear.

"Nope," she said, shaking her head. "It's really jammed." She looked thoughtful for a second; then, looking around, she picked up a stout branch, testing it against her leg before wedging it into the catch mechanism.

It was hard work for a child, and once her makeshift lever broke and had to be replaced; but at last, with the sound of rending wood it gave. The door panel swung slowly forward.

Sweating from the effort, the girl stepped back. She half-expected the Ya-man to turn on her, but after all that she was too tired to care. The creature only sank slowly to the ground with a small whistling noise. Exhausted, Caselin sat down next to it, feeling clammy, dirty, and sore. *What now?* she thought, as she looked around at the thickening dusk. It was too late to go back, so she just sat there.

When she had rested a little, she knelt up wearily to examine her companion's shoulder. The bleeding had stopped and the wound was crusted over. *That's good*, she thought. Margali had told her that you could die if you bled too much. When she laid her hand gently on the creature's chest, she could feel that its heartbeat was strong and slow, and its breathing, though still somewhat labored, was easier. She wished there was something more she could do for it, but without even a stream or spring nearby, she couldn't do so much as fetch water for it.

That thought wakened her own thirst, and with it, hunger. Judiciously she looked about the clearing. There were berries in plenty, so food would be no problem. She rose, slowly so as not to alarm her patient, and began stripping the darkish globes from their branches and cramming them into her mouth. The sweet sticky juice ran down her chin, its moisture easing her thirst as the berries filled her stomach. When she had eaten her fill, she scooped some extra handfuls into her skirt, taking them to the Ya-man. It made wistful sounds as it scented the fruit, and allowed her to feed it. This was a slow process; but Caselin kept to it patiently, as she supported the bird-creature into a semi-sitting position. It was surprisingly lighter than it looked.

When they were finished, it lay back down, and she went to sit huddled against a tree where she could watch the creature. By now the clearing was quite dark and cold. With a shiver, Caselin drew the sack cloak closer and sat back to wait out the dawn, listening fearfully to the sounds that haunted the night.

Caselin woke to the sound of a whistling call, with the misty light of morning in her eyes. She sat up suddenly as she realized that the Ya-man was standing over her—but its attention was elsewhere. Groggily she stood up, shaking out her skirt, to be startled by another of the birdlike cries, this one from outside the clearing. She stood, statue-still, hardly daring to breathe, as a second gaunt and feathered figure entered the open space. Obviously an adult, the newcomer stood fully seven feet tall, and was as terrible as the ones that had attacked the village. She remembered watching them through a crack in the shutters as they had ravened and howled outside. This one, seeing her with its wounded nestling, seemed fierce indeed.

Terrified, Caselin would have run, but the young one she had tended grasped her arm in its taloned hand. Frail as it looked, it had the strength of a fully grown human. Calmly, it issued a series of hoarse trills. The elder answered, eyeing Caselin with what she now thought was a certain amount of curiosity. She was breathing easier now, and when the youngster dropped its hold on her arm she made no move to flee, but watched with wonder as it joined the adult. Both looked at her then, bobbed their heads in a curiously human gesture, and turned to go, the taller supporting the smaller, whose one arm hung limp. They walked with a weaving gait.

"Good-bye," Caselin called softly after them, her wonder cresting to regret at the parting. She stood for a long time, just looking after the way they had gone, then at last she too departed the clearing, turning back the way she had come.

The sun was strong, and she felt sure she would have no trouble finding her way to the forest's edge by following its guide. She walked boldly, without the fear that had dogged her steps the day before. There was beauty in that strange dark place as well as danger, and she knew that someday she would return—perhaps even see her strange companion of the night once more, though she doubted that.

I wonder, she thought as she walked, *who would believe my tale? No one, probably,* she decided, *except Margali.* Nor would she even tell her foster mother, for she knew deep inside her that what had passed between herself and the birdling was best left untold, a secret thing she would keep and treasure always.

She thought again of her foster mother and hurried her steps. Margali would be worried, and there was so much to do. As she looked about at the brooding giants of the forest she couldn't suppress a light trill of laughter at her new-found freedom. With luck, she would be home in time for lunch. Lightly she pattered on.

Probably the finest single writing talent uncovered by the Friends of Darkover is that of Patricia Mathews. She lives in Albuquerque, and is another of the women mentioned in the introduction who manage to juggle housekeeping, young daughters, full-time paid work, and an attempt at a writing career.

In this story she uses her concept of the Free Amazons to clarify her own view of the world we live in, and the place of women in that world and all other possible worlds. One of the main functions of science fiction, as I see it, is to experiment, in safety and on paper, with the designing of other worlds and mockups for society. "There Is Always an Alternative" took its title, and its theme, from a brief interchange in *The Shattered Chain*; the heroine, Magda, has encountered a group of Amazons, who are discussing the punishment given to a couple of prostitutes who attempted to pass themselves off as Free Amazons, thus possibly casting discredit on the Amazons.

Magda said "I have always heard that a *grezalis* follows her trade because she is too stupid to learn any other, so it may have been a lesson wasted.

"You were too hard on them," Sherna said, "It is the foul old pervert who runs that place that I would have treated so."

"On the contrary, I think you were too easy on them," said Jaelle. "Shaming such women is useless; if they were not dead to shame, they would never have been in such a place."

"All women are not made harlots of their free will," Sherna argued. "They must earn their bread somehow."

Camilla's voice was harsh, rasping like a file. "There is always an alternative," she said, in a voice that effectively shut off comment.

In this story, one of the very few openly feminist statements made about Darkover (for most serious feminists regard Darkover as too stiflingly

40

patrist a society for their attention) Mathews tell of the panic reaction suffered by the narrowest kind of man when women step out of their traditional role; and suggests one of the ways in which the Guild of Renunciates, also called the Guild of Free Amazons, might have come into existence.

THERE IS ALWAYS AN ALTERNATIVE

by Patricia Mathews

These were hard times to be a Guardsman, I reflected as we drove the screaming mob back. Their leader, a wild-eyed, shaven-headed freak, stood on a box howling obscenities which dribbled into incoherence as the sorceress reached into his mind for the archetypes that had most power over him and reflected them back in their most potent form.

What did they want? The destruction of all society, of everything good and decent, of everything which made us great, that's what they wanted, I reflected sourly as we cleaned up after the mob. It would be good to get home, to see my little brother again and to take my boots off. I'd heard he was married, a girl of good family from somewhere off in the North, whose house had fallen on hard times. That's what he said; I only hoped it didn't mean she had a pack of greedy kinfolk. We aren't rich, but we do very well.

I saw the work finished, and headed for Rafe's home without sending any word ahead. I wanted to surprise him, and if you must know, didn't want to spare the time; I was bone-weary and home-hungry.

He had a house halfway between the center of the city and the outskirts, a good solid house with a heavy carved door and well-tended plants around it. Either he had a good gardener, or a good wife. The house, and everything I saw, was neat and clean and looked comfortable; I was looking forward to resting in this new sister's domain.

A small child was the first to meet me. "I'm Maellen," she said, and looked at me with the grave eyes of four. "My mommy's coming right away."

The next one down was a woman I couldn't believe I was seeing here. My mouth opened, I would have spoken, but my brother followed her, looking as happy as a puppy. "Dan, Dan, my wife Annilda and her daughter Maellen. She was a widow," he added. Well, she had to tell him something, I imagine.

Annilda is not a common name. You hear it on the sea-coast, and that was where I met her. If she was a widow, she was certainly earning her own bread.

I watched Annilda throughout supper while Rafe chattered on, oblivious; he thought she was a good woman; he thought she was a good wife. She certainly was a good actress. Her talents even extended to pretending to make a good home and be a good mother to the bastard brat she'd foisted on him. I watched, and listened, and heard her answer in the tones any wife would use, and take pains to include me in the conversation like any hostess. She even advised him on business matters. I thought I would be sick.

"What's wrong with your brother, dear, he's so silent?" she asked, while my head shrieked, *Liar! Liar! You know damn well what's wrong, whore, are you going to brazen it out now?*

I caught her alone sometime during the evening. She gave me a cold and haughty look. "Take your hands from me," she said in a soft voice.

"Where do you get the right to tell any man to take his hands away, Mistress Annilda?" I asked, accenting the title so she could not mistake it.

As cool and brazen as all her kind, she said, still softly, "Because I have always loathed it—sir." Her hand moved in something she could only have learned on the waterfront, and in a blaze of pain I reached for her.

"Dan, are you mad?" my brother exclaimed, taking my arm. "Annilda, please excuse him, he's on the front lines of this strange civil war our world is fighting, each fragment against the other; I sometimes think the only thing that keeps us from rending each other in shreds is the family."

"Everybody is in revolt except the women," Annilda said with a strange smile.

Rafe laughed indulgently. "You women have nothing to

revolt against or for! Except more loving attention from your poor negligent menfolk!"

I saw Annilda's face, as bitter as an old whore, mocking, suddenly smoothed over with sweetness as she touched Maellen's hair. *Whore! Liar! Brat!*

I cornered her the next day, blazing in outrage at the way she had wormed her way into my family, determined to expose her for what she was. My poor brother! She didn't whimper or plead for mercy; she did, of course, try to deny it. After all, her whole easy life here was riding on it.

"I'll say your sufferings have turned your brain," she said, still softly, though at dinner her voice was not noticeably soft. "I'll say it was a chance resemblance that misled you. I am not uncommon in looks."

"And I, Mistress, can produce ten Guardsmen anywhere to swear to what you are."

"Were. Was once. And now I am not, not in deed and not in spirit. Are you what you were at eighteen? Can people not change? Must they forever be locked into what they loathe?"

"Were, then, if you so prefer. And when my brother learns of this, it will break his heart. I offer you the choice, Mistress. Disappear, make up some tale, or force me to tell."

"From now on," she said in a heavy voice, "I do nothing unless forced. Speak, you vicious beast; destroy his happiness and mine; force a helpless child to lose mother or father."

"I doubt that brat you've foisted on him knows who her father is," I snarled, determined to put the defiant wretch in the place she rightfully deserved.

The scene was one I would never wish to repeat. Poor Rafe begged, stunned and shocked. The whore he had married said in that soft voice she had only used with me hereto, "It was that, steal or starve. I tried all three. I worked as a maidservant; the only work a woman without kinfolk to employ her could get. I was chaste; have you ever heard of a chaste maidservant? Now I know why you have not. The rough jokes, the brutal handling; I cried out against it and was dismissed, with sneers and scorn, as a little troublemaking slut. Then there was Maellen."

"Your nameless brat!"

"Is there a name for *Child of an Armed Guardsman?* Oh, I was in a trap, and unless I killed both her and myself, what way out was there? Oh, yes, it's true. And it seems I can't put it behind me as I long to do."

Maellen went over to Rafe and begged, "Don't cry, Dada!"

He shoved her backward, howling, "How dare you teach your whore's brat to call me Dada?"

Annilda gathered Maellen to her, then, in one quick motion, snatched my dagger. I gaped and cried out, "Are you mad?"

"To cut her throat and mine before you? I should do it; what else is left? We should have been men and boys to . . . does your serving lad have an extra shirt and breeches? Rough work clothes." She took the sword and began to hack the child's hair.

These tales of women cutting off their braids to serve as bowstrings ignore the long time such a move would take. My brother, moving like a walking dead man, handed his false wife a scissors; she finished the job and began on her own while I retrieved the sword. Rafe came back with the clothes, and, from heaven knows where, a set to suit a child. They were ragged, such as labourers wear. She stripped before me and put them on. Rafe was shocked.

"My brother, Annilda!" he protested.

"He can see what he's flung down a penny to use," she snapped. "Merciful Avarra, what a vile hypocrite you are, Danvar of the Guards; contemplate your daughter by a whore, stripped and bleeding and used by every passing brute, and spat upon by those same brutes later, dream of it at night, for somewhere, within a few years, that dream will come true, and you will know the details beyond all forgetting."

She dressed herself and the child, stripped off all her ornaments, and went, barefoot, out into the world. My brother broke and wept. I went to comfort him

"Get out! I never want to see your face again," he told me, snarling, weeping. "Oh, you did what you had to, but—get out!"

I left, weeping myself inside my soul, for the younger brother so betrayed. Gods above, the woman acted as if she were the one wronged, not us! "What will become of me?" she whined, like any whore, "What will become of my child?" As if that was anything to us! "What can I do, what could I do? Tell me how I may escape this." she said. Then, "At least, this assures your kind of an endless supply of desperate maids for your brutal use! But not me, never again, *never again!*"

And she laid the curse on me she did, as if I had ever had a daughter, or should ever have one.

I saw her once working alongside a gang of men, acting like a lad and taken for a lad, and my gorge rose. I went to the gang boss and told him what she was; she came to me later and snarled, "Why are you persecuting me? Are you that determined to keep me in the cesspool you created for me?"

Her curse had been working, and I said, "Whose child is Maellen?"

"Mine! Maellen daughter of Annilda, none other. Now go; I have a knife and on the waterfront I learned to use it! Ay! A pig!" she cried out, and three of the most hideous women I have ever seen came up behind me, armed with knives. One was a tough, muscular fishwife with a disfigured face; one a raddled whore in men's clothes. "My roommates," she said succinctly. I went.

I heard rumors later that some woman was down in the lowest quarter of the city, taking in drunkards and addicts and whores, beggar-girls and their like, and organizing them. Most of the men thought it was a good joke, and teased about the consequences of the city's whores going on strike. They knew, of course, exactly how to break the strike, and so did I. Besides, with all the other movements abroad these days, all with destruction their aim, nobody was going to take seriously the babblings of a handful of women—and that sort of women, at that!

Then, the tales had it, they were forming a society of Amazons, to live without men, and revenge themselves on men for all they had suffered at male hands. *They* had suffered! Consider how one of their number had shattered the only family I ever had, and broken my poor brother's heart! What sort of vindictive, merciless bitches could they be?

I was sent North again soon; my commander told me it would be better for all concerned. I didn't come back for two years, and then it was to another riot. Women were marching down the street, housewives in plain gowns and fishwives in rough work skirts and tunics, and few gentlewomen in riding dress, and many, many of them in men's or boys' clothing or a strange wonderful compromise between the dress of women and that of men. They were singing.

"What's all this about?" I asked the senior man on duty.

"They want to rule with men, and be hired out on jobs with men," he said, looking at them, "and be free from rape, seduction, and men's rule. That bunch is in no danger."

In truth, they were not an attractive lot. None of them had painted their faces or adorned themselves with jewelry, and the general expression was that of an angry foster mother with a rod in store. I shivered.

"We want our rights, and we want them now," they chanted, *"We want our rights and we don't care how!"*

Then, as we charged, they started throwing rocks. The sorceress began probing the mind of the leader, a tall, magnetic-looking woman in man's clothing. Suddenly she tore off her veil, crying, "Oh, no! Oh, my sisters!" and ran into the street. No one could hold her; no one would touch a sorceress.

We broke up that mob. Not the next. How do you charge a mob of women?

It ended with Annilda herself invited to talk to the lords of the land, to present her demands, and I shuddered at the thought of a whore sitting in the high councils of our government. That was when I turned in my commission and retired to our family's landholding in the far mountains. Let the world turn upside down without me!

And why, when Annilda left the Council chamber, did she nod to me, and say, "We have Captain Danvar to thank for this, too, my sisters." Why?

I swear the woman must be mad.

Eileen Ledbetter was one of the first Friends of Darkover to write apocryphal Darkover fiction. "Darkover Summer Snow," was an attempt to recapture the first meeting of Lew Alton and Regis Hastur, characters in *The Heritage of Hastur*. She had so deftly recaptured my own view of these characters that the story was weirdly compelling even to me; I had to remind myself that I had written the story of their meeting otherwise, even though it had never been published. And now, in spite of myself, Eileen's story has become so much a part of "my" Darkover that when I think of Lew and Regis, I find myself taking it for granted that their meeting, and their early friendship, may indeed have happened exactly as Eileen said it did!

Of course, my earliest admonition to Eileen, when some months later she visited San Francisco and paid me a call, was that she should begin working on her own stories, rather than writing into someone else's world. She had done so; but while she was writing a story (which I haven't yet seen) laid in her own fantastic imagination she wrote me, one day, and said, in effect, "Look what I found." I giggled nonstop as I read Eileen's story of Durraman and his donkey . . . based, of course, on a proverb quoted once or twice in the stories, to the effect that something, or someone, was as stupid—or as dead—as Durraman's donkey.

In my mind, of course, the proverb had been only a way of evoking alien color; I had, as I'd admitted once in an article on the Darkover books, "No idea who Durraman might have been, or why he kept donkeys." Later, my husband, Walter Breen, suggested to me (and I think it found its way into the Darkover Concordance) that the stupid and long-dead Durraman's donkey might have been the one who starved to death between two bales of hay because he couldn't make up his mind which one to eat first!

Eileen had another idea, and that is another story . . . which I'm delighted to present here!

47

About Eileen, personally, I know only that she is in her middle twenties, that she is a pretty, dark-haired and vivacious young woman, and that, at one time, she was a stewardess for Allegheny Airlines. She is active in Darkover fandom's first council, Arilinn, located in New England, and attended the first Darkover convention wearing the costume of a Free Amazon.

And I know, too, that she has the gift for telling an amusing story! All too many of the young writers who try their wings at the writing of apocryphal Darkover fiction are given to grim tragedy, even melodrama. This is good in its own way; but I feel that a gift for humor and the light touch is rarer and almost priceless to a writer, and I certainly hope that Eileen keeps on writing; a gift like this shouldn't be wasted!

THE TALE OF DURRAMAN'S DONKEY

(As it is told to the Children of the Domains by their Nurses)

by Eileen Ledbetter

Carry false coin for thieves

—Traditional proverb

Many years ago, in the land of the Seven Domains, there lives a young Comyn lord known as Damar Aillard. One day, a rumor reached his ears concerning a remote village at the very edge of the Domains known as Candermay. It was a lovely, picturesque place where Damar had spent many happy hours as a child on hunting trips with his father; but it was whispered there was trouble now in the peaceful village. Damar was grieved to hear it; and so, being a brave and resourceful young lord, he decided to undertake the long ride to Candermay to offer whatever aid he could to the afflicted town.

It was a long, hard journey, but at last the little village came into view. Damar reined in his steed and stared ahead in shock and dismay. What had once been a lovely, prosperous town was now a place of poverty and ruin. The pretty little shops and houses were shabby and in disrepair, the gardens lay untended and choked with weeds, and little children, barefoot and ragged, played with mangy puppies in the muddy streets. "What has happened here!" cried Damar to himself.

As he rode into the village, handsome and resplendent in his Comyn finery, with his red hair blazing in the sunlight, the children stopped their games and stared up at him in silent awe. He felt suddenly ashamed of his wealth and good fortune, and thought, *I will do everything I can to keep these good people, for surely some ill luck has befallen them.*

He heard doors clattering open, and in a moment all the men of the village came running from their homes, up the streets, toward him. They were as ragged as the children, but they came jubilantly, welcoming him with outstretched arms, hope dawning in their anguished eyes for the first time in many days.

Damar recognized a familiar face from his childhood and beckoned the man forward. He was Ferrick, the elected mayor of Candermay.

"Ferrick," Damar said, "explain to me quickly what terrible thing has happened here, for I remember how the beauty of your town was your greatest source of pride."

"Oh, Lord Damar, it is dreadful—simply dreadful!" cried Ferrick, wringing his hands in despair. "For many moons now, we have been at the mercy of an evil, terrible man, called Durraman of the Dry Towns—may Zandru send a thousand scorpion whips to sting him! He calls himself a trader when in truth he is a thief, a pirate, a plunderer! He rides into our town with his great gang of men and takes what he will: our food, our wealth, even. . . ." The poor man's voice broke. "Even our women. And we can do nothing to prevent it. His men are cutthroats, trained in the fighting arts—while we have always been a peaceful town, secure in our remote location. The second time he came, our men tried to take a stand, but we were reduced to half our number in less than a minute and forced to surrender. And still he comes again and again, as if to squeeze blood from a stone! We can go on no longer, *vai dom*, and now— now. . . ." Ferrick grew even more agitated and his voice rose in pitch to near hysteria. "We have reports that Durraman and his gang ride this way again and will be here before the afternoon. Oh, *vai dom*, what shall we do? You must help us! Please!"

As Damar listened to the story, his mouth set in a hard, tight line, and a light in his gray eyes glinted like steel. "Yes, I will help you, Ferrick, and with pleasure! Here is what you must do." He raised his voice and spoke to the waiting men. "All of you, go to your homes; take your women, children, and animals, and lock yourselves in. Do not come out until the word is given. Ferrick, pick two of your men and go to meet Durraman as he rides into town. Tell him a Comyn Lord has come, alone and unarmed, who will meet with him and give him anything he desires in exchange for leaving the village at peace. That should be enough of a prize to whet his greedy appetite! Tell him I will meet with him in the yard of the old inn, and he too must come alone and unarmed. He has my word as a Comyn Lord there will be no ambush. Tell him his men may hold the three of you hostage until their leader returns unharmed." He smiled at them reassuringly. "Trust me in this, dear friends, for I have a plan and perhaps you will be free of this Durraman once and for all. Now go quickly!"

The men did as they were told, scattering toward their homes, scooping up children, puppies, and clucking fowl on the way. In moments the street was deserted except for old Ferrick and Damar.

"Before you go to choose your men, old friend," said Damar, "answer me one question, as strange as it may sound. Is there in the village an animal—perhaps one old and useless, doomed to slaughter?"

Ferrick thought for a moment, looking puzzled; then suddenly he brightened. "Aye, there is at that, *vai dom!* Piedro the trapper has an old donkey he planned to butcher for food for the dogs. I cannot understand your interest, for the beast could be of no other use to anyone. Since the day it was born, it has had a vile temper; and now that it is old, blind and lame, its disposition has grown even worse. Yesterday, it lashed out with its hooves at a young boy and broke the child's arm. Piedro knew then that the time had come to do away with it. It is so old, I doubt the creature has many days left anyway. But why do you ask, *vai dom?* How can an old donkey possibly be of any use to you?"

A slow smile spread across Damar's handsome face. "Why, this is better than I had hoped! I will answer all your questions later, Ferrick. For now, just make haste and procure that donkey for me. Bring it to the inn yard where I will meet you, and tell Piedro I will pay him well."

Ferrick ran to do as he was told, but Damar saw his puzzled worried look and thought, *The poor old fellow thinks I have gone mad. I only hope my plan works.*

A short while later, Damar was camped in the inn yard with all the possessions he had carried with him spread around him. Suddenly a fearsome braying assaulted his ears, and looking up, he saw Ferrick coming toward him, leading the sorriest looking creature Damar had ever seen. It was a gray shaggy donkey, knock-kneed and rheumy-eyed, with long evil-looking teeth protruding over slack lips, and ridiculously sway-backed.

"He is all yours, *vai dom,*" said Ferrick, handing him the lead rope. "But by the Blessed Cassilda—*why?*"

"Later, Ferrick, later," said Damar, laughing. He reached out and patted the shaggy beast's neck, keeping well back from the wicked teeth. "Well, old fellow," he whispered into the drooping ears, "perhaps you can be of one last service to us yet. . . ."

The sun had reached its apex when Damar finally heard a boisterous commotion out on the street, and knew the infamous Durraman had arrived. He did not have long to wait before a huge, sandy-haired, rough-looking man strode through the gates into the courtyard, sneering and bellowing, "I've heard there is a Comyn Lord here to bargain with me!"

"Here, Dry Towner!" Damar stood and faced his adversary, tall and unfearing.

Durraman looked him up and down, then his ugly scarred face broke into a distasteful grimace. "So this is a great Comyn lord! Why, you are hardly more than a beardless boy! Did they think to send a boy to do a man's job? Where are the rest of your men . . . lord?" He spoke the word as an insult.

"There are no other men, Dry Towner. I came alone to this village as you have been told. My word is good, and I wish only that you deal with me and leave the rest of the village in peace."

Durraman's eyes glinted suspiciously. "I have heard something of you Comyn. It is rumored that those of your caste are part sorcerer; but I have always had too much intelligence to believe such superstitious drivel. But what of that, my lord? Is there truth to the rumors? Perhaps you mean to kill me with some sorcerer's trick?"

Damar smiled gently. "I do not intend to kill you, Dry Towner, and I doubt I could even if I would, for those of my kind possess more science than sorcery, I fear. I wish only to bargain with you for the freedom of this town. Their plight has touched my heart." His voice grew suddenly stern and harsh. "It is a wrong and wicked thing you do here, Durraman!"

Durraman's fists clenched into huge beefy knots. "I am not in the mood for your moralizing, Comyn pup!" he snarled dangerously. "I can do my own! The power commands the right—I have the power, therefore I am right. Simple, isn't it?"

"Yes," said Damar, and his voice was very low. "I have divined the rules of your game, Dry Towner, and I mean to play by them."

Durraman's face lit up in gleeful contempt. "Then, since we are in agreement, let us proceed to business. I believe I am going to enjoy this! Now, what wealth has a foolish Comyn lord to offer me—for foolish you are indeed!"

Damar pointed to his possessions spread out on the ground. "As you can see, I have a great deal of copper, and I could procure more. Jewels I have also, and a fine steed. All together, more wealth than you can extract from this threadbare little town, Dry Towner; and you may have it all—all, that is, except for that old gray donkey tied over there in the corner."

Durraman stared for a moment in amazement, then he threw back his head and roared with laughter. "Now, what would I do with that miserable creature, Comyn?" he finally managed to gasp through his mirth. "Have you taken leave of the little sense you may have?"

"Oh, do not be so quick to laugh, Dry Towner," Damar said very seriously. "It so happens this 'creature,' as you say, possesses a most marvelous secret."

Greed suddenly hardened Durraman's face. "What secret, Comyn?"

Damar shifted uneasily. "I am not supposed to tell it."

"Why not?"

"My family has forbidden it. They would not have the knowledge of their hidden strengths and talents bandied about."

Durraman loomed over the younger man threateningly. "Nevertheless, I think you will tell it!"

Damar chewed nervously at his lip and dug at the ground with the toe of his boot. At last he sighed, "I see the position I am in. Very well, Dry Towner, I will tell." He glanced furtively over his shoulder, as if he knew spies lurked in every shadow; then he leaned forward, almost to Durraman's ear, and whispered, "It flies."

Durraman shot him a suspicious penetrating glance. "What was that, Comyn?"

"I said, the beast—it flies."

Once again, the huge Dry Towner threw back his head and howled. "You expect me to believe that! Why, that knock-kneed, broken-down old creature can hardly walk! You are even more stupid than I first thought!"

Damar shrugged and turned away. "Very well, don't believe me, then."

As quickly as a striking snake, Durraman's hand reached out and closed over Damar's wrist. His grip had the strength of a vise. He yanked the younger man close and hissed into his face. "You think you can play tricks with me, Comyn? You have spoken your fine words, now prove them!"

Damar drew back in consternation. "Truly I cannot! The secret of its power has been in my clan for years. I cannot reveal it—I am sworn!"

"You will reveal it, Comyn, or at a word from me, three men will die—and you will follow close behind."

Damar's eyes narrowed and his mouth came up in a thin tight smile. "You are a hard and persuasive man, Durraman—I expected no less from you. It appears I have no choice. Very well. But you must watch closely." He strode quickly to the donkey, untied his line, then backed slowly away, intoning in a solemn voice, "Dry Towner, the lineage of this beast extends back through fine and noble stock—raised and trained for years in the secret places of our Domains. Its talents are not to be taken lightly! Hear me as I speak the three magic words!"

Durraman, his greedy eyes fixed on the donkey, did not notice Damar's hand as it crept up toward the front of his

richly embroidered shirt, reached inside, and cupped there a
jewel that glinted with a strange blue light against his breast.

"Evanda arise Avarra!" the young lord cried.

And before their eyes, the donkey slowly began to rise in
the air, higher and higher, until its four legs dangled three
feet above the ground. The stupid beast began to bawl and
thrash madly, while at the same time it began to move forward in a wide circle around the courtyard. It whirled faster
and faster until nothing could be seen but a gray blur spinning high above the ground. It was a most wondrous and
awesome sight.

Durraman's eyes were wide and incredulous. He stood his
ground as the donkey went spinning past, but furtively, he
made a superstitious sign with his fingers. At last, when the
poor beast's braying had reached a deafening pitch, Durraman clapped his hands over his ears, crying, "Enough! I've
seen enough! You are a sorcerer, Comyn!"

"Avarra descend Evanda," said Damar, fingering the blue
jewel. The donkey slowly stopped spinning, then fell back to
earth with an audible thump. It stood panting and swaying
slightly, then it shook itself indignantly, and ambled away,
ears twitching irritably.

"I did not believe you at first, Comyn, but now that I have
seen its talent, I realize it is truly a marvelous beast," said
Durraman, still too intent on the donkey to notice Damar's
pale and sweating brow. "I have underestimated you, perhaps. Well, no more games between us." He licked his lips
greedily. "You said you wished to bargain for the town. Is
your word still good?"

"Of course. You waste your breath asking."

"Then I want the donkey."

"But I asked you to take anything but the beast!" Damar
gasped.

Durraman laughed. "What are your copper and jewels,
Comyn? With this beast I need never want for a fortune
again. This is my bargain; give me the donkey and the town
goes free—forever!"

"Oh, I am loath to do it!" cried the young lord. "My clan
will disown me if I return without the beast! And yet—I
would see this town set free from a brigand such as you!"

"Watch your words, Comyn! I hold you—now—in some
respect, but do not forget, I also hold three men!"

"Well, perhaps I am a fool. But I will take you at your
word, Dry Towner. The donkey is yours, Durraman, in ex-

change for the town; but do not try to take more than we bargained for. My family will accept the beast's loss in this cause, but any further treachery and my kinsmen will be down your neck with a vengeance!"

"I know when I am well off, Comyn," Durraman replied. "The bargain is struck, then. But tell me more about this wondrous animal! What does it eat?"

"The same as any other donkey; but as you can see, it is well on in years, so you must treat it with respect, and not burden it too heavily. More than your weight it could not carry easily in flight. And you must never use its gift lightly. It must rest between demonstrations. A few hours, though, and it will be ready to use again. And remember, the words are 'Evanda arise Avarra,' and 'Avarra descend Evanda.' "

"Ah, Comyn," cried Durraman heartily, and a beefy hand descended on Damar's shoulder, gripping it hard, "it has been a pleasure doing business with you! I had taken all I wanted from this town anyway, and only a strange hunch made me turn this way again! I see it has been a lucky day for me, and a sadder one for you—although we both have what we want, at least! Farewell, Comyn! May we meet again—but not too soon!" Laughing boisterously, he seized the donkey's halter and led it triumphantly from the courtyard.

Damar watched him go, then slumped forward wearily in relief. A few moments later, Ferrick and his two men rushed into the yard, panting and babbling in disbelief. "They are getting ready to leave, *vai dom*," cried the mayor, "with only the gray donkey and no other spoils! And Durraman—Zandru take me to his coldest hell if I am lying—Durraman is laughing as if he would never stop! How did you do it, Lord Damar?"

"It is a long story, Ferrick," said Damar, wearily passing an arm across his young face. "But come! I find I have need of strong refreshment, and I will tell you all about it!" He threw his arm around Ferrick's shoulders in a warm gesture of fellowship. "My friend, I think soon we will all be laughing at Durraman. For if ever two deserved each other, it is Durraman and his donkey!"

When Durraman emerged from the courtyard with only a knock-kneed, mangy old donkey, his men, of course, thought he had gone mad.

"Where is our treasure, Lord?" they cried, looking about them.

"Why, have you no eyes in your heads, you stupid pack of
he-wolves?" Durraman snarled. "Here is the treasure! And, I
warn you, the first man who raises an ill hand toward this
beast will find his head on a pole!"

"Yes, Durraman," they whispered deferentially, for they
had long ago learned to respect his temper; but some of them
made the sign of the cuckoo at each other behind his back.

They took their leave of Candermay, and set out on the
trail, Durraman in the lead, the donkey following behind,
braying belligerently at every step. But when the men saw the
direction they were taking, one of them came forward and
said, "Lord Durraman, are we not going on to Trilltan as we
planned?"

"Of course not, fool! I have no need to plunder more
towns! I have all I want. We will return to Shainsa immediately." He raised his riding-whip threateningly. "Are there
any objections?" There were none the man cared to voice out
loud, of course, and he retreated silently.

The way was steep and treacherous, and at Durraman's insistence, they traveled at a slow pace to keep the old, blind
donkey from putting a foot wrong. Twice it sat down in the
middle of the trail and refused to move until it had rested,
and when the men tried to prod it, it lashed out with snap-
ping teeth.

The men began to grumble and fret, muttering, "At this
rate, we will be caught on these high trails by the winter
snows!" But they dared not speak to Durraman again, knowing that somehow this miserable donkey had softened their
leader's head.

Stopping and starting, they managed three days travel.
They were well into the fourth day, walking along an uneven,
narrow ledge, when, almost under their feet, the trail
crumbled and disappeared, leaving them on the edge of a
rocky precipice; and it was a drop of a thousand feet into the
valley below.

The men bunched up at the brink, milling and cursing.

"The ledge has been washed away!"

"Look, the trail begins at the other side—too far to jump!"

"Now we must retrace our steps!"

"By all the gods, I knew we would never reach Shainsa before the snows!"

Then Durraman began to laugh, and to his men, it was a
frightening, demoniac sound. "You might not reach Shainsa
before the snows—but I will be there tomorrow, warm and

rich!" He signaled impatiently to one of the men. "Bring me my donkey!"

The men watched in awe, their jaws hanging slack, as their leader—who must, they thought, now be truly mad—led the ugly gray donkey to the very edge of the precipice and leaped upon its back. It was a ludicrous sight: the huge, bearded Dry Towner, his legs dangling almost to the ground, atop the sway-backed ignoble donkey. Their jaws dropped even farther, and their eyes grew round, as they saw Durraman raise his whip and bring it down hard on the donkey's rump three times, crying, "Evanda arise Avarra!"

With an outraged bray, the donkey bucked once, then leaped forward—out over the abyss! For a moment it seemed to hang suspended in space; then both beast and rider plummeted like a stone toward the valley below—and it seemed to the men standing on the cliff that they could hear a hysterical voice screaming "Evanda arise Avarra!" over and over and over. . . .

They stood in silence for a few minutes, listening as the last echoes died away. Then, as one, they shrugged their shoulders and rode back the way they had come, never once looking back.

All this happened many years ago; but they say, if you pass the prosperous little village of Candermay on a cold winter's eve, you can hear them, as they sit gathered around the fire, telling the tale of the fine young Comyn Lord who outwitted a Dry Towner with the help of a useless old donkey. No doubt the story grows each time with the telling; but they call it the tale of Durraman's donkey, and they are laughing still.

Susan Shwartz says of herself that she "started reading mythology when I was seven and SF when I was twelve." She grew up in Youngstown, Ohio, which does not sound, offhand, like a center for SF, but she was acquainted in youth with a sister of Edmond Hamilton; and the discerning reader will sense, in this, her first published story, the influence of the writer who was called affectionately by his fans "the old world-wrecker." She attended Mount Holyoke College—"as close to the Free Amazon Guildhouses as I could get," graduating in 1972, and spent several summers at Trinity College, Oxford; then studied for a Ph.D. in English at Harvard, doing her dissertation on the prophecies of Merlin. Currently she is an assistant professor of English at Ithaca College, in upstate New York, teaching Chaucer, Arthurian Literature, and courses in fantasy and science fiction, trying, as she says, "to introduce my students simultaneously to literary criticism and to fandom." She also commented that she would "read anything that didn't get her first," including fourteenth century manuscripts!

Perhaps, then, as a medievalist, it is not surprising that Ms. Shwartz has chosen to deal with the "medieval history" of Darkover and the Ages of Chaos. The theme of "The Fires of Her Vengeance" comes from *Spell Sword* (p. 96) where the Keeper is called Mirella Hastur; in *The Heritage of Hastur* Lew Alton tells virtually the same story, calling the Keeper Marelie, (which shows how oral traditions are passed down, altered by repetition even over a few generations.) Shwartz adds about her story:

"What you have to be aware of, is this; the story of Marelie Hastur is really in verse, and demands *rryl* accompaniment and a good lyric performer. I've translated it into Terran Standard English prose of the late twentieth century and adopted the romance form of Gottfried von Strassburg to do it. Any faults are those of the translator, not of the original singers of tales from whom Damon and Lew originally heard the

58

story. If I can ever get into the Archives at Comyn Castle to study the *MSS*, I'll try to bring out a variorum edition. Now if only I can get a travel grant from the Interstellat Endowment for the Humanities! I can just see them approving a voucher for a return trip starship berth to Cottman IV. . . ."

To which we can only say, "We'd like to come along when you do!"

THE FIRES OF HER VENGEANCE

by Susan M. Shwartz

"Marelie, Marelie! Woe if you cannot kill! And woe, woe, if you should ever wish to!"

"Cleindori!" Marelie cried. The name husked from between lips bitten and fouled with sickness. "Don't leave me."

But the apparition of the old *leronis* who'd trained her guttered out. There were only trees and the snow, clouds and the savage light of the bloody sun. Blood defiled the snow. Hers: well had Cleindori predicted that Marelie Esyllt, princess of Hastur and Lady of Arilinn, could not kill, not even to save herself when *he*, the black-bearded one, dragged her away from the rest of the Kilghard bandit pack and . . . and. . . .

"Now show yourself to the Hali'imyn as a sign of their doom!" he had shouted.

The Keeper who could not, or would not defend herself against rape, people would whisper. *Keeper now no longer.*

Marelie retched dryly, tasted blood, dirt, and snow. Her eyes burned with unshed tears and her cheeks felt feverish with an outrage beyond humiliation. Still she lay face down on the icy ground. Her groin ached. Each muscle felt strained from the fight she had put up (though she had quailed from summoning the lightnings), a fight ending when a blow to her jaw had knocked her senseless. And once she was safely unconscious, he had raped her.

Merciful Evanda, forgive me. How could I use laran to kill?

Contemptuously someone had flung a cloak over her before the bandits had retreated to their Kilghard *forst* and the warleader who had been raiding Arilinn. Zandru wither their manhood! Marelie loathed owing her life to their charity. But why not? Rape the Keeper and the woman is disarmed. No need for her to freeze to death.

Only a dawn ago Marelie had ridden with an escort of City Guardsmen toward the ashes that once had been a village sworn to Hastur. Survivors, so badly burnt that their flesh charred from their dying limbs, moaned of flames leaping from nowhere to ignite their homes. Then the bandits had attacked, bandits who grinned as they forced children trying to flee back into the flames. And over the crackling of the flames and the wail of the dying had come the mad, damned laughter, "Like Naotalba, *vai leronis*, as she twists in Zandru's arms!"

This was no common war. Someone possessed one of the giant artificial matrices and a matrix circle skilled and perverted enough so to misuse it. Most of the matrices tenth-level or stronger had been destroyed; a few, monitored and largely idle, remained insulated in the Towers. Still, the Comyn had always feared this: an illegal matrix surviving the Ages of Chaos and falling into the power of a *laranzu* mad enough to use it for war. Marelie, sworn to defend the Domains with her life against such attack, rode out to investigate.

The bandits had lain in ambush, as if their leader had ordered them to expect her. Brandishing knives and torches, they pounced. The torches spooked the *chervines*, seared her guardsmen. As they writhed on the ground, the bandits had stabbed them. Several others had overpowered her own mount and flung her to the ground to await the pack's captain.

Screams, burning, burning her ears, and shrieking over them the mad damned laughter . . .

Someone had known that the ravaged village and the abuse of *laran* would draw her. And without her, Arilinn—well, Janna, its other Keeper, had nowhere near her strength. Arilinn lay as vulnerable as she had after the beastmind of her attacker had flamed into rage and his hard fist cracked against her jaw.

Who could wish to destroy Arilinn? Marelie thought in desperation. *The Lords were at peace; it must be a madman,*

*an outcast, Zandru savage him! But could even a madman
wish to level the Towers and lord it over devastation?*

Aldones! Were the Ages of Chaos come again?

Such a man was one Marelie wished to kill. Even more,
however, she wished to flee back to Arilinn.

With one rigid arm, she levered herself up. It was the
hardest thing she had ever done. She studied the hills, the
beaten track which ran through the forest. Arilinn lay *that*
way. In fact, she realized, just over that rise loomed the city
gates. Oh, the bandits had been sure, sure that they had disarmed and destroyed her.

Marelie forced herself to sit. She coiled her legs under her,
the throbbing ache in her torn flesh making her a little dizzy.
As she had mastered other pain in the long discipline of her
training, she mastered it. The wind blew and she shuddered.
Despite her revulsion, she forced herself to pull the cloak
they'd left her—heavy, colorless wool bordered with shabby
fur—over shivering shoulders. She would need its warmth in
order to walk to Arilinn. And she craved its concealment: it
was not fitting that the Lady of Arilinn walk abroad in her
Domain with bodice torn and skirts bloodied.

But was she Keeper any longer?

Ah, she exulted, her enemy's ignorance would destroy him
yet! A time of seclusion, time to heal, to forget a little, and
once more Marelie, Lady of Arilinn would twist to her will
the energon rings. Janna the Underkeeper, and Felizia, her
cousin and Arilinn's *rikhi,* would restore her to herself.

Anguish caught her in the belly, doubled her over. Air
forced itself in a tiny keen through tightened lips. The burning, the burning! So many bodies had lain unburied in that
village. With trembling, fumbling fingers Marelie drew her
matrix (*praise Avarra they'd not taken it or she'd have died
in shock!*) from the tatters of her robes. Almost afraid to
look into its flickering depths, she cupped her fingers about it.
The starstone warmed, pulsed to her touch with the rhythms
of her heartbeats. She gazed into it, seeking to visualize her
desire. Arilinn.

The Tower—besieged! Shaken as she was, she could not
penetrate the locked screens of its defense. So far then,
Arilinn stood. But now for herself. She scanned her body
quickly, suppressed a gasp of dismay as she watched the
nerve channels and nodes in her pelvic region pulse red and
sluggishly. Once clear as befitted the purity of a virgin
Keeper, her channels were now tainted It was not fair. She

had not consented, but still her channels were overloaded from the trauma of the rape. The world, she sighed, went as it would, not as she would have it. Nevertheless Arilinn stood. Soon she would be home.

Marelie Esyllt, Keeper and Lady, compelled herself to her feet. How odd her steps felt on the frozen ground. They jarred her ravaged body, but she forced herself to walk. As befitted sorceress and princess she held her head high as she entered the gates of Arilinn. The bloody sun glowered lower on the horizon, touching the distant peaks with flame. A guard shouted, and she flung the noisome cloak's hood back from her face: carven, pale features under the lambent fire of her tangled hair. The challenge died on the man's lips. On she walked.

I am Marelie Hastur, I am not shamed, she chanted to herself. Gladly she would have sobbed like a wounded child in the arms of her foster mother, but she was Keeper and Keepers do not weep. Arilinn's Veil, the rainbow haze so deadly to enemies, shivered before her and she passed through it, feeling the hair on her arms prickle in fear lest the Veil should turn against her, a Keeper no longer virgin, and crisp her with its lightnings.

Footsteps echoed, firm, rapid, deliberate on the stairs of the Tower. A man's footsteps. Despite her knowledge that a man in Arilinn Tower could only be her kinsman, sworn to her, Marelie shrank into a corner. The man's *laran*, however, betrayed her presence to him.

"Marelie! Oh, thank the Lord of Light you're safe!" Amaury Ridenow-Elhalyn, son of a prince, strode toward her, hands outstretched as if to embrace her. She was Keeper: no man might touch her. As she backed against the wall, he remembered and stopped. Marelie raised her hand, touched his fingertips.

"Bandits kidnapped me," she said softly, the crystalline tones of Keeper addressing technician. "My guard was killed, but I managed to escape."

Evanda, let him not doubt the word of a Hastur. Amaury was a technician, ranking just below herself, Janna, and young Felizia. Let him just scan her and he would know instantly. She must distract him.

"They have an unmonitored matrix, tenth-level or stronger," she told him. "Have they used it against the Tower?"

"Oh gods, you could not have known," Amaury groaned.

His face went pale. "We fought, how we fought. Janna—you would have been proud of her. But Janna's . . . she's dead, burnt herself out and we couldn't restore. . . ."

Then there could be no seclusion, no Keeper's aid for Marelie. What Marelie required Felizia alone could not supply. And in conscience Marelie could not withdraw her from the circle in order to try and fail to heal herself: against a tenth-level matrix circle, Arilinn needed its Keeper.

"Avarra grant her peace," Marelie murmured. She saw the fatigue that shadowed Amaury's eyes. "But the others—Felizia, Damon, Arnaud—"

"When Janna collapsed, Arnaud took a lethal back-flow trying to save her," Amaury reported. "The monitors tried to pull him clear: they're still unconscious. We hope they'll survive. But the gods help us tonight if they attack again. I'm, I'm *afraid* that they will."

Prince's son, technician, proud like all the Elhalyn, Amaury *looked* at Marelie. *Be strong, oh be Keeper and protect us*, the gray eyes begged. They were reddened, burning. . . .

Marelie glanced aside, politely ignoring his self-betrayal.

"The city. Tell me," she demanded. Soon she could retreat to the sanctuary of her own rooms, rid herself of the stained robes she wore, bathe, and rest. But her first responsibility was to those sworn to her, circle and city.

"Captain Marius died in the first onslaught. The bandits attacked while we were . . . distracted by the enemy circle. Duvic, *teniente* of the Guard, commands now," Amaury reported. His eyes flashed; he too had been a guardsman once, warrior before he'd turned warlock. "He speaks of *geilt*. . . ."

The word from an obscure Heller dialect was new to Marelie. Amaury translated. "Berserk. They fear nothing, feel no wound, no pain. Hack off the sword hand and they draw dagger with their right. The men are almost unnerved, but Duvic's trying to rally them for an attack again tonight."

He shook his head, dashed a hand through the long copper-gilt hair. "Until you returned, Janna being . . . gone, we hadn't much hope of maintaining the Veil or Arilinn itself." His voice faltered. "It was like a challenge between Towers, lady. Aldones, are the Ages of Chaos come again?"

Marelie, shrinking even from the fingertip touch required, brushed his shoulder. She too had asked that question. But Amaury looked to her to answer it. "I pray not, kinsman," she said. "We will hold them here. No bandits rule in the Domains."

At a run Damon entered the room, his face lighting like the sun when it strikes the pass at Scaravel after a blizzard. Two men in the room! Marelie held herself rigid, suppressed fear and then the relief she felt as Felizia entered after him.

The girl, her brother's eldest daughter, gasped and would have run to her.

"Hold, child!" Marelie commanded. "A Keeper controls herself." Felizia's mouth worked, her face twisted as she attempted to check her panic and relief. They were too much for her, and she burst into half-hysterical sobs. No one touched her: Keeper, sacrosanct.

"Kinswoman, the Guard must know of your return," said Damon, a mechanic with the sturdiness of an Alton backing his trained skill. "The men will fight the better. 'Higher our thoughts, our hearts more keen, our courage sterner as our strength lessens,' he half-hummed, half-quoted from his favorite ballad. May I tell. . . ."

"Yes," said Marelie. She drew herself up, a tall, slender woman, imperial with the *presence* that made the children of Hastur, son of Aldones who is the Lord of Light, seem more than human. "Say to Duvic and our brave Guardsmen that Marelie Esyllt, Lady of Arilinn—"she breathed deeply despite the sobs that would cramp her throat—"sees them and blesses them They shall not be overcome, this I vow!" She raised a grimy hand. "The gods witness it, and the holy things at Hali!"

"Your words brighten the sky, *vai leronis*," Damon whispered the ritual response, bowed deeply, and left.

Do I have a choice? she thought. *I am sworn to defend the Tower and the Domains with my life. And now my life is no longer than a candle's span.*

"Go, Amaury," she said. "Ready the circle. When Liriel rises in the sky, we will gather for war in the matrix chamber. Felizia, *chiya*, retire to your room to meditate and calm yourself. With Janna dead, I must rely upon you."

"But you are tired," Felizia dared to protest. "See—you're limping."

Marelie paused on her way to her rooms. "I need neither your assistance now nor your disobedience," she told the girl. "The *kyrri* will supply what I require."

Someone—probably Amaury—tried to touch her mind. She blocked contact, remembering the brutishness and the pain, the explosion in her jaw that had shattered her consciousness. Nothing showed in her face; the damage, she knew, lay deeper. Her channels were contaminated, and, burning in her heart, twisting in her belly like a firedrake smoldered the urge to kill.

Though the room was now empty, Marelie seemed to feel in it the *presence* of Cleindori, so long dead, who had ruled Arilinn before her, and to hear her words:

"Woe, Marelie, should you wish to kill!"

The *kyrri* pattered out into the Garden of Fragrance where Marelie stood under a tree. Snow and the violet petals from its blossoms drifted down onto her disheveled hair. The nonhuman indicated that her bath was ready.

"Thank you." With the high empathic rating of its kind, the *kyrri* stared at her, something like concern in its green eyes, before it turned away.

Marelie drew one dirty hand to her mouth. A blossom lay upon it and she touched it gently. *Nevermore to see, to smell her garden in flower. . . .*

She had promised to assemble a circle of war in the matrix chamber. Keeper, but no virgin: her channels tainted, but no chance, no time, to clear them. Not with Janna dead and Amaury—she could not expose to Amaury what that beast-bandit had done to her. She was alone and very much afraid. The power of the energon rings generated by the matrices of her circle flowed through her into the screens and relays, power that she alone must forge into a weapon. Using *laran* to kill was dangerous at any time, but now especially . . . now she thought she understood Cleindori's prophecy.

Marelie wanted to kill. But it would mean her death. Only a virgin's channels could handle the energy a Keeper must wield. Oh, certainly, there were stories, fragments from the Ages of Chaos, myths to while away the long nights before Midwinter Festival, of Keepers who turned from their lovers to their work in the circle. But the ritual virginity of the Keeper had been sacrosanct since women, centuries ago, had replaced the *tenerézuin* of Varzil the Good's time: no one thought of disbelieving it. The unchaste Keeper was no Keeper at all. Marelie, despite her resolution, was terrified.

And she was so cold, so dirty.

She entered her rooms and undressed, hastily throwing cloak, torn crimson garments, and her underlinen into a bundle.

"Burn these," she told the *kyrri*, and watched it leave.

The bathwater was warm, delicately scented, and infinitely welcome to her battered body. It even soothed the pain between her legs. She lay full-length in the tub, scrubbing and soaking as if she could remove memory as well as dirt. The *kyrri* came in to attend her, but she waved it away. Naked was vulnerable. In the few hours left to her, Marelie, princess of Hastur, refused to be vulnerable again. Her starstone, freed from its silk and leather sac, lay between her breasts under the water, and she stared at it.

Fire, fire in its depths.

What else could she expect? A battle and victory: but she desired to live and face no woman's pity, no man's whisper. Nor would she leave the Tower she had saved. Hasturs took oath lifelong. Marelie had sworn to be Lady of Arilinn unto death.

After a time she rose and dried herself on the heavy, warmed towels the *kyrri* had left for her. She wrapped herself in a robe, and found food waiting on a small table by the fire. Mechanically she sat and ate. Hunger kindled, and she savored the food as she had not for years. Bathing, eating, and resting, propped against pillows for an hour of meditation, assumed almost ritual significance.

For each, the last time. . . .

The bloody sun was an ember behind the Kilghards when Marelie Esyllt began to dress. Sweet, perfumed oil on her chafed skin, fresh linen, and, over it, the crimson robes of the Keeper. Red for blood, red for fire. The copper and gilt of the embroideries and ornaments at neck and waist glinted like sparks; the gem on her brow flamed. She allowed her starstone to blaze at her throat.

I am fire and air, she whispered to her reflection in the silver mirror. The gray eyes burned back at her as she brushed her long hair. Static made it crackle about the brush; it drifted in red clouds over her slim shoulders. Bodies were of importance to Keepers only as the means of sustaining and accomplishing their work, but Marelie, outraged, going to her death, looked upon herself.

She was beautiful. Beautiful as the Flamehair before the son of Hastur had chained her. Now she, Hastur's daughter, must invoke the burning.

She brushed her hair back, pinned it, and rose. Liriel glowed over her quiet, sealed garden. It was time.

Marelie Hastur's slippered footsteps echoed in the silence of the vaulted matrix chamber.

"I set the dampers to guard us," she heard Felizia say. "But with Arnaud dead, there are no fit monitors, and we can spare no one from the circle."

"Then we shall not have monitors," Marelie said. A monitor would detect the turmoil in her channels, know what had been done to her, stop her, pity her: she would not bear it. She dared not allow it, not with Arilinn to be protected. She raised a hand, quelling protest.

"Damon, the Guard?"

"Duvic can hold the gates against the bandits for a little time if no sorcery is sent against him."

"We shall relieve him quickly."

The violet night shone through the clerestory beneath the ancient wooden vault. Below it only the eldritch flickers of the matrix screens and lattices lit the room, embers in the dark that Marelie's circle must fan to violent life. She raised a hand and the overlight glimmered from her six fingertips, danced madly in the giant artificial starstone she unveiled and set upon the massive table.

She took her raised seat, watched the others join their hands, then convulsively looked away. The werelight of matrices and lattices glanced over the dark woodwork of the cupboards, throwing the figures carved on them into high relief. Marelie found herself studying the figures intently and wrenched her eyes away.

"Begin," she commanded.

The circle's nine survivors, a pathetically small group to master the great matrix, fell into rapport like the layers of a crystal struck by flint to product sparks. In what had always been the only intimacy of her life, Marelie touched each mind.

She raised her left hand. Her mind expanded, focused to receive and seize the energon flows from the rapport circle. Deep within the giant crystal the blue flame began to quiver and pulsate. The ancient screens awoke to violent life.

Then Marelie's mind soared from her body like sparks from a resin tree in flame.

Below her teniente Duvic fought. His sword was notched, reddened to the hilt. He stumbled and fell. In an instant, bandits heedless of their wounds leapt upon him and the white-lipped cadet who bestrode his body. . . .

Flying above the battle, Marelie stretched forth a "hand."

From it leapt the lightning, the lightning. Bandits shrieked as they burned. Again! And the men lurking in reserve jerked and yammered as the lightning consumed them too.

Then Marelie was flying over the gates and the forests. Past the accursed place she had lain—she suppressed memory before Felizia could detect it—*into the foothills. Past the charnel remnant of the village the mad matrix had burned.* She suppressed a moan of anguish at the charred bodies, the smoking roofs below her. A bolt of blue flame obliterated them. Soon the snow would cover the place.

She sought for direction. *To the east.* The bandits—her attacker and their *laranzu*—had a *forst* in the eastern crags. She aimed her thought-self east, felt her "body" grow warm as it rushed through the unresisting night air.

Not yet! she prayed.

Question troubled the circle and she flashed it reassurance.

Again she skimmed over hills. Beyond the foothills towered the Kilghards: stunted trees and, looming over them, crags and peaks. There the kyorebni wheeled and the banshees screamed in terror of the blue-lit forst that glowered beside an abyss. Marelie's eyes maddened and she hurled her lightnings. Again and again. She laughed, the fiery hair of her thought-self shaking in the wind. Now who would laugh last, herself or her enemy?

Walls shattered. In the forst's inmost keep the outlaw circle clasped hands about a great jagged matrix. Keeper in the circle was a flame-haired emmasca. Even through the trance of concentration with which the emmasca sought to defend his circle and destroy the Domains, Marelie saw hate and madness etched into his face like acid burning, burning. . . .

Pressed near him among a throng of entranced followers who loaned him their strength, their belief, stood a man, bulky with muscle, his bearded jaw blue in the matrix fire. Marelie recognized him. Marelie demanded his death.

Briefly she returned to her body in the circle at Arilinn. Lightnings crackled and flashed from matrices to screens, screens to lattices. Ozone and alarm sharpened the air, threatening the calm of matrix trance. She scanned herself, saw the damage the energon flows left as they seared through her body, ravaged her nerves. Her neural ganglia looked like hot coals. She could not live long.

No matter, no matter.

No! It was Amaury's thought.

Yes! she commanded him. *We must end this.*

Woe, woe, a mental voice keened in the heart scalding coronach. Cleindori's voice again, or Amaury? She looked at the technician. In his mind was a truth she had never before noticed. *No time now.*

Again Marelie exploded from her throbbing nerves and body, extended her hands over her enemy First the laranzu, *then the others. First of them, her rapist. Then, one by one, slowly, slowly, all the others, wasters of her Domain. . . .*

Flame speared the *laranzu's* chair. Blackjaw screamed, his clothes afire. He plunged for the outside and the safety of a snowbank, but fell over the cliff. Marelie felt the speed of his fall as if it were her own. She heard him scream against the cold and she exulted. *Was this what Sharra had felt in the instant before Hastur's son bound her with burning chains?*

Marelie laughed, a beautiful savage sound that echoed in the matrix chamber. The fires of her vengeance seemed to glow on the rapt faces of her circle. How still, how beautiful they were! Her laughter rang with triumph; she, defiled, defeated, she had saved them. Satisfaction tossed her consciousness, like a spark in an updraft, high above Arilinn. All around the old city, soldiers straightened, content to be alive. Marelie laughed as she drifted down toward her body.

Then her flesh knew the agony of the burning; but even then, in the last seconds of exultation, she knew that Arilinn was safe.

I made the acquaintance of Elisabeth Waters under circumstances which will be told later, in speaking of the title story of this anthology, *The Keeper's Price*; and since that story comes later in time sequence, I will leave it to that time.

In our recent contest for the Friends of Darkover, for the best-written short story, "The Alton Gift" was one of our prize-winners. Stories were rated and judged on three counts; ten points being allotted for fictional technique, ten for authenticity to the Darkover background, and ten for sheer enjoyability. Of the five judges, three (including myself) rated this story with a full thirty points, indicating that by each of these criteria, they rated the story as highly as possible on a one-to-ten scale. The story lost the first-place prize by a narrow margin of two points (the first prize winner is printed elsewhere in this volume) because *one* judge confessed to a distaste for the grim and macabre ending. Even she gave it high rating for authenticity and technique. No other story drew a "30" rating from more than two out of five judges.

To say anything about "The Alton Gift" would be to lessen its impact. It is a story from the darkest days of the Ages of Chaos; that time of tyranny in which the great families of Darkover, who later became the Comyn, were breeding for the *laran* gifts which later became so essential to their power.

I should add that all stories in the Friends of Darkover contest were submitted anonymously, with the names and addresses of the authors inside sealed envelopes opened only *after* all stories had been judged and the prizes decided upon. Lisa Waters had gone to the trouble of using a typewriter different from the one she used for her letters, and of having the story mailed by a friend in a distant state, so that no postmark on the envelope would reveal the authorship to the judges, two of whom (myself and Jacqueline Lichtenberg) were her close personal friends. I can't speak for Jacqueline; but I was visiting Lisa Waters after the stories had been judged, and asked her, offhand, what story she had written. I ought to say that I had told her that, although the level of revealed *talent* in the contest was high, the general level of technique was *deplorable;* and then I said that there was one story which, for sheer impact and masterly technique, was so far above all the others that I thought it was probably a guaranteed winner. I must compliment Lisa on her powers to dissemble; she kept her face absolutely straight and had just the right note of wistfulness as she wondered aloud who could have written a story with an odd name like "The Alton Gift" . . . later, on that same visit, I said that since the stories had all been judged, there was no harm if she told me what story she had written. When she said, "The Alton Gift" I literally fell over into a chair and gasped.

"You didn't! You're kidding!"

I'd known the talent was there; after "The Keeper's Price," I'd never doubted it. But the original of "Keeper's Price" had been, although powerful and gripping, almost unplotted and chaotic, a mere fragment; I had no idea that Lisa could create a compelling story, masterfully handled, in such a compact space. The worst amateur fault is trying to write a novel in seven pages; the ability and skill to handle a very short story usually comes only with long experience.

I still don't have it; already this preface is almost as long as the story it describes.

THE ALTON GIFT

by Elisabeth Waters

Caillean Alton finished lacing her dress and started to braid her hair, rather awkwardly because this was only the third time she had tried to do it herself. Her hair had been cut short and offered to Evanda the day of the festival which marked Caillean's becoming a woman, and now that it just touched her collarbone and was long enough to braid again, she was considered fully grown and old enough to marry—which, Caillean thought bitterly, was the polite way of saying that now the leroni would decide where they wanted to fit her in their breeding program, and she would be given to the man as if she were a cow or a sheep—and they would call it "her duty to kinsmen and clan." Merciful Avarra!

Her mother entered her room just then, unannounced. Bianca Alton had borne nine children, five of whom had survived infancy and only two adolescence, and she overshadowed her children to the point where disobeying her never occured to them. Caillean really wished she would knock or at least make a little noise in the hall instead of appearing suddenly and making people jump, but she knew that nothing was ever going to make her mother change.

"Caillean, how long do you plan to take to braid your hair?! You're already late for breakfast, and your father wants to talk to you right afterwards!"

Caillean hastily picked up her clasp and tried to fasten the end of the braid, but her hands slipped, and the whole mess began to unravel.

Muttering something Caillean did not quite catch about Durraman's donkey, Bianca quickly and efficiently braided her hair and slipped the clasp into place. "There! Come along, child, don't keep your father waiting."

After a hasty breakfast, Caillean found herself sitting opposite her parents in her father's study.

"Well, Caillean," her father smiled at her, "I'm sure you will be pleased to hear that a husband has been chosen for you. You will marry Dom Bertin Serrais next month."

"You are a very lucky girl," Bianca said. "Fine family, lovely estate; it's an excellent match."

"But, Mother, I don't like him. And I don't really want to get married."

"Nonsense, every girl wants to get married! And it doesn't matter if you like him or not—what does that have to do with marrying him?"

"I don't want to live the rest of my life with someone I don't even like!"

"Why do you *think* you don't like him?" Her father was obviously trying, with limited success, for an attitude of patience with girlish folly.

"He kissed me last midwinter night, and I didn't like it and I wanted him to stop and he wouldn't even listen to me!"

"You should be flattered that he finds you attractive, child," her mother said sharply. "That will be a big help when you are married."

"But I don't want to marry him—or anybody! Look at what happened to Rafaella! She got married, and less than a year later she was dead!"

"Your sister was always sickly; you know that. Most women survive childbirth perfectly well; I always did. Now, Caillean, calm yourself; it is perfectly all right for a bride to be a bit nervous, but you must not make such a fuss that you bother Dom Bertin when he arrives."

"Mother, I am *not* going to marry him!"

"Don't be so childish, of course you are! Really, Caillean, you should be very thankful for your good fortune. It's not as though your *laran* were anything really useful, it's just something the *leroni* want to experiment with—and you're getting a very good husband out of all this, so I expect you to hold your tongue and behave like a properly brought-up young lady!"

"Why can't you ever listen to me! You don't even care how I feel—all you care about is yourself! I can be bred to Dom Bertin as if I were a sheep or something, and if I die the way Rafaella did, well, that's just too bad; you don't even care!" Caillean was screaming now. "I hate you! I wish *you* had died in childbirth!"

Bianca gave a slight gasp and suddenly slumped over, falling off her chair onto the floor. Caillean stood there, staring in astonishment, as her father bent over her mother's body. Then he turned his head and looked in fury at her.

"She's dead! You spawn of the cat-men, what did you do to her?"

Suddenly Caillean understood. So this was the *laran* that wasn't "really useful" but that the *leroni* wanted—the ability to kill with an angry thought. "That's abolutely all they need, another weapon for their continual wars! No! I won't let that happen!"

"What did you *do* to her?!"

"Nothing very difficult, Father," Caillean said quietly. "Only this." And she reached inside her own body, and stopped her heart.

Most of the writers in this anthology are known to me, at least by correspondence or through brief meetings with the Friends of Darkover. Kathleen Williams is the exception; she may possibly have been at a meeting of the Friends at some convention or other, but she has not made herself known to me—much to my regret. On the very last day allowed for considering submissions to this anthology, this story was handed in, in my absence, at my front door. I wrote immediately to the writer (an attempt to reach her by telephone was unsuccessful) for permission to use the story, and asked her to send along a brief biography; but at this writing it has not reached me, and so I must judge Kathleen Williams only by her excellent and gripping story of Alindas, a young monitor in the Ages of Chaos, who rebels against the policy of her circle, wishing to use her *laran* for the unknown art of healing.

CIRCLE OF LIGHT

by Kathleen S. Williams

Alindas's feet found the dim, white puddle of her hastily thrown off monitor's robe and the velvet house shoes beneath it before the urgent mental summons died away in her mind. Twisting a hastily caught up scarf about her disordered, blonde hair, she hurtled down the corridor with none of the decorum and grace with which three years of residence in the Tower of Hali might have been expected to endow her.

Concentrating on her matrix, she shot up the elevator shaft so quickly that she fetched up hard against one of the walls as she stopped. Struggling for the composure she knew she would need in the minutes ahead, Alindas moderated her pace down the corridor to the centermost of the three insulated working chambers.

In a tight cluster around their fallen Keeper, the circle

awaited her, senior by talent among the monitors of Hali. In resigned silence, they were pouring their own failing energies into the effort to ease the passing of Damon Leynier, Senior Keeper of the Tower of Hali.

Lips tightly compressed, Alindas sought the eyes of each member of Damon's circle. She looked up at Mhari, monitor of this circle and long-time companion and lover of its Keeper, who returned Alindas's stare defiantly. "We ease his passing, Alindas, as he wished us. You were called only because he wished to see you before he passed on." Mhari's voice softened, her amber-colored eyes filling with tears. "He loves you, *chiya mia*, as do we all, and wished to spare you his passing, knowing well how deeply you would feel it." Beckoning Alindas to Damon's side, she knelt down herself.

Alindas crept to his side, unable to answer from her darkly churning mind. Summoning every technique of self-control she had ever learned, she extended her hands out over Damon, her sensitive mind tracing nerve channels, the flow of blood and vital substances to the organs of his body.

Hovering over his heart, she knew that what she had long watched developing had finally come to pass. The large vessels feeding his heart had become more and more constricted, until the trickle of blood through them was no longer enough, and before her, she had watched his heart die; now she watched his body follow. Sinking her consciousness into his, easing his breathing and pain, she listened to his last thoughts to her: "Grieve not, my daughter, for I have long known the time and manner of my passing. Do not disturb the peace I hold in my heart, but take my love and let me pass gently beyond the Veil." Mutely accepting, Alindas eased his pain, and when he had finally passed beyond her ability to aid him, she softly chanted the song to guide him to the side of the Lord of Light.

She rocked back on her heels, tears streaming down her cheeks, and unleashed the violence of her pain and rage. "I could have helped him, saved him," she wailed. "You all know I could have." She raged out of the chamber, racing from the Tower in such a storm that she would never know which route she had taken. Mhari moved to follow her, but Lerrys, the circle technician, held her back.

"She will not be comforted," he said gently, "nor will she believe how much we would have truly wished to save Damon. Her *laran*, if it is truly a new talent, is untested, and such healing goes against our beliefs. With these facts, she must herself come to terms. He led the weeping Mhari away from the still-stunned circle, and left her to be tended by her own servants.

Through the protective Veil of the Tower, away from the glittering lake, Alindas fled the backlash of her own pain and the shell of one whom she saw almost as a father. A *nedestra* of the large Serrais clan by a captured Low-Land Ridenow woman, Damon and Mhari were the only family she had known.

She knew that when she regained control of herself, the pain she had caused Mhari would haunt her. But grief fed pain, rage, and frustration until Alindas felt that she would spin apart under the stress of her emotions, spreading a network of throbbing nerves over the face of the world.

She topped a steep rise some distance from the tower, then descended into a small, tree-lined hollow. There she paced for a time, her heart racing, her muscles knotting, and her gut twisting as her own body absorbed the destructive emotions she would have liked to pour out on the other members of the Tower.

Suddenly, a golden hawk swooped into the hollow, snatched a rabbithorn from where it had been sitting unwarily by its burrow, and winged off, its golden plumage darkening to the brown of old blood against the rising, red sun.

"*Survival of the fittest, the strongest, say the old ones*," she thought bitterly. *Are we but animals, to spend our days rending sustenance from forest and plains, never to look up and see the light of day?*

"A somewhat outworn lesson, but perhaps not without value," said a firm, scholarly voice from behind her.

She turned to see Krist, who would now be Senior Keeper in the Tower of Hali. Tall, slender, seemingly ageless, he was an *emmasca* of the Hasturs, and half-brother to the present King.

Seeing the one who could have persuaded Damon to allow her to heal him, Alindas felt her fury return with full force and lash out at him.

"Peace, *chiya*," he said, deflecting her blow with some difficulty. "Damon truly believed in the old ways, and if what you have been able to tell me about your *laran* is true, a cooperative patient is necessary. Also," he said, raising a hand to dispel her coming protest, "you belittle his strength of mind and purpose if you think he could have been swayed by others, even by me, in this decision. Think on what you can do, my child, and have some patience with the wheels of civilization. Do you think you are the first born with the power to heal with the matrix?" Alindas' surprise and chagrin at not being unique were too comic even for Krist's gravity. His pleasant, full-bodied laughter filtered gently through the gray-green firs of the tiny amphitheater.

"I have known at least four, in my admittedly long life, besides you. They return eventually to their homes, to husbands and wives and babes, seeking in their own ways the extent and strength of their talents. They do this knowing that some day their children and grandchildren will be able to shift that balance, that not just men of great value such as Damon will be saved, but that there will be longer and healthier lives for all men and women of the Domains."

Alindas stared at him, honestly appalled at his attitude. "But can't you see how much more we could do, could learn, if we worked together? How can you send such people away to breed babies on farms, when they could do so much? Why, a circle with one good healer to each Tower could help thousands of people a year."

"Do you really know what you can do, Alindas?" Krist asked severely. "Who does know? Who could teach you? What if you can't do what you think you can? Who do you suggest we let you practice on? The time is *not* now, my child. Cultivate patience, learn to know, and control, yourself. Come now, you have extended yourself enormously this morning; you must spend the day resting and meditating, so you are strong and well-controlled for tonight's work, which is also very important to our people." He turned and walked up the hill with graceful, athletic strides.

"Mining," Alindas spat contemptuously at a boulder, as she followed him reclutantly back to the Tower.

Krist sat vacantly at the desk in the corner room he used as an office and study for administrative matters and the occasional visitor to the Tower. His mind wandered in a pleasant, relaxed manner as his slender, six-fingered hands fondled the soft wood accessories on his desk, casually sensing the thoughts of previous Keepers and savoring the tactile pleasures of old, well-used wood. The late afternoon sun had turned the translucent blue stone walls a deep, warm, amethyst, and stained the etched sandstone tiles to the red of very old wine. The late summer breeze carried the spicy smell of nearby forests and the exotic, indescribable scents of the lake to his expanded consciousness.

He paused in his reflections to consider the girl, Alindas. In her fifth year now, in the Tower, she had finally made an uneasy peace with the strictures of Tower living, and his own policy about her *laran*. She had still not outgrown the adolescent desire to mold society to meet her own expectations, and would, occasionally, for no apparent reason, become moody and depressed, but Krist was personally encouraged by these signs. The proper balance between self-confidence and humility would make her an unusually strong person, and make the exploration of her all-important *laran* more fruitful.

Krist allowed his mind to drift back to those painful months and years when he had had to come to terms with his own *emmasca* state, accepting that he would never be Lord of his Domain—the Kingdom which, from his earliest memories, he had been raised and prepared to rule; that no matter how good a King he might have been, the twist of Nature that had robbed him of a definite sexuality had also robbed him of his birthright. Although he acted and felt like a male, he frequently wondered if he *really* knew what it was to be man *or* woman, or if he merely acted in the way everyone seemed to expect of him.

Abandoning that line of thought, he sped a silent wish to Alindas that she would learn to cooperate with nature and man, and cease wasting herself in a fight she didn't understand. "Accept," he prayed, "the wonder of your gift, my child, and let us work together to make what use of it we can."

A silent bid for his attention was accompanied by a soft knock on the frame of his doorway. "Come in," he called, curious about an interruption at that time of day.

One of the newer monitors entered, discreetly accompanying Regis Estaban Alton-Hastur, Prince and heir of the Seven Domains. Krist rose and bowed, surprise apparent in each gesture. "You lend us grace, Your Highness. How may we serve you?"

Regis' broad grin lent brightness and charm to his thin, almost emaciated face. "I thought such formality did not exist in the Tower of Hali, Uncle. If I had known it would be expected of me, I would have contrived a more spectacular entrance!"

"I must confess that surprise got the better of me. Kinsman. Your father insists, and rightly so, that you be treated at all times as our future King, and the habit dies hard, even in a tower." Krist gestured his royal nephew to a chair, and asked the girl to send up refreshments.

He surveyed the boy, hiding the sadness he felt. Weak and fragile from birth, Regis was the only one of four man-children to survive the first ten-day after birth. He was to be fourteen soon, and confirmed as heir to a still unstable kingdom, but Krist seriously doubted the boy's ability to survive to father an heir. Even if he could, had he the strength to hold together a kingdom in almost constant turmoil? Krist's brother, Stephan, was the eighth King of the Seven Domains which comprised—supposedly—the seven major families of Darkover, those possessing the all-important *laran*. Yet he was the first to hold fealty from all seven at once, and this only through the expedient of marrying a princess of the Altons, the family that had fought amalgamation longest and hardest. Loss of the only legal heir of both Hastur and Alton blood would plunge their world into violent turmoil.

He had once seriously considered asking his brother to allow their half-sister, Melora Hastur-Elhaylan, a healer of great potential strength, to see if she could help the boy, but the consequences of failure were, frankly, too great. "Well," he thought gloomily, "as long as he lives we may hope for the best." Forcing down his fears, he turned to the boy, who seemed to be becoming somewhat apprehensive.

"How may I serve you, Kinsman? I am certain your father didn't allow you just to trot over for a visit, in these troubled times."

Regis licked his pale, bluish lips nervously. "I have come to be tested, uncle," he blurted out, obviously expecting a great ordeal.

Krist chuckled softly, and was relieved to see some of the stress leave Regis' face. "Well, then," he said, "you are certain you are fully over your threshold sickness?"

"Oh, yes, uncle. No more dizzy spells, strange voices, or . . . strange feelings," he finished in a rush, blushing violently. "And when my father mind-speaks to me, I can hear him quite clearly. My mother, also, I can hear, and they both say they can hear me back quite well. But they will not let me try with anyone else, not even Cathal, and we are *bredin!*" he finished, somewhat resentfully.

"Your parents are wise in this, Regis. An untrained telepath with the high potential of a Hastur can cause great havoc in the thoughts and emotions of others. Cathal hasn't been tested or trained himself, has he?"

"No, kinsman, I'm sorry," he said slowly. "I had no idea I could hurt Cathal with my mind."

"I understand that, Regis, so don't worry about it any more. The first thing we will do is to give you a matrix. Once you have done what we call keying, matching the resonance of the crystal to your own resonance, you will be able to hear thoughts at will, without danger to anyone. You will stay here for a few ten-days, for in addition to learning how to use your *laran*, there are certain courtesies and habits among telepaths that you must learn to respect."

"My father said that I was to put myself completely in your hands, and stay as long as you feel it is necessary. How soon can we start?" Regis asked, unable to control his eagerness.

"At once, of course, kinsman. I wouldn't think of delaying you," Krist laughed. "Since the Hasturs take to *laran* like a rabbithorn to the snow, it might even be dangerous to delay you!"

Joining in Krist's infectious laughter, Regis moved to the closer chair his uncle indicated. Krist was frankly excited. Both Stephen and his Queen, Camilla, could draw more than the usual power from a matrix, as could Krist himself. If Regis had this *laran in* double measure, it would be wondrous to see what he could do.

Krist knelt before Regis, taking the boy's head between his hands, and began to match resonances with him. "Just relax, Regis, and let yourself float on a sea of warm, quiet water. Breathe slowly and deeply, relax." With very little difficulty, their resonances came together. Taking a blank gemstone from his pocket, he held it before Regis' eyes. Krist was elated as Regis reached out instinctively and brought the stone into their combined consciousness. Slowly, with infinite care, Krist allowed his own resonance to ease out of phase, and stepped away from a Regis who sat spellbound by the matrix he held cradled in his hands. He touched Regis lightly on the shoulder. "Kinsman," he queried gently, "are you all right?"

Regis looked up, his face radiant in the pale, blue glow of the matrix. "It is more wonderful than I ever dreamed, uncle. I . . . I can feel the whole world pulsing with life!" He stared into the gem, rapt in his contemplation of the new world he was discovering. Krist left him alone for a while, as the sunlight finally began to fade from his study.

He brought Regis back to the reality of the darkening tower room with an infinitely gentle mental summons. Regis blinked several times, still awed and startled by what he had seen and felt in the thrall of the matrix.

"Pay attention, now, Regis," Krist said, "and I will give you your first lesson in how to use that matrix." With the barest flicker of concentration, Krist lit every candle that stood in his chamber.

Regis gasped, dumbfounded by this simple yet spectacular demonstration of the everyday use to which a matrix could be put. "Was that an easy or difficult task, kinsman?" he asked, seriously concerned that the extent of his power would be lighting candles, as awesome as such a task seemed at first.

"That," said Krist solemnly, "will depend on your own personal power level. For some, it requires much more concentration than it does for others. Obviously, I would not do it myself if it took much effort, since my duties require that I conserve my strength for work in the circles. A testing of your power potential is what we will do next. Regis twitched, unable to contain his desire to begin.

"Now listen carefully." Krist tapped his desk with a long forefinger and assumed a lecturing stance. Regis leaned forward intently, ready to play the student to the hilt to get the information he craved. Krist smiled slightly at Regis' obvious attempt at tolerance, deciding he'd better proceed quickly.

"The brain of a human being is capable of many things, most of which we know little or nothing about. But when our forefathers first came to this world, the Wise Ones of the Forest gave them the star stones, what we now call matrix stones. And as they sometimes came together with our people, children were born who taught us how to use them. We rarely see the Wise Ones any more, but their gifts to us live in our people and in the stones themselves. For some of us, those who are kin to the Blessed Hastur and Cassilda, children of the Seven Domains, these gifts are strong, and often different in each of us. But the thing that is most important, and which will be expected of you at all times, is that you respect this gift of power, being ever mindful that it has been given to you in faith, as part of your heritage, and must never be abused. Every person who enters this Tower, and leaves with a matrix, takes with him also the oath, not only to use his own power in good faith, but also to protect others from those who would turn this power to ill. As our future king, this burden will lie especially heavy on you, never to use the power offensively, and to join the Towers in punishment of any who might abuse it."

Regis sat very still, tension in every line of his thin, bony body, an expression of intense concentration on his face. "To turn such a wonderful thing to evil strikes my mind strangely, uncle," he said seriously, "but my knowledge is still small. In this, I will depend on you to guide me, as I know Father would want me to, and as I truly wish you will also want to." He ended with a questioning lift of his left eyebrow, a gesture which strongly reminded Krist of his brother.

Krist sat down suddenly, struck by Regis' response, so strong and adult in his grasp of, and solution to, this problem of which he had previously been entirely unaware. Krist was struck again with an almost uncontrollable sadness as he reflected on Regis' health. This child—no, this young *man*—showed the promise of a great king in the making. Regis smiled hesitantly at his uncle, and Krist forced himself to relax and smile back. "I will always be yours to command, kinsman," he said softly.

"Well, that formality out of the way," he continued briskly, "it is time to see what you can learn to do with that piece of rock!" Regis grinned and jumped to his feet, pleased at his uncle's response, and glad to be getting on to the real business.

Krist brought out a small lattice work made up of four of the personal-sized matrix stones—the largest he had been able to synthesize and control so far—and set it on his desk. If Regis could energize this lattice, it would mean that he had inherited the Hastur ability to augment power and handle more then one matrix at a time in full measure.

"Now," he said, "I want you to concentrate on this lattice. Don't try to direct the power or do anything with it. You don't have the training or experience. Just relax, match resonance with your own stone as you did earlier, and try to do the same with this larger arrangement of stones. Do you understand what I want you to do?"

"I think so, Uncle. You just want me to activate the structure as you activated *my* stone for me, is that correct?"

"Precisely, Regis," Krist said, excited and pleased by the Prince's rapid comprehension of the technique. "Now I will step back and let you concentrate." Taking out his own stone, he established a light contact, to monitor Regis' life signs and stop him if he started to weaken.

Regis stared intently into his stone. For what seemed a long time, he just concentrated on the matrix crystal, its pale radiance spreading over his whole body. Krist felt the breath catch in his throat as he sensed Regis starting to reach mentally for the matrix lattice.

Slowly, the lattice began to glow with an intense brilliance that seemed to defy limits to its expansion. Krist watched enthralled, as the power level shot beyond anything he had ever before experienced. The throbbing glow increased beyond the upper limit of human vision, and a vague, disconnected part of Krist wondered if he would be permanently blind, as he desperately tried to break the hypnotic link between Regis and the lattice. In that instant, the limits of the lattice were reached, and it burst into a thousand blackened fragments, flying in a jagged rain around the room. The backflow struck both of them like a mountain falling on them, and with his last dregs of strength, Krist broadcasted a frantic cry for help.

Krist was aware of a vague return to consciousness as Alindas burst into the room, followed by six others.

Noting Krist's weak gesture toward Regis, she signaled one of the junior monitors to attend him, and went directly to Krist. "No, *chiya*," he whispered, "attend our Prince first."

Surprised, but not slow to understand, Alindas reached the young man's side in what seemed like one movement. He was very close to death. Quickly, she grasped his left hand, extending hers to the other monitor. Linked together, they poured strength into the prince, while she monitored him with another level of her mind. When his breathing returned to normal, and his skin color and heartbeat were as normal as Alindas suspected they could be, she dismissed the other monitor to rest and regain his strength, and turned to Krist, who was stretched out on a divan, looking the color of new snow.

"You look as though you're hardly still alive. Is this the best Mhari could do for you?"

"I sent her for food. I don't want too many people around when Regis wakes up. He is going to have a lot of mental backlash pain." He looked anxiously to where Regis had been placed on another divan.

"You mean *if* he wakes up, don't you?" Alindas asked.

acidly. "What were you thinking of, Krist, to let someone in his condition do . . . whatever it was you two were doing?" Her look of disgust took in the entire, blasted chamber.

Krist clutched her wrist with a strength that belied his appearance. "What do you mean, 'someone in his condition'?" he asked worriedly. "He has always been sickly, but he didn't appear ill today."

Alindas looked at him in surprise. "I don't understand, Krist. Haven't you ever monitored him? I'm frankly surprised he is still alive. He won't be much longer, you know."

Krist lay back on the divan, tears gathering in his clear, gray eyes. "Yes Alindas, I *have* monitored him. But I honestly don't know what *is* the matter with him. He has always been weak, and frankly, I never expected him to survive so long. I hope that since he *had*, perhaps Evanda would spare him for our Kingdom which needs him so much."

Alindas looked at him with great sympathy as he cried weakly, his head in her lap. The depressing aftereffects of heavy matrix work draining away the last of his control. "I am very sorry, Krist. I know how much your Domain and family mean to you, but he will not survive much longer. The monitors at Neskaya frequently attend the births in the area, to ease the pain and calm the babe. When I went there to study for a season, I discovered that newborn babies have holes between the chambers of their hearts. "At first," she remembered wryly, "*I* thought the children were in imminent danger of death. I learned, however, that these holes close up, like a wound closing, within a few days after birth. Lauria, whose *laran* is much like my own, said she had seen a babe whose holes didn't close die before he was a ten-day old, because his heart couldn't pump blood to the proper places in his body. That was why I was surprised that the Prince still lives, for the holes are still open in his heart."

Krist looked at her in utter amazement. Even though he had always believed in her abilities, to see them thus demonstrated surprised him beyond belief. "If he could live this long, why can he not continue to do so?" he asked, with an almost detached interest.

"He is still quite young, Krist. When he gets his adult height very quickly, as all young men his age do, the body will, for a time, grow faster than his heart. His heart can barely keep his body alive as it is. When this sudden growth occurs, it will strain his heart past bearing and he *will* die." Alindas' sorrow and pity were a palpable texture in the shattered room. She gripped his hands very hard, giving him what strength she had left to give. "I will leave you both now, to rest and eat; he should awaken soon. Call me if there is anything I can do." She left quickly, not wishing to exacerbate Krist's grief by the reminder her presence would bring.

Krist leaned back, staring at a sliver of blackened matrix buried in the blue stone above his head, "Such power," he grieved, "so much young, untried wisdom." He fell into a deep, troubled sleep; peopled by the distraught figures of his brother and the Queen. The Queen was being forced to return to the Alton Domain. Lord Alton was preparing for a war being pressed on him by his sons and the other families of the Domains. His brother stood in a freshly plowed field, dirt trickling between his fingers and tears streaming down his cheeks. "My kingdom, my son, both gone," he muttered over and over and over again, beating a painful cadence in Krist's mind.

He awakened to someone knocking on the frame of his doorway. Wondering why someone in a tower was doing something as barbaric as knocking, he sat up quickly, followed a split second later by the heavy, bloated head he had left on the pillow. He fought with nausea and the memory of the night before. "No one in his right mind would bespeak me in this condition," he thought dully. Croaking permission to enter, he staggered over to where Regis lay, looking down on him worriedly.

"Go and lie back down, Krist," Alindas said, looking unusually fresh and pretty this morning. "It's afternoon," she said, reading Krist accurately, "and I've been watching him. He'll awaken soon, and we will probably have to force feed him. Now you eat." Krist went obediently back to sit down, and looked distastefully at the food before him. Not wishing Alindas to take it into her head to nag *him,* he dug in with a gusto he did not feel. The enormous meal did, however, soon have the desired effect; his head and stomach began to feel as though they would stay where nature intended them, and he lay back with a real feeling of relief. Meanwhile, Alindas had managed to force a weakly resisting Regis to put away an equally large meal, and he was already asleep again. She came over, kneeling beside Krist and taking one of his hands in hers.

"Are you feeling any better now?" she asked.

"My body feels much better, *chiya.* I'm afraid my heart

may never recover." With a joint will their eyes moved to where Regis slept.

"Krist," Alindas probed cautiously, "I know very little about the politics of the Domains. Frankly, there have been too many things that interested me more. This difficulty, however, has caused me to wonder. I know how much you love the Prince, yet I sense there is much more to your fears than his death alone. What do you fear?"

He looked at her, very surprised, and then sighed. "It is hard, sometimes, to realize how little attention people pay to the state of their own kingdom," he confessed. "It is thus, Alindas: since Damon-Aran Hastur tried to bring peace and cooperation to all of the Seven Domains, believing that the divine plan of Hastur and Cassilda was for their descendents to live together as one family, the Alton Domain, and, at one time or another, almost all of the other Domains, have resisted the will of Hastur. By taking Camilla, the Princess of the Alton Domain, as wife, my brother, with old *Dom* Lerrys Alton, believed they could bring about a lasting peace among all the Domains by providing an heir of both Alton and Hastur blood. All three have worked very hard to make this peace work, for *Dom* Lerrys's sons would raise the Domain of Alton to war at the slightest excuse, and there has been constant unrest in various parts of the Kingdom. This very fragile peace will go up like a puff of smoke if Regis dies before producing an heir; even if he does, the fight for the regency may be just as bad as no heir at all," he sighed heavily. "That is the important thing, but there is also what happened here last night."

"What did happen here last night?" asked Alindas seriously, still reflecting on what Krist had told her.

"Regis boosted enough power from a four-matrix lattice to blow it to smithereens," he said dryly, anticipating the disbelief in her eyes. "He may be able to figure out how to build large, artificial matrix lattices and teach us how to use them, with his kind of *laran*." His voice trailed off as he dwelt on never seeing this, or many other dreams, come true.

Alindas sat in silence for a long time, next to Krist, brooding on factors and implications that had never touched her in her twenty-two years, but which might, in the future, mean a great deal to her, and all the people to whom she was close. Grasping Krist's hand firmly, she looked up at him, determined to try once more.

"Do you believe what I told you last night?" she asked him with her customary directness.

"*Believe* you, Alindas? Why should I not? You have never given me cause to doubt you. Why do you ask such a question?"

Taking a deep breath, Alindas faced him fully. . . . "He has so little time, Krist, and he is so badly needed. Could it truly hurt anything for me to try to heal him?"

Krist stared at her blankly, struggling to suppress the hope that sprang up in him. "Do you truly think you can do this thing, Alindas? If you could, I think I could persuade my brother. He and Camilla have tried everything they could think of, hoping something would help."

Alindas jumped up angrily, glaring down at him. "You know better than anyone that I can't promise anything. I tell you the holes close like any other wound, and you yourself have seen me heal those. But this is much more complicated. I *feel*, deeply and honestly, that I can help, but you, of all people, should know I can offer no person of whom it can be said that I healed him!"

Krist pressed her hands, trying to calm her. "I know that, Alindas, I only wished to see how confident you felt. Do you realize that if you *do* heal him, it must be kept a secret? That you could never work in a circle again, for fear of the knowledge getting out? I am sure I can convince Camilla; she has worked as a monitor, and to some extent, she will understand what we propose. Between us we may be able to convince my brother, for his son and his kingdom mean everything to him. But the Domain Lords are another story entirely. It took nearly one hundred years to convince them to let us heal external wounds and monitor childbirths, and we have had those concessions a bare twenty-five years. It must be a secret. Can you live with that?"

Alindas was devastated. "Leave the Tower forever? Where would I go? I have no family, my mother died soon after bearing me, she but a captive Ridenow, my fosterage was paid for, and they were most grateful to give me to a Tower. The Tower is the only family I have!"

"I know this is so, *chiya*. Believe me, I would do my best for you, but it would still be imperative for you to leave."

"Well," she said painfully, "I have already seen what must be done. All that is left now is to do it. I think I can, Krist, and somehow, I feel that if I can, I must. As you have often

said, the gift is given in trust. I would violate that trust by
not doing what I could."

Krist kissed her gently on the forehead. "The Lord of
Light will bless you, Alindas. Now," he sighed, "you must
make traveling arrangements for me at once. My old bones
say that we may not have much time."

Alindas smiled tremulously, both thrilled and saddened by
this opportunity. "Rest a while, my Lord, for *my* old bones
say traveling arrangements will take some time."

Alindas stared thoughtfully at the fluffy, pink clouds
floating on the beams of the rising sun, that were the only reminder of the night's light rain. As her usually staid stag-
pony frisked in the fresh, fragrant morning air, her mind
sought endlessly for arguments to present to the King and
Queen that would persuade them to permit this unorthodox
treatment of their son.

She eyed Krist, still pale and weak from his ordeal, wondering if they weren't both after all on a fool's errand. The
prohibition against meddling with Nature in any way had
been with them, as far as they knew, forever. The few people
who had studied the scant records of their race could find no
reference to a time when such healing had been allowed.
Krist was the only person Alindas knew who believed what
he had told her, that the matrix power was new to their race.
Everyone accepted that the stones had been given them by the
Wise Ones of the Forest, but most believed that *laran* was a
gift of the Lord of Light, that the offspring of the God's own
son, the Blessed Hastur, fathered seven sons of his own, each
gifted with a particular *laran*, and that these sons were the fa-
thers of the present Seven Domains. She was sure that the belief that their race was relatively newly come to this world,
and that *laran* was both taught and given them by the Wise
Ones, was not held by many. She was not even sure she believed it herself.

Krist had a strange aspect to his *laran*, wherein during moments of expanded consciousness, time spread itself out before him in both past and future aspects. These moments
were brief, and, Alindas knew, frequently frustrating to him.
He was certain, however, that he had seen a time when there
had been *no laran* or starstones among the humans of
Darkover. He was often tantalized by a black area of the
past, beyond which he could not see, and he knew, or per-

haps only felt, that this was the time before the coming of his race to Darkover.

Alindas did not know what she believed, but felt with her whole heart that it was what Stephan and Camilla Hastur believed that could someday prove a turning point in the history of their people. She could not accept that the Lord of Light—or the Wise Ones of the Forest, for that matter— would have gifted her with a talent that she was not intended to use. In her more bitter moments, she had thought many things, including that she was being punished for some obscure reason, or that she was a freak of nature, like a two-headed stag-pony foal, and would be better destroyed. Fortunately, Krist always watched her closely during these times, not allowing her to dwell in these doldrums of her own making.

Alindas's stomach sank and twisted at the thought of not being close to Krist any longer. He had become central to her way of life, and she felt lost and confused at the thought of living forever apart from him.

"It will not be as bad as all that, *breda*," he smiled softly, for he had been following her thoughts for some time. "You will find someone you will truly love, and he and your babes will give your life much new meaning. People rarely stay in the Tower forever—you must have known that some day I would find a suitable husband for you and send you forth. Your *laran must* be preserved, even if it cannot, now, be used." He grasped her hand firmly across her saddle. "I have only delayed this, *chiya*, for we have had need of you, and you, I think, had an even greater need of us.

"My kinswoman Melora has often asked for me to send you to her, for she became quite attached to you when you visited her a season ago. She is eager to discover what you two can do together, and, I think, she secretly hopes you will look with favor on one of her sons, and wish to stay with her always. Is this a plan you would approve? It will not be the same as a Tower, but in many ways, it may be better. Since she is married to the heir of Elhaylan, the day may come when, at least in that Domain, you may be allowed to heal more freely. And between you, who knows what you may be capable of?" Krist searched Alindas' face closely, for this plan had been carefully considered, not dreamed up overnight for the sake of expedience, and he hoped desperately for her good that she would agree. If she chose another way he could not see how to provide for her future happiness.

Alindas looked at him consideringly, taking time to absorb the ideas he had offered her. Suddenly, she laughed softly, "You have always wanted me to do this, haven't you, Krist? Lady Melora was most kind to me—more kind, I would think, than the *nedestra* (and she gave the word the obscene inflection meaning, truly, 'bastard') daughter of a Serrais lord and a captive woman with no *laran* would normally be offered. But," she held up a hand to ward off Krist's expected protest, "after a time, we *did* become close, more as sisters than as mother and daughter, and I am sure she meant her offer kindly, so I shall go to her, for the time being. I do *not*, however, promise to marry one of her sons, of whom I have not met even one!" She looked at Krist with a trace of defiance in her green eyes and a firm set to her jaw—she would die a shriveled old maid before she married just to please him!

Nodding, more pleased than he was willing to admit, Krist mutely accepted her decision. In companionable silence, they rode on toward Castle Hastur as the sun rose toward noon over their heads and the filmy lake along which they rode began to stir in its warmth.

They arrived in the early afternoon, riding into a bustling courtyard. Impressed by a visit from their sovereign's brother and, more importantly to them, a Keeper of Hali, the grooms took their ponies and the *coridom* saw that they were shown immediately into the presence of the Queen.

Camilla Lanart-Hastur, Queen of the Seven Domains, was a stunningly beautiful woman in her early thirties. Tall, slender, with dark auburn hair massed in heavy braids around her head, very fair skin, and eyes of a gray so dark that they often seemed black, she was a lady of great presence and aristocratic bearing.

So riveted was Alindas by her appearance, that it took her some time to notice the elegant, dim chamber in which she stood. Soft, amber light filtered into its soft greens and other earthy colors, with thick fur rugs and more pieces of shining, dark wood furniture than Alindas had ever before seen.

Fortunately, the time it took Krist to greet the Queen formally allowed Alindas to collect herself. She curtsied shyly as the Queen looked at her intently.

"You have come about Regis," she said, apprehension very evident in her voice. "Is he well?"

"He is resting now, Camilla." Krist spoke with an intimacy granted to very few people. "You would have been very proud of him. He has more power potential than anyone I have ever known of. Because I was not aware of how much power he was capable of activating, he took a very large backflow, but is recovering well from that now. I am going to ask Alindas to explain to you why we have sought you out today, for she understands it better than I." Krist motioned Alindas forward.

Alindas was struck dumb and motionless. Krist wanted *her* to explain to the Queen? Alindas felt, suddenly, very old. More than shyness before the Crown, awareness that Krist was letting her take the responsibility of the explanation kept her tongue-tied. Responsibility was not a strong point of hers, and this frightened her more than anything she had ever faced before.

"Come, child—Alindas—what is it you wish to say to me?" Camilla pressed patiently.

Alindas, feeling as though she were lost in an unlit mountain cave without even a glimmer to guide her, gathered what courage she had, and dropped to her knees before the Queen. "Your Majesty," she said breathlessly, "I think I may be able to do something to improve your son's health!" Afraid to meet the eyes of the woman sitting rigidly before her, Alindas stared fixedly at the Queen's feet.

Before Alindas could understand what had happened, the Queen had thrown herself to the floor, grasped both of her hands, and was drawing the information about her precious son's condition, and what Alindas might do for him, directly from her mind. After a short, instinctive struggle against this invasion, Alindas relaxed, letting every fact at her disposal flow into Camilla's anxiety-ridden mind. She learned with awe how much fear Camilla Hastur lived with every day, every time she gazed upon her fragile, only son.

"So, Krist, what you hoped, what we all hoped, may yet come to pass. I cannot yet think clearly," the Queen said, dropping back into her chair with an expression of such hope on her face that Alindas felt her own body start to tense in sympathy. Their rapport had been very deep, and remnants of it still overlay the atmosphere of the room. "Krist, please, as someone who knows much more of these things, tell me what *you* think." Camilla was visibly struggling to keep her hopes in check.

"All that I can say, Camilla, is that I would not have brought Alindas here if I didn't think there was some chance, however small, that she can do what she says. I have no doubt that her evaluation of his condition is accurate—she is by far the best monitor I have ever known. What healing she can do will probably be on an instinctive level, and how successful that will be, I cannot say. Her conviction that she can help him is the best guarantee we will have, for there is not enough time for her to prove herself on someone else."

Camilla sat thoughtfully for several moments, then sent a page to ask the King to come to her. "Krist, would you and Alindas wait outside, please. I think it is best if Stephan and I discuss this matter privately." Krist nodded silently, then bowed; Alindas curtsied, clumsy with wariness, and they departed the chamber.

The next two hours would be the longest of their lives. They neither ate, nor slept, nor talked, but occasionally one or the other would pace for a few minutes, largely intent on not accidentally eavesdropping, audibly or mentally, on the intense discussion going on in the royal chamber.

Camilla and Stephan finally emerged, both looking too exhausted to be still upright. Stephan's grim, red-rimmed eyes swept past his brother and settled on Alindas. "We will permit you to try this thing, for we truly believe it to be our only hope. You must both understand, however, that *no one*, other than ourselves, must know about it. The Council will never allow Regis to rule if they know his body has been tampered with in any way."

With a calm she would have believed impossible from herself, Alindas met the eyes of her King firmly. "Even Regis need now know about it, if you wish it so, Your Majesty. If you and your Lady are willing, the four of us can provide enough power, and no one else will ever learn of it."

Stephan's tense body relaxed considerably, a slight smile tilting his lips. He bowed deeply to Alindas. "We are grateful for the risk you take in trying to help our son, my Lady. Know that we are *very* grateful." He turned to Krist, "Camilla tells me that you have already arranged for Regis to return, following you. We all, I think, should get what rest we can, that we may start as soon as he has arrived and rested." Taking the arm of his Queen, he walked down the corridor, leaving Krist and Alindas to the care of his household.

Nearly a full day later, Alindas sat on the leather-padded seat of a bench set deep in a window embrasure. The setting sun cast the distant, violet mountains into black, sleeping giants. She laughed a little at that whimsical thought—her foster brother had liked to frighten her with stories about what happened when the mountain giants were aroused.

Suddenly, she longed desperately for even the uncomfortable safety of her foster home. She was not made of the stuff of a decision-maker. Praying to see this night well passed, Alindas vowed to live, forever and meekly, wherever her fate dictated. Newly perceiving the complexity of her world, of which she had never before been aware, she suddenly felt unable to cope with it. She squirmed at the memory of her angry impatience with the ways of the world, not realizing until that instant how little she knew of it.

It was time, now that the sun had set, to go to Regis. They had decided to let him sleep as much as possible after he had arrived the night before, but soon the time would come for them to join their secret circle, to take their deadly risk.

Warmly and comfortably dressed, they gathered at Regis' bedside. He looked at them with some amusement at their palpable concern. "I am not all *that* damaged, you know," he grinned up at them engagingly. "Not that I mind having my favorite people hanging over me, you understand." He included Alindas in that smile, and she thought, irrelevantly, that he could charm the snow off the Hellers with it.

Camilla explained gently, "We have merely asked Alindas and Krist to give you a good check over before they return to Hali, just to reassure us that you are all right. It was no small thing you did, after all, and you will need to be stronger before you can return to study at the Tower." Though the trained telepaths in the room picked up her fear with no difficulty, Regis was still too inexperienced to sense how frightened his mother really was.

With a patience uncharacteristic of a young, chronic invalid, he lay back and looked up at them all expectantly.

Taking the initiative, Alindas knelt on the bed and took both of Regis' hands in hers. "I am going to match my resonance to yours, Regis, just as your uncle did the other day. After a few minutes, you will not be aware of much, but don't worry. It is only a trance, a light sleep, that will make it easier for me to monitor you." This was not precisely true, but Alindas had promised the King and Queen that Regis would not know what was being done to him, and this seemed to her an explanation he would accept. She was apparently correct, for he relaxed completely, concentrating on his own matrix and half affecting the match himself.

As they watched the trance deepening, the other three

linked, waiting to feed Alindas the power she would need, at her signal.

When the trance was deep enough to keep Regis unaware of his family, Alindas linked with them, testing the power at her disposal. She felt Camilla closest to her, keeping a strict monitor on both Regis and Alindas. She was grateful for the gentle concern in Camilla's mind, a little surprised that she could be so concerned for a stranger when her own son's life hung so perilously.

Taking much comfort in this, Alindas began the first step: concentrating on the weakly beating heart, she began the slow process of reducing the number of beats until Regis's heart was only beating about twice a minute. Knowing that her time was now very short, Alindas reached for her instinctive affinity with the cell structure of Regis' body.

First she sought the edges of the small slit between the two upper chambers of the heart. With infinite delicacy, she accelerated the rate of cell growth along the edges. Like a seamstress with a needle, she wove the long, flexible cells of the heart muscle back and forth. Three times she was interrupted by the pulsing of the heart, nearly losing her mental grip on the delicate cell structure. With a deep sigh and a slight wavering of concentration, she turned her mind to the slit between the lower two heart chambers. Finding it easily, she again began darning with newly generated cells, only to lose her grip entirely with the sudden beat of his heart!

She nearly lost concentration completely when she realized what she had done: by restoring the upper chambers first, she had increased the flow, with each beat, in the lower chambers. Exhausted, she grasped frantically for contact again, realizing that the closure would have to be strong enough to resist the next beat. Sensing it coming, she increased her mental grasp, concentrating on holding the slit closed, as the heart beat again. This time, she did not lose her hold, again weaving, drawing more and more power in an effort to close fully before the next beat. In a few seconds, the slit was completely sealed. She watched for two more full beats, to assure herself that the repairs would hold under full pressure. Then, slowly, tenderly, feeling Camilla's strong encouragement, she relaxed her hold on Regis' life-force, allowing his heart to establish anew its own rhythm.

Phasing out of Regis' resonance was a painful snap in Alindas' mind, and she soon passed completely into welcome unconsciousness. Unable to muster enough power to arouse

Alindas, nor, themselves, to ascertain the condition of the Prince, the others of the circle ate hurriedly and settled to wait in a deep, healing sleep in various chairs around the chamber.

Alindas' return to the world was as slow and gentle as awakening. Seeing that she had been stretched out on Regis' large bed, next to him, she slid quietly away from his side and stood watching him carefully. Trying to extend her conscious mind to monitor him, she found herself, to her anger, too weak to do so. She stalked around the room, gathering up leftover food and eating ravenously.

Camilla, sensitive to her mental turmoil, also awoke, gathering a depressed, and now sobbing, Alindas into her arms. "Do not cry, *chiya*," she chided gently, "you did your utmost, and although I have not your measure of talent, I think you succeeded. Come and look upon him."

She led an unresisting Alindas to her son's bedside. "Do you not see how pink his cheeks are, how red his lips, when he has always been pale and blue? Can you not feel how strongly his heart beats?" Alindas pressed her hand against the Prince's chest, feeling a slow, normal rate of beating.

Bemused, she looked up into Camilla's warm eyes. "You believe it *worked*?" she asked in an unbelieving voice. For the first time, she heard Camilla's warm, vibrant laughter, and Krist and Stephan scrambled to join, Regis also awaking.

"All finished, are you?" he queried, even his voice sounding deeper and more robust to their weary, hopeful ears. "You know, Mother, I am feeling *very* well this morning— are you sure I can't return to Hali when Uncle Krist goes back?"

"Well, my lady," said the King, bowing deeply to Alindas, "what say you?"

Surprised by Stephan's deference, Alindas was a little slow in answering: "Definitely not, Your Majesty," she said firmly. She appealed to Camilla, "I think he should stay abed at least a ten-day, till we are sure he has suffered no ill effects."

With visible disappointment, Regis accepted their combined strictures on his activities and went back to sleep as the circle separated to their own chambers, and rest.

Two days later, Alindas rode from the courtyard of Castle Hastur, this time bound north, toward Nevarsin and her new home. In her ears echoed the thanks of the royal couple: "You will always have a claim upon us. We will think of you with fondness of a daughter, which is little enough for what you have done for us. Remember, always, that our prayers and thanks are with you."

"But it is I who should thank you," Alindas thought, the pain of this new parting still with her, "for you gave me as much a new life as we, together, gave Regis. For my doubts are gone, and my heart finally free." Alindas considered, again, with wonder, the relaxed serenity of her mind and body. "In each way, we give what we can, do what we are able, and take joy in the life the gods gave us."

With a last glance at the dawn-tinged castle, she rode out of her old life.

One thing an editor learns quickly is that cliches have a reason for existence. In putting this introduction together, I tried for a long time to avoid the statement, "No anthology of Darkover fiction would be complete without a story from Jacqueline Lichtenberg" and finally gave up because it's true, exactly the way the cliche has it; no such anthology *would* be complete without, *et cetera*. Second only to my editor, Don Wollheim, Jacqueline was the one single person instrumental in making me realize that Darkover had its own independent existence and that I *should* continue writing. Jacqueline and I differ on almost everything one can imagine, from the aesthetic value of mathematics (I'm con, she's pro) to the quality of the TV show *Star Trek* (and we won't go into that, thank you.) But, while with all these differences, one would imagine she would absolutely *loathe* the Darkover books, she likes them; in fact, she once paid me the compliment of saying that a copy of *Star of Danger* had "saved her sanity" when she was marooned overseas without access to American science fiction.

I also think of Jacqueline, with pardonable pride, as a protégée; I read reams of her earlier amateur fiction (and ripped the hide off of her in long bleeding strips for the usual amateurish mistakes, having made them all myself, and worse.) Therefore I was delighted when her work began to assume professional and publishable quality; she has now sold four novels in her own series, and has begun another, and I couldn't be prouder if I'd written them myself.

Jacqueline is one of the few fans who have become not only professional writers, in their own right, but personal friends. She is still very active in fandom (as am I) has recently taken on the managership of the SFWA Speaker's Bureau (a sort of rent-a-writer service for fan clubs, universities and the like) and is the kind of dynamo hard worker who appears likely to succeed at all of them. Personally she's small, dark, dynamic, and while all the writers in this anthology are manic types who juggle writing, careers, house-keeping and often children, Jacqueline is one of the few people I know who appear to handle the whole thing with dynamic energy and competence, instead of succumbing to the harried-woman syndrome. She seems to *like* trying to crowd twenty-eight hours into an ordinary Terran-length day!

However, she has one fault; she can't seem to write anything shorter than a hundred-thousand-word novel. Which is why I welcomed her collaboration with Jean Lorrah. Jean is a college professor of English in Kentucky, and well known in *Star Trek* fandom as the author of several highly literate and intelligent short stories and novelettes. Jean and Jacqueline have sold a novel in collaboration, *First Channel*, to Doubleday and now Jean has sold the first novel in her own "Savage Empire" series. You'll be hearing more from both of them, separately and together. "The Answer" is only a sample of their work.

And again, like many inventive people, they have turned to the Ages of Chaos for their story; a period in Darkovan history of which little "written history" survives, leaving the writer free to create whatever she wishes.

THE ANSWER

by Jacqueline Lichtenberg

and Jean Lorrah

It was cold.

That one fact was all reality to Velana Hastur as she fought to remember what she was doing here, her mind frozen, numbed beyond thought, beyond memory—

No. She must remember. She was inside the glacier, seeking the way to destroy it, to send it back beyond the Wall Around the World for as long as men dwelt in the valley.

Year by inexorable year the glacier had moved toward their home, imprisoning the highlands in ice and finally, this very winter, threatening Velana's village. Now, with the spring thaw heralding storms, an immense block of ice hung suspended above them, ready to crash into the village where Velana and her friends had grown up, burying her home beneath inpenetrable ice.

They had packed last fall to move, to brave the disease-ridden lowlands or, if they could not survive there, to fight for the fertile lands held by others. All the battles would have to be fought again, but they had been prepared to do so . . . and then had come the coughing sickness.

All through the winter people came down with fever and a hacking cough that would not let them eat or drink or sleep, wasting their strength for weeks on end, leaving adults debilitated, weak as babies, while the children. . . .

The children were dying.

Every house seemed to have some little one coughing his life away, and the parade of small coffins to the burial ground was hideous to contemplate. Velana and the six women she had gathered around her used their starstones in healing, working day and night against the disease—but they lived on the edge of exhaustion, every success greeted by a new critical patient.

Then just this morning Velana had emerged from Jekker and Marta's house after bringing their son through crisis, to a glorious spring day. As she dropped her shawl to let the sun's warmth penetrate her stiff shoulder, hope surged through her. She lifted her head high—and caught the glint of the sun's rays off the glacier.

It had moved! In the weeks that Velana had been so busy, the mass of ice had continued its steady motion until now a monolith hung suspended over her home, awaiting only the proper moment to break free to destroy them!

It would be weeks before those who had survived the coughing sickness would be strong enough to be moved, while others were still in the throes of illness. But the very warmth of the red sun, with its promise of spring, now threatened to send that ice mountain tumbling into the valley. Something had to be done.

Ignoring both her tiredness and the pleas of villagers to come help other sick people, Velana hurried back to the great house of the Hastur family. She was ravenously hungry, as work with the starstone always left her, so she substituted a hearty meal for the sleep she needed, and then hurried to her room.

There she calmed herself, sat down in a comfortable chair with a fur robe about her, and drew her starstone from its pouch. It lay in her hand, glowing like a living thing as she stared into its depths, concentrating on the glacier. *I must seek within the glacier. Only thus can I learn how to stop it from destroying us.*

Slowly, the starstone expanded, enveloping her in blue crystal . . . blue ice. She was walking through solid ice as if through air. At the periphery of her vision stars flashed, disappearing if she turned to look at them. She could feel the pushing strains, the cracking, the fluid flow of pure solid.

At last she came to the center of the glacier. The strain was gone. There was no up or down, east or west; she was suspended, immobile, herself part and parcel of the living ice, contemplating the luminous purity of bright blue crystal. She would remain there forever, enveloped in beauty, herself that beauty. . . .

Something moved. A bird of the same blue crystal was flying through the ice toward her. She put out her hand. The bird lighted on it—and the ice crazed! The crystal purity shattered into an infinity of cracks, the glacier, the bird, Velana herself.

And she was cold, frozen, unable to move or see now through the opaque ice. *I must remember.* But she could think of nothing but the absolute cold. *How can I help my people if I cannot help myself?*

Suddenly there was a flash of light—then another. Velana was suspended under an arc of stars—or were they glowing starstones? They glowed in perfect symmetry at even intervals, forming an arc above her that might be part of a circle surrounding her completely, if she could move to look.

Her numbed brain tried to focus. This was important. . . .

The endless cold was leaching her life away. The starstones glowed, but gave no warmth. Velana yearned toward them, and they glowed brighter, brighter—

A blinding flash of searing pain, and when she opened her eyes she was back in her room, looking into the worried gray eyes of her cousin Ellonie.

"I'm sorry!" Ellonie said. "I didn't know how else to bring you out of trance—I feared you were dead!"

Velana realized groggily that Ellonie must have touched her starstone. "I almost had the answer!" she said peevishly through chattering teeth.

"And what good would it do you if you were dead?" Ellonie snapped. "Just look at you!" She pulled the younger woman to her feet and sat her on a bench before the fire, wrapping blankets around her, and then her own arms after she had rung for the servants to bring a tub and hot water.

It was only when Velana lay in the bath, warmth at last seeping back into her limbs, that she could begin to think again. "I wish you hadn't interrupted me, Ellonie. I know—you were afraid for me, and I love you for wanting to take care of me. But I'm not one of your children, Breda."

"Sometimes you act like a child," Ellonie chided. "Coming off by yourself to perform some starstone experiment—"

"I almost had the answer. I know I would have had it in just a little more time."

Ellonie's eyes widened. "The answer to how to cure the coughing sickness?"

"No," Velana said impatiently, "the glacier! I was inside the glacier."

"No wonder you almost froze to death. Glaciers, indeed, when our children are dying. Find an answer for *that*, daughter of the gods!" The gray eyes flashed, and Ellonie paced away in anger. From the back, in her tartan skirt and heavy shawl, she looked far sturdier than she was, her copper curls escaping as usual from the butterfly clasp that was so precisely their color that it disappeared against her hair. Ellonie was only two years older than Velana, but she had been married at fourteen, and had three children, so that she seemed another generation to the younger woman.

Shame burned through Velana, and she rose from the tub, wrapping herself in a heavy robe. "Ellonie, I'm sorry. Your son—how is he?"

"I came to tell you," her cousin said without turning, "that Kyril has passed the crisis."

"But that's wonderful! I'm so glad for you."

Ellonie turned, fighting back tears. "My children may survive, thanks to your skill with the starstone, and what you have taught me. I'm sorry I was angry with you, cousin. It's just—they're so weak. I don't know if Kyril can survive being moved, while the other children. . . ."

"I know," said Velana. "You're exhausted, too, cousin. And hungry, I'll warrant. I'll send for something to eat."

"And you must sleep." Ellonie sighed. "Why do you do these things, Velana? The only answer to the glacier is to move away from it, and before we can do that we must heal the sick. You may be the granddaughter of a god, but that does not give you the right to run off to satisfy your curiosity, when your abilities are needed for an immediate crisis."

"But the glacier *is* an immediate crisis! We can't move now until the spring thaw, and by then it could fall—"

"And what does it matter if ice fills the valley if we are all dead of coughing sickness? Now you've exhausted yourself so we will lose your help in healing while you sleep. How many will die because you were not available?"

"There isn't anything I can do with a starstone that can't be done by others."

"But there are only seven of us! Ever since this epidemic started, we have hardly slept at all. Velana, your discoveries have saved many lives, but this is no time for experiments."

Velana knew what her cousin was saying, but Ellonie could not understand. She had never gone out from her body into the heart of a glacier, seeking an answer—"

"Wait!" Velana cried. "I *did find* an answer! A *circle* of starstones!"

"What?"

"We've been working one by one, *breda.*"

"Of course—and even so there are not enough of us for all who are ill."

"But suppose we all worked together? Doneva!" she cried to the servant who entered just then with a tray of food, "Go down into the village. All the sick people are to be brought together into the great hall!"

"Velana—what are you doing?" cried Ellonie.

"Gather the women, cousin. The seven of us, in a circle, as I saw the starstones in the glacier. *Hurry,* Ellonie! Run—find the other women and bring them here while I get some clothes on—"

Velana's reputation with the starstone was such that by the time she came downstairs, the great hall was rapidly being turned into a makeshift infirmary. When all was ready, Velana gathered the six other flame-haired women about her.

"We have all touched one another through the starstones," she said. "Now we are going to work together through them. We'll join hands, and thus join strengths. By lending strength to one another, we may be able to go deeply enough within a person's body to heal completely, and not have to withdraw because we're tired, or because we fear getting lost."

There was fear among the women, especially from fourteen-year-old Callina, who had been pressed hurriedly into developing her talent during this terrible winter. Looking into her starstone, pulsing with the beat of her heart, Velana sent her mind out to touch Callina reassuringly, gathering the girl gently within her influence. The girl's fear slowly melted as one by one the other women joined in the rapport. They were not actually sitting in a circle, but in Velana's mind they had become that circle of starstones she had seen within the glacier. Lines of glowing force leaped across the circle, welding them into one unit. Velana envisioned the most critical patient within the circle, all the lines of force penetrating his body. It was old Mordek, who had worked for the Hasturs since long before Velana was born. Like the children, the very old were hardest hit by the coughing sickness; Mordek's wife had died of it at midwinter.

Mordek was wracked with coughing, his body convulsing as he expelled air, gasping and choking weakly. Three different women in the circle tried at once to soothe him, and met with a clashing sparkle. *That won't do,* Velana told them. *Lend me your strength, and let me do the work.* She seemed to feel Ellonie's arms about her, supporting her, although neither woman had moved. Warm encouragement came from the other women as Velana sought deep within the fibers of old Mordek's body to the nerves carrying the impulse to cough. She found the sparkling network, and for the first time, with the other women caring for her body, she had leisure to explore thoroughly, to watch the flow until another spasm of coughing began, and she could trace and block the impulse.

With the coughing stopped, Velana turned to the healing they'd been doing all along, encouraging the flow of blood to carry away the fluids from the lungs. Unable to cough, the man would drown unless she could speed the drying of his lungs. Already in contact with the patient longer than she had ever dared before, Velana went even deeper, down to the cellular level, encouraging the walls of the man's lungs to absorb the fluid and cast it into the bloodsteam to be disposed of, and then to draw extra oxygen from the air to enrich the blood for its work. . . .

In each separate sac, it seemed, Velana had to start the process afresh. Would it never end? Would it take forever to set just one patient on the road to recovery? Just as she was despairing of having time to heal all these people by this slow process, the old man's body suddenly took over. Spontaneously, the process she had set in motion continued. Velana withdrew slightly, carefully removing the nerve block.

Mordek coughed once, turned on his side, and fell into deep, healing sleep. Velana swam up to consciousness, to the awed murmurs of the other women.

"It's taken two days to reach that stage before!" cried Felina.

"And we all saw how it was done!" said Ellonie. "Velana, do you need all of us? If we divide three and three we can do twice as much, and the one left can watch both groups for signs of weakening."

"You're right," Velana agreed, and so they separated into three's, and later into pairs, one working, one supporting, the odd woman carefully watching each couple to see who needed help, or rest.

Velana's excitement faded, and with it the false strength it had lent her. As she moved from one ill person to another, they began to blend together, men, women, children—all patterns of nerves, veins, arteries, meaningless. . . .

She found herself on the stone floor, Ellonie bending over her. "You fainted."

"I'm needed—"

"No. It's all right now. Listen."

Velana listened. "I don't hear anything."

"That's right. No coughing. We've won, Velana! Everyone's resting now. Sleep, *breda*."

Velana slept, on a pallet on the floor of the great hall. She woke up once, when someone brought steaming soup. Several patients around her were also eating, and she heard only an occasional light cough, none of the deadly wheezing. Ellonie was sound asleep just a few paces away. Callina sat at the far end of the hall, concentrating on her starstone, keeping watch. Velana let herself sink back to dreamless sleep.

A crash of thunder woke her. At the same moment Velana sat up, heart pounding, others all over the great hall were doing the same. Children began to cry.

Ellonie scrambled up to comfort her four-year-old son, who was screaming, "Mama! Mama!"

The little boy clung to his mother as she murmured, "It's all right, Kyril. It's just thunder."

Watching those two curly heads, one copper, one gold, Velana smiled at the picture, herself comforted. Just thunder. Nothing to be afraid—

"Oh, no!" she gasped as lightning flashed and another peal of thunder shook the hall. The spring storms! The glacier! The shaking caused by the pounding thunder!

"We've got to go now!" she cried. "Everyone—gather what you can and run! The glacier!"

Palpable fear animated them, but Ellonie turned to Velana crying, "We can't! Velana, many are still too weak to travel."

"And there's still snow blocking the high pass," reported one of the men. "A strong man with pack animals can't get through—no way can we move women and children."

"We're trapped!" someone cried. Eyes turned to Velana. "Help us, daughter of the gods! You stopped the coughing sickness. Help us!"

Velana stared into the pleading faces. It was one thing to encourage a person's body to heal itself, quite another to turn back a glacier. Yet had she not been seeking just that? Had she not almost found an answer?

"Ellonie—gather the other women. We must go up to the glacier."

"What? But—why?"

"Because the answer is there! The day I explored the glacier through my starstone, I kept seeing something from the corner of my eye. It's there, cousin—but we must go there to find it."

With nothing else to depend on, the villagers pinned their hopes on Velana and her women. The ablest mountaineers came to help the women in their climb; other women packed food, and helped to dress the seven who would brave the glacier in layer after layer of warmest clothing.

Nonetheless, by the time they reached the edge of the field of ice, Velana and the other women were chilled through. The animals could go no farther, so Velana instructed the men to pitch camp, while she and the other women climbed up to the glacier.

The drizzling rain of the lower elevations had turned to sleet here, ice coating the rocks as they scrambled painfully upward, Velana leading them toward—what? Thunder rumbled in the distance, and she raised her head. "Look! A cave!"

She remembered her vision of walking within the heart of the glacier. Was this what it meant—a cave in the ice? For it was a cave of ice, not rock, that the women entered, grateful to be out of the sleet even within frozen walls.

They looked around in awe at the translucent ice, magnificently beautiful, white, opaque, crazed as Velana had seen it in her vision. *I must find that pure blue ice again,* she thought, and looked deeper into the cave.

Some trick of light threw a veil of shimmering rainbows across a narrower passage some distance back. There was no sunlight today . . . it was as if that veil were somehow lit from behind.

"I'm going in there," said Velana.

"We'll go with you," Ellonie replied.

"No—I must go alone. I had the vision, Cousin. I must find the spot alone."

"Velana—you can't do everything. At least let us join you through the starstones."

Remembering her vision, Velana said, "Yes—join with me through the circle, but stay here. Don't come any farther unless I call you—no matter what happens!"

The women took out their stones. It was only when the gentle touch of six minds eased her fear that Velana realized just how afraid she was. Nonetheless, her starstone twinkling in the palm of her hand, she moved determinedly toward the mysterious veil of rainbows.

It was insubstantial as it appeared, but she felt her breath stopped, every pore of her skin leaping with pain, and she stumbled forward a few steps until, as if bursting free of a bubble of illusion, she emerged into a huge crystalline cave.

In that instant, all contact with her circle died. Her starstone, glowing so brightly, went ashen gray, opaque—*like the ice in my vision!*

She turned, saw the women beyond the veil looking up at her in shock—they had felt the loss of contact. "No!" she called as they started toward her. "Stay there!" She waved them back, and they stayed, although she could see the concern on Ellonie's features. The last glimpse she had of them was in silhouette, backlighted by a flash of lightning. The thunder that followed rumbled through the ice mountain, and Velana turned, knowing her search must reach its goal soon, for the approaching storm would surely dislodge the glacier.

With her starstone dead, she felt naked, blind . . . and yet somehow it was not dead; she was still attuned to it . . . or to something. Following a sense she had never known before, she moved through the cavern. It was an ice crystal palace, wakened to exquisite beauty by some source of light she could not fathom. There were pools of frozen blue—the crystal blue she sought—amid magnificent white ice sculptures.

Suddenly, as in her vision, there was a flash at the corner of her eye. But this time when she turned she saw a frozen waterfall, streaked with cobalt blue and fiery red as varied as the hair of the women in her circle.

To see the top of the waterfall, she knelt, looking up into blue starred vaults above her. At the high, center peak of the curving ice ceiling, a point of light began to glow starstone blue, then deep gold, brightening as she looked at it.

It was a starstone, caught up from its birthplace within the living rock and carried by the glacier into the cave, frozen there eons ago—waiting for this moment. It was huge, easily two handspans, the biggest starstone Velana had ever seen.

And it's mine! This is what drew me to the cave, the power in that stone that I alone can use. As she watched, the flickering depths of the huge stone shuddered and changed, and began to pulse steadily to the beat of her heart. At the same moment, the small stone in her hand rekindled to life, and she felt renewed contact with the six women in the cave entrance. Their relief and curiosity almost broke her concentration, so she told them, *Support me. Don't interrupt. I have the answer if you'll let me alone to use it!*

That huge glowing starstone carried within it the memory of the formation of the glacier. If Velana could get at that ... she would know how to unform it!

Eyes riveted on the starstone, she concentrated, leaving the other women behind, flowing into the stone, pure blue crystal once again, one with its structure, one with its memory. Down she sank through the center of the crystal to its very structure—to the structure of each ice crystal of the glacier. She *knew*! She could destroy the glacier with one flick of a finger—except that she was frozen once again, unable to move, that terrible cold numbing everything, even her thoughts. ...

But for one spot of glowing warmth, the small starstone in her hand, glowing with the love and support of the other women. Now she knew what her vision meant. The large starstone was to unite the circle, to join their minds together in a matrix far more powerful than the sum of all their abilities combined. But all must share. It was not Velana's stone—it was the circle's.

Help me! Join with me!

Six minds joined with Velana's, and she was at once deep within the crystal and in the cave entrance with the other women, howling wind tearing at hair and clothing, thunder and lightning crashing about them.

She drew them into the frozen silence of the crystalline structure, showed them how that structure could be destroyed. Then seven minds became as one; the power of seven became infinity through the one huge crystal, all the other starstones joined, pulsing as one, surging as one to change, to end, to disrupt, to destroy utterly that mountain of imprisoning ice.

A searing, flashing CRACK lanced upward from the center of the circle, which was the center of the immense starstone. For an instant all was blackness, a void that hollowed out their nerves.

Then, with a slam that threw her on her belly on the rocks, Velana was alone again in her own body, the circle broken as the mountain shook and rumbled, the women tossed and rolled in a floundering cascade down into the camp.

The men, unable to keep their feet, shouted as the pack animals screamed and reared while the earthquake spattered loose rocks down on them, dropping boulders, animals, people in careless abandon.

When it was over, three of the women lay dead, and four of the men as well. Everyone else hovered on the brink of madness, for when they looked up above them, in the intense flashes of lightning from the retreating storm, they saw the glacier was completely gone.

Velana dragged herself to her feet, feeling a tug at her long skirts, pinned under fallen rock. As she pulled them free, she pulled the huge starstone free as well, unbroken, still pulsing to her heartbeat. *Mine?* she thought. *No, not mine, but my responsibility.*

She returned her own small starstone to its pouch, and looked for something to cover the large one, for the men were beginning to look her way and wince. Ellonie, attuned to her cousin more than ever, it seemed, came limping up to her and in businesslike fashion reached under her skirt to take off a silken petticoat. "Wrap it in that," she said. "I don't think I ever want to see it unwrapped again!"

Velana sighed, not yet ready for tears for those who lay dead, still caught up in the fact that the rest would survive. "You'll look at it again, *breda*," she said. "You were right—

this is not something for one person alone. We must teach others, form a circle again."

"Lady Velana!" called one of the men. "Lady Ellonie! Rafeo is hurt, and I can't stop the bleeding!"

"You see?" said Velana, as she and her cousin hastened to tend the wounded man. "This is what it is to be daughters of the gods. We must share the burdens or we will all die beneath them."

"Yes, *breda*," said Ellonie, and Velana knew that in her heart her cousin had known the answer all along.

From the very inception of *Starstone*, we have received more stories about the Guild of Free Amazons than all other subjects put together.

That is not surprising. Many readers of the Darkover stories are women; and the Free Amazons, more accurately called the Guild of Renunciates, is the honorable alternative for women who do not fit accurately into the stereotype heroines of a society repressive of women. It is easy for women who have suffered, and are still suffering from the limitations placed on women in *our* society, to identify with women who suffer from the limits of *theirs,* and are actively doing something about it.

However, most "Free Amazon" stories are more cathartic than creative, expressing the dissatisfaction of the women who write them, and most of them are far too grim and bitter to make good fiction. This is not, of course, surprising. The very existence of the Amazons, and the restrictions surrounding women who wish to join them, is structured in such a way that every Amazon, with few exceptions, has her own story, and most of the stories are tragic without qualification.

And, as with most tragic stories, most of them are humorless and totally lacking in a sense of perspective. Not so Linda MacKendrick's "The Rescue." When I saw it, I said, rather resignedly, "Oh, dear, another Free Amazon story," and set myself down conscientiously to plow through another searing confession, hoping to find a scrap of talent which I could encourage. Instead, I soon discovered myself giggling so hard I nearly rolled off the sofa! The story of the young Amazon, Elana, and the hunter Chadris, may err a little from over-optimism; but it's a delight, anyhow.

Linda MacKendrick is young, fair-haired, and, in Darkovan costume, has graced many get-togethers of the Friends. She is active in the Arilinn Council, and is also an aspiring artist and illustrator.

THE RESCUE

Linda MacKendrick

Chadris leaned against his bow, breathing in the scent of
last year's leaves crushed underfoot. He was enjoying this
brief patch of sunlight in the forest. The beginnings of spring
always distracted him. Slowly he shifted his feet and turned
back toward the trail. In two or three more days of traveling
time he would be deep enough in the forest to start more
serious hunting.

Patches of snow lay hidden under some of the under-
growth, while in other spots flowers were already in bloom.
He moved amid the new growth leaving barely a trace of his
passing. The sun was still climbing the sky when he came
across the signs of several people trampling through the underbrush. This was not a common way, particularly not for
so many to be using it. He decided to follow cautiously. Not
all strangers are to be mistrusted, but it is wiser to know who
else travels the forest paths. The tracks looked to be nearly a
day old. At least he could test his tracking skills. A warning
bell of caution sounded in his head when later he found the
remains of their encampment, left a few hours before and
very near the main route through these hills. Too many an
ambush had been perpetrated in that area. He had no wish to
be a stumbling bystander.

When he reached the main trail, to his dismay, his suspi-
cions were confirmed. The people had fanned out and paced
the trail, two men on one side and three on the other. Now
he moved very carefully, wondering what he would find.
Their movements were those of bandits. Perhaps an hour
passed before the signs proved him correct. Whoever had
been ambushed seemed to have joined with the attackers after a brief scuffle. At least, the two horses they had been riding were now being led by the attackers. The victims would,
no doubt, be held for ransom. Now that he was sure of the
bandits' purpose he did not want to risk meeting them. He
turned off the trail to the right, intending to proceed in that

111

direction, when something odd caught his eye. It was a patch
of bright red, like a flower, but in the midst of an area of
snow. It was red, blood red, and deep in the shadows was a
figure, thrown into the drift to die. Blood was still pumping
out of a head wound, but the cold must have slowed the
bleeding. It didn't look good, but it was impossible to tell;
wounds of this sort always seemed to bleed excessively.
Gently he moved the inert shape out of the snow, tied a
pressure bandage to the wound, and began a careful inspection for other injuries. It looked to be a young boy; what
he was doing here was puzzling. Why should they take one
and not the other? The inspection showed, beyond the head
wound, only a few bruises and scrapes. With a self-deprecating smile, Chadris realized, *my eyes aren't as good as
I thought they were—this young boy is a girl! I should have
known, her attire is that of a Free Amazon.* That, at least,
explained why she had been left for dead; she had probably
been the guide. Looking about, Chadris realized they were
too close to the trail; he would have to risk leaving her to
scout a more sheltered camp. Ten minutes later he returned
and carried her to a protected spot near a small stream.

He was now very wary of whoever else might be moving in
the woods. He had no wish to attract any unwanted attention.
Even so, she would need warmth and food if she were to survive. Considering her needs above caution, he built a small
fire. It would be a long wait before she regained consciousness. He moved to the stream, remaining within sight of her,
intent on catching some fresh fish. Time passed while, with
long patience, he caught, bare-handed, several small fish. After cleaning, they went into a stew, to simmer on the side of
the fire, while he waited.

Daylight deepened into twilight and then evening before
she stirred. At first when she opened her eyes she seemed
only to stare, then she focused on him and the fire. Her eyes
were an almost unheard-of deep blue, well complementing
her dark hair and small frame. In a vague, soft voice she
asked him, "Where is the Lady Marissa? What have you . . .
done with her?" For a moment she looked as if she would
pass out again, but she retained control and repeated her
questions.

As gently as he could he told her, "Whoever attacked you
left you for dead, and, I assume, took the Lady Marissa with
them. You were hit on the head and lost some blood. The
best remedy I can offer for your injury is to keep your head

as still as possible and to try to regain your strength by eating something." With what he hoped was an encouraging grin, he added, "I've made some stew. It's not the best, but it should be nourishing."

She raised herself up on her elbows, too quickly—stopped short, put one hand to her head and one to her stomach, and started retching. It was mostly dry heaves, which stopped soon after they began. Swallowing with difficulty, she said, "I don't think I had better eat anything."

"If you take your time in moving, you won't get so dizzy." Offering her the stew, he added, "Try a little. I'll help you." He put his arm behind her neck to support it, and steadied her head.

After two full spoonfuls she asked, "What is it? It's awful!"

Feeling relieved that she was well enough to protest, he replied, "Stew." Then, knowing the type of cook he was, he added, "All I had was beef jerky and fish; I thought it made a good combination." She was encouraged to take a few more spoonfuls for nourishment. Chadris had intended to wait but his curiosity was strong, so he asked, "Why were there only two of you navigating the Kilghard trail? There are a multitude of local marauders up here."

She took his question as a rebuff to her abilities, answering sarcastically, "And two women can't take care of themselves without a man's help, I suppose?" In a strong, firm voice she stated, "I'll have you know I'm a Free Amazon, a licensed guide and bodyguard. I'm well able to take care of myself."

He sighed. "Which, I suppose, is why I found you in a snowdrift bleeding to death? *Anyone* can be ambushed up here, which is why most people take the precaution of adding to their numbers to make it seem less desirable. Why were you traveling through here, and who attacked you? Then we can decide whether there any others of that group lurking nearby. I don't want a second ambush."

"I don't know why we were attacked," she answered. "They didn't stop to introduce themselves." Then, with a slightly tilted head and narrowed eyes, she added, "But I don't know who you are, either, or why you helped me."

Sitting cross-legged in front of her he replied with a smile, "My name is Chadris, formerly of the City Guard of Thendara, and currently a hunter for my mother's household near Braemore. I'm helping because I found you and you were alive. I would hope you'd do the same for me. Now, what is your name?"

She lifted her head slowly, but with pride. "I'm Elana n'ha Mhari, licensed guide and bodyguard of Fendale House. I was hired to protect and guide the Lady Marissa Cuerva on her return journey to her father's estate."

At the mention of the lady's name he frowned, started to say something, and stopped, considering. Once in Thendara he had met the Lady Marissa Cuerva—during a street riot. She was a very proud, arrogant woman, and had insisted on going through the midst of the rioters, simply because it was on her way and she would not detour. She had succeeded— alone. Why, he had never understood. It was possible that such a woman had chosen to travel with only one guide, although he would have expected a large retinue. He would not have thought that her Comyn pride would allow Free Amazons as guards, either, but he kept that to himself. Smiling at his charge with an almost mischievous grin, he said, "If you're going to regain your strength, you'll have to finish that stew no matter what you think of it."

She looked up suspiciously. "Have you had any of it?"

"Of course. It's one of my better efforts."

She groaned, but continued eating. Didn't even gag this time. When she finished she leaned back to rest; he gave her his pack for a pillow and propped himself against a tree to stay on guard through the long night.

The next morning she had greatly improved; the blow couldn't have been as bad as she had originally feared. She moved about with ease and even enjoyed a breakfast of fried fish. He studied her awhile before asking, "Do you plan on reporting to your Guild House, or to the Cuerva estate, first, about the kidnapping?"

She looked up, startled. "Neither. I intend to recover the Lady and fulfill my contract of employment."

"What?" He couldn't believe she was serious. The Amazons taught practicality; one person does not go up against who-knows-how-many. "Not alone."

She sounded totally calm. "Naturally. I'm trained by the Guild House to handle any situation. If I wish to remain a bodyguard, I'd better recover my charge."

Attempting to explain his initial reaction, he said, "Your motivations are admirable, but you can't do it alone. You no longer have any supplies or weapons, and you'll be facing the five men who jumped you plus any others who might be at their hideout." Sensing that he had made no impression, he continued, "What tracking experience do you have? Tracking someone through this forest can be deceptively easy, but I've seen good mountain trackers lose their quarry in these woods." Attempting to explain further, he added, "There is an overabundance of wildlife here. They can leave many false trails crisscrossing the tracks you're following and it's very easy to start following one of these false trails instead of the one you intended to follow."

"I'm an Amazon, trained by Fendale House and Fionella, expert guide."

"I didn't ask who trained you, though her competence is well known. I asked what experience you had." *Aldones, she sounds young, and what's worst, new to the Guild. I just won't feel right unless I know she can handle it.* Aloud to her, trying to sound as reasonable as possible, he said, "There is a great deal of difference between education and actual practice. How many jobs have you had?"

"Several." She tried to look as convincing as possible, but she would not look directly at him. "I know what I'm doing."

Her reluctance to look at him made him sure she was evading. "How many?"

"Three. I was Fionella's finest student."

"I'm sure you were," he tried to placate her, "or Fendale would not have allowed you to take employment as a lone guide and guard. The Guilds have stricter standards than those who do the licensing." Trying to think of a way to explain his feelings without quoting the old cliché, *Survive the blizzard only to feed the Banshee,* he added, "The problem is that the odds are against any one person, however competent, finding the hideout and the Lady, and then getting out with her. You've been injured; a concussion can temporarily throw off your sense of balance and timing, a difference which would be crucial. Now will you please get help?"

She sat on the ground, staring at a small toad which had moved into her line of vision. She took her time answering. "I have no choice. If I went for help I would lose the trail. Besides, I said I could do this alone; I staked my future reputation on being able to guard her. I must go."

He sighed, pushing his auburn hair out of his eyes. He still felt somehow responsible. "Would you like a companion, at least part way? I had intended to do some hunting in the deep woods, and one direction is as good as another."

"This is my job, not yours!" She was aware of the set look of his jaw, his arms crossed on his chest. She smiled and took a different tack. "If you wish to come, you must understand I am in charge. I will lead and all decisions about what is to be done are my responsibility. Do you agree?"

"Of course."

She looked shocked; obviously her tone of voice would have exasperated most of the men she knew. But she regained her composure. "We should get started."

During their talk, he had cleared the camp; not even the remains of the fire were detectable. All that might show their presence were some bent blades of grass, which would quickly spring back. They returned to the main trail where he had found her, and picked up the trail of the kidnappers. Nearly a full day had elapsed, but fortunately the kidnappers had been clumsy and overconfident. The signs of their passage were quite distinct. Elana took the lead and by midday they had made good time. So far there had been no deviation from the main trail. It appeared that even with the two horses, the bandits had taken their time, perhaps going at an easy pace because of Lady Marissa. Chadris suggested a noon break and received a rebuff from Elana; she had, she told him coldly, no such need of pampering. An hour later she was looking very pale and a bit wobbly on her feet.

He sat down on a log, opened his pack, and pulled out dried meat and journey bread. "You can continue if you want to. For myself, I'm tired and hungry. I'm not moving until I've eaten something." He hoped she would stop too; she looked as if she needed it.

She looked tempted but instead turned and continued down the path, pride in every movement. A few yards farther she tripped over a root and fell full length. He was there even before she hit the ground.

"Will you please stop being stubborn, and take care of yourself instead? Keep on like this, and I'll have to carry you out of these woods; something which, I am sure, would offend your dignity far more than resting." He held her up and moved her to the log he had vacated. "Do you seriously believe that being a Free Amazon stops you from being human, with human fallibility? All it really does is give you a good education, skills, and the right to choose your own destiny." He stopped, then added in a more thoughtful tone, "I realize I have no right to yell at you. I simply become upset when I see a waste of intelligence and life. I do not mean you shouldn't be proud of being an Amazon; that is something worth every ounce of pride you have." Gently smiling, "But even Hastur and Cassilda needed to rest now and again; the wisdom is in knowing that, and accepting it. Now will you please sit down, rest, and have something to eat; after all, you have to be fit enough to track."

She was confused by his attitude but sat down and took some food. "I don't understand you. You don't act like the men I've known." She spent a long time slowly chewing her food, occasionally looking at him, a slight frown on her face. Finally she said, "I've never known any man who cared about me, just as a person. For my father, women were meant to be kept pregnant; my mother spent all her adult life pregnant, until she died in childbirth. All so my father could have five sons and a daughter to rule over. And my brothers, every one of them could do their father proud." Her voice was sad and bitter. "When I became old enough to marry, each of them found a suitor for me. Oh, they all had special qualifications, they could each advance the ambitions of one or another of my brothers. But the one all five finally agreed on was fat, bald and seventy." She shuddered, remembering. "He would paw me at every opportunity with those old puffy white hands of his. And my brothers—" she was having difficulty speaking, "My brothers *encouraged* him. All because he had land and no heirs. To be put to bed with that!" Her voice was close to breaking. "I loved them. I trusted them." She stopped, blocking out the old hurt, and composed herself.

In a firmer voice she continued, "I didn't learn any self-respect until I joined the Free Amazons at Ferndale Guild House. There they taught me self-defense, and I discovered I had a natural ability for tracking. I became a person of worth because of my own abilities. That means a great deal to me." She looked directly at him, her head cocked to one side. "You seem to think somewhat the same way as the Amazons, which I feel is unusual for most men. Why are you like that?"

He said with a gentle shrug, "I am like that because my family believes the individual is very important. My parents believed very strongly in learning our strengths and weaknesses, and in respecting each other's differences. We lived near Braemore Guild House, and shared our land with them. My father wanted us to have as much education as possible. In exchange for the use of the land, the Amazons taught us to read and write, and even something of the use of medicines."

Elana had been watching him speak, her eyes wide, her head tilted to one side. Considering her background, Chadris thought what he said must have sounded incredible. He laughed softly. "I have four sisters, so it was really not so odd that they helped educate us. After all, you just said that one of the Guild's objectives is to teach women a sense of their own individual worth. As for myself, my aunt Sybil n'ha Linnea taught me how to hunt; she's my mother's sister and a licensed guide. My sister Carla also became an Amazon; she chose to spend her life at medicine." Watching her, he continued, "The other girls are more romantically conventional, but woe betide any man who tries to make unwanted advances to any one of them."

"But your father, he doesn't object to your sister and her Amazon principles?" She looked lost, as if she had only half understood what he said. She pulled herself together, having answered her own question, "No, he doesn't object, as you don't. That is something very new to me." She looked up toward the sun. "We should continue while there is still some light. Who knows how long this good weather will last? If it changes, we might lose the trail." She stood up, smiling, offering to shoulder the pack for awhile. They traveled till dark.

Two more days passed uneventfully. They climbed higher into the Kilghard Hills, following the kidnappers' crushed path. On the afternoon of the fourth day, the tracks ended in confusion. Trails went off in several directions. Here was a true test of tracking skill. Chadris leaned on his bow, silently awaiting her decision. Elana knelt down, investigating the ground. At last she straightened and indicated the more disrupted path to the right. There were no actual prints; she seemed to have decided that only their heavy-footed friends could have trampled the ground so much. She took the lead. Chadris shrugged and followed. For perhaps half an hour they trudged through the disturbed brush, until they came to a bare patch of ground, softened by melting snow. The cloven hoofprints of staghorns were clearly visible. Elana's face turned scarlet. They had not followed men and horses after all. She looked up at Chadris. He was attempting to keep a straight face and failing; his eyes sparkled and he was forcibly holding down the corners of his mouth. She tried to take offense at his mirth and couldn't. She started laughing and he joined in. "At least I could help you with your hunting," she laughed; then, with a little frown, she realized, "But you knew we were following staghorns. The brush all looked about the same on the ground. How could you tell?"

Chadris grinned. "Two reasons. The first is that I've hunted staghorns, and the one very distinctive thing about them is that their branching antlers clear a path high off the ground—" he indicated with his hand an area some feet above "Something like an inverted triangle. Men with horses are the reverse of that."

"And your second reason?"

"That's easier," he teased. She was waiting for the rest, and refused to react as she would have a few days before. He continued with a rueful smile, "I've followed the wrong tracks myself. The most embarrassing time was when Aunt Sybil first let me lead a hunting party. For half a day I followed another group of hunters instead of the staghorns—we walked right into the other camp. Sybil allowed me to do that, knowing it was the only way I'd truly remember."

With a greater sense of camaraderie, Elana spoke. "Now that I've had *my* lesson, let's find where I led us astray."

Retracing their steps, they found the true path. By nightfall they could smell the smoke of cooking fires; the stronghold could not be far. Rather than blunder into their quarry's camp, they spent the night huddled against a hillside. It was too cold to sleep; Elana told him of her mountain home and how, when she was younger, she and her brothers would hunt falcon's nests for the local lord's mews. Chadris spoke of his days in the City Guard in Thendara and how much he preferred the clear air of Braemore and the Kilghard Hills.

Birds roused them to a wet dawn, and a vision through the trees of an ancient stone fortress. The outer walls were tumbled in several places and had been down for centuries. Plants, even a tree or two, had taken root in the debris. Wreckage blocked the front gate. There was a side gate, still intact, and, by the signs, well used. A guard half-dozed against the wall, groggy from the long night. They circled the building twice, looking for a safer access than that gate. By mutual consent they climbed the rubble farthest from the side gate and took up their station in a tree. The tree was absurdly perched on what had been a battlement. During the day they counted no more than ten men moving about the courtyard. What kept drawing their attention, though, was the building itself: impressive, and most assuredly once belonging to a Domain lord. It could have housed over one hundred fighting men, and most of their families. For reasons that were not apparent, it had been abandoned long ago. Marks on the outer walls indicated that it had at least once been threatened by fire.

In this isolated area it would probably support no more than twenty outlaws at a time. They wondered at the men; discipline seemed erratic. Though the outlaws had been well organized for the ambush, they had made no attempt to cover their tracks. (Granted, the only one they might have expected to follow had been left for dead.) But even here in their stronghold, only one guard was posted at the gate and the condition of the courtyard was most unmilitary. Stable refuse was piled along one wall, and garbage from the kitchens had been added. Only the cold climate kept it from being a pesthole. With such a lax attitude, it might prove easier to get in, though escape with Marissa might not be as easy.

At dusk they ventured across the courtyard, avoiding the more noisome areas. Fortunately no bandits were in sight. When they reached a long running split in the wall, Elana led the clumb; her mountain-climbing training found handholds and footholds for the less experienced Chadris. What seemed to him an eternity ended when they climbed through a deep window, forty feet off the ground, into a disused room. Dust of decades of neglect made them wish for the clean air of the forest again. The door of the room was stuck part way open. They entered a dark corridor. Elana took the lead, one hand to the wall, and shuffling her feet so as not to trip over anything. Though they were high up in the building, it seemed more as if they were exploring a cavern. Thirty paces, then a turn to the left, fifteen paces and an open door, then at another turning they found a disused stair. Elana nearly fell down it as it unexpectedly dropped away from her right hand. Chadris reached out quickly, steadying her.

"Thanks, I wasn't expecting any stairs here. Let's follow them." Cautiously they moved down the narrow staircase to a closed door. It took their combined efforts to open it; the grating noise of its opening sounded deafening to them, though it was barely above a whisper. They had now reached the inhabited area. Every breath felt loud to them as they sneaked stealthily down the corridor. Voices could be heard vaguely echoing out of an archway at one end—one was feminine. They crept toward them, through the archway, out onto an old balcony overlooking what had once been a banquet hall.

It was magnificent. In its former days, this hall would have suited a Hastur. Huge tapestries hung from the walls, so ancient only shadow shapes could be seen. The floor was polished blue stone, and in its center was a long table made from petrified wood. Pulled up to it was a huge carved wood chair, practically a throne; and seated in the chair was a large muscular man, tanned even at this season. He was dressed in flamboyant colors, copper chains about his neck, jewels flashing on his hands; his glossy black hair and short beard added to his rakish look. He was eating from a plate of meat, picking up each piece with his fingers, letting the grease run down his arms to his elbows. Next to him was the Lady Marissa, her hands as red as her tangled hair. She was complaining, "I have never before had to do anything so disgusting as cook or wash dishes. I married you to get away from becoming a baby factory like my dull relatives, not to become your servant. Corwin, you may be an excellent lover, but I am a *Comynara*, and I *demand* that you get me servants befitting my station!"

He lifted his head, took a swig of wine, wiped his mouth on his sleeve, and belched in her direction. He looked at her with contempt. "Woman, my mother was capable of washing dishes and floors, sewing, cooking, and raising children without any help; it didn't hurt her any. Do you claim to be better than she was? Consider your answer carefully; my mother was a saint."

She stared at him, paused, and in a sly sweet voice answered, "I never met your mother, so I can't say." And then, as if she had just thought of it, "How old was she when she died?"

"Forty." A puzzled frown crossed his face.

"She could have lived many more years if she had had servants to help her. You wouldn't want me to die young, worn out before my time."

Returning to his plate, he grunted, "When you have seven children I'll get you a servant. Till then, learn. You can start with these dishes. Complain, and I'll have you clean the stables." Looking up, he commanded. "*Now*, woman!"

She stood sullenly and left the room, without the dishes. Corwin leaned an elbow on the table and swore. She returned, and with a disdainful air picked up the dishes. "Corwin, I will clean the dishes, not because of anything you say, but because I refuse to eat off filthy plates." She turned and sauntered out. Muttering, Corwin carried his wine bottle to an area under the balcony, where the heat and flickering light came from a huge fireplace.

With a gesture, Chadris indicated that they should move back to the corridor. A whispered conference decided them that an interview with the lady was necessary. To Chadris the necessity of her rescue seemed dubious: she had married the man, it seemed, freely. She might lack a pampered life, but probably no more than many other ladies in the Domains— or, for that matter, Free Amazons. But Elana was adamant; Marissa should be offered escape and freedom.

Eventually their search disclosed a suite of rooms intended for the Lord and Lady of this household: the best cared for of all the rooms they had seen. One of the three rooms should be Marissa's, where with luck they could speak to her alone. Outside the windows was a weed-choked inner court-yard where even after decades of neglect flowers still bloomed. From there a private staircase wound up to the inner room of the suite, its doorway carved with flowers and the figures of Hastur, Cassilda, and Camilla. Even the walls and floor were in fanciful tesselated patterns. Against an inner wall was a huge fireplace, its fire now banked; behind that wall was the Lord's bedroom. It contained some of the original furnishings, including a bed built into the wall that backed up the fireplace. Chadris grinned. *Clever, these old lords. How cozy for a winter night, especially with plenty of bed partners.* A search showed that the room contained nothing that could belong to Lady Marissa, even if she slept there. In the adjoining bedroom they found articles Elana recognized as Marissa's, brought on the trail, along with unfamiliar feminine paraphernalia probably stolen from wayfarers to be given to Marissa. Elana and Chadris chose inconspicuous corners to hide; they did not wish to startle Marissa into a scream or, worse, be discovered by Corwin.

Perhaps two cramped hours passed in hiding before Marissa appeared, wet and dirty. She had yet to master the art of dishwashing. She pulled off her outer dress and was about to remove the rest when Elana stepped forward.

In a reassuring voice she spoke. "Lady, it's me, Elana. Your guide. I'm here to take you home."

Marissa turned toward the voice and demanded, "You? What can you do for me?" Then she frowned and looked at Elana. "How did you find me? I thought we left you for dead!"

"I recovered and followed you here. My contract of employment was to take you to your father's estate. My duty was to protect you from your kidnappers."

"My kidnappers?" She sounded highly amused. "You Free Amazons are incredible!"

"What do you mean, my Lady?"

In her sweetest tones, Marissa said, "All that I wanted for this job was someone incompetent, who could be easily overcome. I expected that a Free Amazon would be perfect for that. I knew my father would never allow my freemate marriage to Corwin; it therefore required some arranging." She seemed to lose interest in the girl's presence and continued as though talking to herself. "As it was, you were more difficult to handle than I expected. I even had to hit you myself." Then, looking around, "Of course this place isn't all I expected. It needs a decent staff." A sly look came over her face as she turned toward the door. "But with a good servant girl it might improve." She inhaled to yell for the men, but Chadris had followed her train of thought faster than Elana, and stuffed a gag into her mouth before she could make another sound.

"Find something we can tie her up with. If she has her way, neither of us will ever get out of here."

They moved quickly; time was now their enemy. Marissa was left on the floor, tied, gagged, out of immediate sight. Corwin would be there soon enough, and they had no wish to encounter him.

This time, to Chadris' relief, they found a lower window to drop through. Watching for the guard, and fearing discovery every minute, they made their way back to the tree, where Chadris recovered his pack and bow, and they headed up a nearby ridge.

Dawn found them several miles away, bruised, tired, and lucky. A lush valley lay before them, new green leaves sparkling in the early light. Chadris looked out over the valley, stretched, and sighed. "From here I can find the trail to Candermay. You can pick up one of the main routes through these hills. Will you return to Ferndale Guild House, now that your obligation to her is over?"

"No, I must first go to the Cuerva estate, to tell her father. It will not be easy, but it is the only way to clear my name. But what about you? Will you take up your hunting again?"

"I am only one of many hunters. I was thinking, perhaps,

there might be a greater need for a pair of guides." Solemnly he gazed at her, a question in his look.

She was startled; never had such a possibility occurred to her. "I don't know. You are different from anything I had ever expected to find in a man. I know now what Fionella meant when she told me that not all people will fit into the categories I had assigned them. You don't fit. And Marissa, though she is a woman, is *not* my sister. It will be difficult to change my attitudes, even some of those about myself." Then, with a self-deprecating laugh, "I have a long way to go before I can work with anyone else. For now, I have to work with myself." Smiling softly up at him, she added, "Perhaps in a different season, we might meet again. "Who knows?"

He nodded in acceptance. "Let us at least journey to Candermay together." There was a mischievous gleam in his eye. "One day I intend to learn mountain climbing, and I will need an expert teacher."

I became acquainted with Elisabeth Waters, first author of "The Keeper's Price," because of religion.

One of my best friends, who started as a fan, and quickly rose from that level to close personal friendship and later to write and sell her own work, is Jacqueline Lichtenberg, who has a story elsewhere in this anthology. On several occasions, visiting New York, I have stayed in the home of Jacqueline and her family. However, Jacqueline is a rigidly orthodox Jew; and I was nervous about spending a Sabbath in her home, not from prejudice—I would have been extremely interested to observe—but out of fear that I might commit some terrible blunder or do something which would infringe upon the strict laws of their observance, and offend her family—Jacqueline, I knew, would put my blunders down to ignorance, but I was hesitant about distressing her family.

And so a friend of hers, whom I had met briefly and casually at an afternoon gathering at Jacqueline's, and who agreed with me that spending Sabbath in a kosher home is an acquired taste, invited me to spend the weekend with her, adding the inducement that we could drive up the beautiful Hudson river country to Peekskill and attend vespers at the convent of which Lisa Waters is an Associate.

During that weekend, Lisa mentioned that she had been fascinated by the briefly-mentioned Hilary Castamir, the failed Keeper in *Forbidden Tower*, and had written a short story about her. As it happened, I too had written a story about Hilary, and we agreed to exchange stories.

"The Keeper's Price" impressed me deeply as a story of tremendous, raw power; Lisa had indeed gotten into the skin of the suffering Hilary. There were flaws in the story; and there were things Lisa did not know about the training of the Keepers which, I felt, would add strength to the story. So, with Lisa's permission, I ran the story through my typewriter, and added a few of these things, making it a little more coherent. The resultant story, printed in *Starstone*, aroused tremendous interest in Hilary; we have received several other stories dealing with her later life, love, marriage, and the like.

But this one, written in collaboration with my dear friend (as she is now) Lisa Waters, is the best of them, and my own personal favorite.

Elisabeth Waters is twenty-six years old, lives in Stamford, Connecticut, and is acquiring an M.S. in Computer and Information Science, meanwhile working full-time as an executive secretary for a local business. And she still has time to write—on a schedule which puts her in the same category as the "jugglers" mentioned elsewhere; a college program vies with young children and a household when it comes to being demanding! When she finishes her Master's degree, I'm really looking forward to seeing what she'll do in the creative field.

THE KEEPER'S PRICE

by Marion Zimmer Bradley

with Lisa Waters

The pain had started.

Hilary was aware of it even in her sleep, but, knowing that her body needed at least another two hours' rest, she tried to ignore it. But the gnawing discomfort deep in her body would not be ignored; after an hour she gave up the futile attempt and threw on a robe, slipping silently down the stairs to the still-room to make herself a cup of golden-flower tea. She knew from experience that it would numb the cramping pain, at least a little.

It might also, she thought, settling back into her bed, make her sleepy. At least that was what the other women said. Somehow it never seemed to work that way with Hilary. It only made her arms numb and her head feel fuzzy, and the room seemed unbearably warm as things swam in and out of focus. The effects of the tea wore off all too quickly, and the heavy cramping pains, contractions, Leonie called them, became worse and worse, moving up from her abdomen to her stomach to her heart, so that she felt constricted and aching, struggling for breath.

She had only to call, she knew, and someone would come. But in a Tower filled with telepath, help would be there when she absolutely needed it. And she didn't want to disturb anyone unless she had to.

After all, she thought wryly, *this happens every forty days. They should be used to it by now. Just Hilary again, going through her usual crisis, disturbing everybody as usual.*

The circle had been mining metal the night before, and everyone had gone to bed late and exhausted, especially Leonie. Leonie of Arilinn had been Keeper since she was a young girl; now she was an old woman—Hilary did not know how old—training Hilary and the new child, Callista Lanart, to be Keepers in her place. For the last half-year Hilary had been able to work at Leonie's side, during the heavy stresses of the work, taking some of the burden from the older woman. She wasn't going to drag Leonie out of bed to hold her hand. They wouldn't let her die. Maybe this month it would be only the cramping pain, the weakness; after all, there wasn't a woman in Arilinn who didn't have some trouble when her cycle started. It was simply one of the hazards of the work. Maybe this time it would subside, as it did in the other women, before she went into crisis, without the agonizing clearing of the channels. . . .

But they couldn't wait too long, hoping it would clear spontaneously. Last time, wanting to spare her the excruciating ordeal, Leonie had waited too long; and Hilary had gone into convulsions. But that wouldn't happen for hours, maybe for days. Let Leonie sleep as long as she could. She could bear the pain till then.

Hilary adored Leonie; the older woman had been like a mother to her ever since she had come to Arilinn, five years before, a lonely, frightened child of eleven, enduring the first testing of a girl with Comyn blood, the loneliness, the waiting until, when her woman's cycles began, she could begin serious training as Keeper. She had been proud to be chosen for this. Most of the young people who came here were selected as monitor, mechanic, even technician—but very few had the talent or potential to be a Keeper, or could endure the long and difficult training. And now Hilary was near to that goal.

Had all but achieved it; except for one thing. Every time, when her cycles started, there was the pain, the cramping contractions quickly escalating to agony, and sometimes to crisis and convulsions.

She knew why, of course. Like all matrix workers, she had begun her training as a monitor, learning the anatomy of the nerve channels which carried *laran*—and, unfortunately, also carried the sexual energies. Hilary had known, from the time she agreed to take training as a Keeper, that she must pay the Keeper's price; ordinary sexuality was not for her, and she had solemnly sworn, at thirteen, a vow of perpetual chastity. She had been taught, in all kinds of difficult and somewhat frightening ways, to avoid in herself even the slightest sexual arousal, so that the lower nerve centers which would carry these energies were wholly clear and uncontaminated, the channels between the centers nonfunctional.

Only, somehow, the channels were *not* clear at this time, and it puzzled all of them. Hilary, who lived under Leonie's immediate supervision, and rarely drew a breath Leonie did not know about, knew that her chastity was not suspect; so it had to be something else, perhaps some unsuspected weakness in the nerve centers.

The only thing that pulled Hilary through each moon, and sent her back to work again in the screens, was her desire not to fail Leonie. She could not leave Leonie to shoulder the burden alone, not when she was so close to her goal. Leonie had been letting her, now, take a part of the burden as Keeper, at the center of the circle, and Hilary knew, without conceit, that she was capable and strong, that she could handle the linked energies of a circle up to the fourth level without too much drain on her energies. Soon, now, Leonie would be free of at least a part of the burden.

Little Callista showed promise and talent; but she was only a child. It would be a year before she could begin serious training, though she was already living with the carefully supervised life of a pledged Keeper and had been allowed to make provisional vows; it would be years before she would be old enough to take on any part of the serious work. There was so much work to do, and so few to do it! Arilinn was not alone in this; every Tower in the Domains was short-handed.

The last effects of the tea were gone. Outside the window it was sunrise, but no one was stirring. Now the pains seemed to double her into a tight ball; she rolled herself up and moaned to herself.

Don't be silly, she told herself. *You're acting like a baby. When this is over you'll hardly remember how much it hurt.*

Yes, but how much longer can I stand this?

As long as you have to. You know that. What good is your training, if you can't stand a little pain?

Another wave of pain washed over her, effectively silencing the inner dialogue. Hilary concentrated on her breathing, trying to still herself, to let the breath flow in and out quietly, one by one monitoring channel after channel, trying to ease the flow of the currents. But the pains were so violent that she could not concentrate.

It's never been this bad before! Never!

"Hilary?" It was the gentlest of whispers. Callista was bending over her, a slight long-legged girl, her red hair loosely tied back, a heavy robe flung over her nightgown. She was barefoot. "Hilary, what is it?"

Hilary gasped, breathing hard.

"Just—the usual thing."

"I'd better get Leonie."

"Not yet," Hilary whispered, "I can manage a little longer. Stay with me though. Please. . . ."

"Of course," Callista said. "Hilary, your nightgown is soaking wet; you'd better get out of it. You'll feel better when you're dried off."

Hilary managed to pull herself upright, to slide out of the gown, drenched with her own sweat. Callista brought her a dry one from her chest, held it while Hilary slipped it over her head; maneuvering deftly, so carefully that she did not touch Hilary even with a fingertip.

She is learning, Hilary thought, and looked with wry detachment at the small scarred-over burns on her own hands; remnants of the first year of her training. In that year she had been so conditioned to avoid a touch, that the slightest touch of living flesh would create a deep blistered burn exactly as if the other flesh were a live coal. Callista's scars were still red and raw; even now she would punish herself with a deep burn if she touched anyone even accidentally. Later, when the conditioning was complete, the command would be removed—Hilary was no longer forbidden to touch anyone, the prohibition was no longer needed; she *could* touch or be touched, with great caution, if it was unavoidable—but no one touched a Keeper; even in the matrix chamber, a Keeper was robed in crimson so that no one would touch her when she was carrying the load of the energons.

And among themselves, even when the conditioning was no more than a memory, they used the lightest of fingertip-touches, more symbolic than real. Hilary, settling back on the clean dry pillow—Callista had changed the pillow-cover, too—wished rather wistfully that she could hold someone's hand. But such a touch would torment Callista and probably wouldn't make her feel any better.

"It's really bad this time, isn't it, Hilary?"

Hilary nodded, thinking, *She is still young enough to feel compassion. She hasn't yet been dehumanized. . . .*

"You're lucky," Hilary said with effort. "Still too young to go through this. Maybe it won't be so bad for you. . . ."

"I don't know how you bear it—"

"Neither do I," Hilary murmured, doubling up again under the fresh wave of violent pain, and Callista stood helpless, wondering why Hilary's struggles hadn't yet waked Leonie.

"I made her promise to sleep in one of the insulated rooms last night," Hilary said, picking the unspoken question out of the child's mind.

"Did you get all the copper mined?"

"No; Romilla broke the circle early; Damon had to carry Leonie to her room, she couldn't walk . . ."

"She's been working too hard," Callista said, "but Lord Serrais will be upset; he's been badgering us for that copper since midsummer."

"He won't get it at all if we kill Leonie with overwork," Hilary said, "and I'm no good one ten-day out of every four."

"Maybe overworking is why you get so sick, Hilary."

"I'd get sick anyway. But overworking does seem to make it worse," Hilary muttered, "I don't have the strength to fight off the pain anymore."

"I wish I'd hurry and grow up so I could be trained, and help you both," Callista said, but suddenly she was frightened. Would this happen to her too?

"Take your time, Callista, you're only eleven. . . . I'm glad your training is going so well," Hilary murmured, "Leonie says you are going to be really great, better than I am, so much better . . . we need Keepers so badly, so badly. . . ."

"Hilary, hush, don't try to talk. Just try to even out your breathing."

"I'll live. I always do. But I'm glad you're doing so well. I'm so afraid. . . ."

"That you won't be able to work as a Keeper anymore?"

"Yes, but I have to, Callista, I have to—"

"No you don't," said the younger girl, perching on the end of Hilary's bed, "Leonie will release you, if it's really too much for you. I heard her tell Damon so."

"Of course she will," Hilary whispered, "but I don't want her to be alone with all the weight of the work again. I love her, Callista. . . ."

"Of course you do, Hilary. We all do. I do, too."

"She's worked so hard, all her life—we can't let her down now! We can't!" Hilary struggled upright, gasping. "The others—there were six others who tried and failed, and there were so many times she tried to train a Keeper only to have her leave and marry—and Callista, she's not young, not strong enough anymore, we may be her last chance, she may not be strong enough to train Keepers after us, we *have* to succeed—it could be the end of Arilinn, Callista—"

"Lie down, Hilary. Don't upset yourself like this. Just relax, try to get control of your breathing, now." Hilary lay back on the bed, while Callista came and bent over her. Light was beginning to filter through the window of her room. She did not speak as Callista bent over her, but her thoughts were as tormented as her body. There must be Keepers, otherwise darkness and ignorance closed over the Domains. And she could not fail, could not let Leonie down.

Callista ran her small hands over Hilary's body, not touching her; about an inch from the surface of the night-gown. Her face was intent, remote. After a little she said, troubled, "I'm not very good at this yet. But it looks as if the lower centers were involved, and the solar plexus too, already—Hilary, I'd better waken Leonie."

Wordless, Hilary shook her head. "Not yet." The cramping pain had moved all through her body now, so that she found it hard to breathe, and Callista looked down, deeply troubled. She said, "Why does it happen, Hilary? It doesn't happen with the other women—I've monitored them during their cycles—and they—" She stopped, turning her eyes away; there were some things from which a Keeper turned her mind and her words away as she would have turned her physical eyes from an obscenity, but they both knew what the quick equivocal glance meant: *and they are not even virgins. . . .*

"I don't know, Callista. I swear I don't," Hilary said, feeling again the terrifying sting of guilt. *What forbidden thing can I have done, not knowing, that the channels are not*

*clear? How can I have become contaminated . . . what is
wrong with me? I have kept my vows, I have touched no one,
I have not even thought any forbidden thought, and yet . . .
and yet . . .* another wave of pain struck her, so that she
turned over, biting her lip hard, feeling it break and blood
run down her chin; she did not want Callista to see, but the
child was still in rapport with her from the monitoring, and
she gasped with the physical assault of it.

"Callista, I have tried so hard, I don't know what I have
done, and I can't let her down, I can't . . ." Hilary gasped,
but the words were so blurred and incoherent that the young
girl heard them only in her mind; Hilary was struggling for
breath.

"Hilary, never mind, just lie quiet, try to rest."

"I can't—I can't—I've got to know what I have done
wrong."

Callista was only eleven; but she had spent almost a year
in the Tower, a year of intense and specialized training; she
recognized that Hilary was fast slipping into the delirium of
first-stage crisis. She ran out of the room, hurrying up the
narrow stairs to the insulated room where Leonie slept. She
pounded on the door, knowing that this summons would
rouse Leonie at once; no one in Arilinn would venture to disturb Leonie now except for a major emergency.

After a moment the door opened, and Leonie, very pale,
her graying hair in two long braids over her shoulders, came
to the door. "What is it? Callista, child!" She caught the
message before Callista could speak a word.

"Hilary again? Ah, merciful Avarra, I had hoped that this
time she would escape it—"

Then her stern gaze flickered down Callista; the robe but-
toned askew, the nightgown dragging beneath it, the bare
feet.

This is no way for a Keeper to appear before anyone! The
harsh reproof of the thought was like a mental slap, though
aloud she only said, and her voice was mild, "Suppose one of
the others had seen you like this, child? A Keeper must always present a picture of perfect decorum. Go and make
yourself tidy, at once!"

"But Hilary—" Callista opened her mouth to protest,
caught Leonie's eyes, dropped her own gray eyes and murmured, "Yes, my mother."

"You need not dress if your robe is properly fastened.
When you are perfectly tidy, go and send Damon to Hilary;

this is too serious for Romilla alone. And I will come when I can."

Callista wanted to protest—*Waste time in dressing myself when Hilary is so sick? She could be dying!*—but she knew this was all a part of the discipline which would make her, over the years, into a schooled, inhumanly perfect machine, like Leonie herself. Quickly she brushed her red hair and braided it tightly along her neck, slipped into a fresh robe and low indoor boots of velvet which concealed her bare ankles; then she knocked at the door of the young technician, Damon Ridenow, and gave her message.

"Come with me," Damon said, and Callista followed him down the stairs, into Hilary's room.

A Keeper must always present a picture of perfect decorum—even so, Callista was shocked at the effort Hilary made to compose her limbs, her voice, her face. She went and stood beside Hilary, looking compassionately down at her, wishing she could help somehow.

Damon sighed and shook his head as he looked down at Hilary's racked body, her bitten lips. He was a slight, dark man with a sensitive, ascetic face, the compassion in it carefully schooled to impassivity in a Keeper's presence. Yet it came through, a touch of faint humanity behind the calm mask.

"Again, *chiya?* I had hoped the new medicines would help this time. How heavy is the bleeding?"

"I don't know——" Hilary was trying hard to control her voice; Damon frowned a little, and shook his head. He said to Callista, "I don't suppose—no, you cannot touch anyone yet, can you, child? Leonie will be here soon, she will know——"

Leonie, when she came, was as calm, as carefully put together as if she were facing the Council. "I am here, child," she said, laying the lightest of touches on Hilary's wrist, and the very touch seemed to quiet Hilary somewhat, as if it stablized her ragged breathing. But she whispered, "I'm so sorry, Leonie—I didn't want to—I can't let you down—I can't, I can't——"

"Hush, hush, child. Don't waste your strength," Leonie commanded, and behind the harshness of the words there was tenderness, too. "Callista, did you monitor her?"

Callista, biting her lip, composed herself to make a formal report on what she had discovered. The older telepaths listened, and Damon went over the monitoring process for himself, sinking his mental awareness into the girl's tormented body, pointing out to Callista what she had missed.

"The knots in the arms; that is only tension, but painful. The bleeding is heavy, yes, but not dangerously. Did you check the lower channels?"

Callista shook her head and Damon said, "Do it now. And test for contamination."

Callista hesitated, her hands a considerable distance from Hilary, and Damon's voice was harsh.

"You know how to test her. Do it."

Callista drew a deep breath, schooling her face to the absolute impassivity she knew she must maintain or be punished. She dared not even form clearly the thought, *I'm sorry, Hilary, I don't want to hurt you*—she focused on her matrix, then lowered her awareness into the electrical potential of the channels. Hilary screamed. Callista flinched and recoiled, but Leonie had seen, and forced swift rapport so that Callista, immobilized, felt the wave of sharp pain flood through her as well. She knew the lesson intended—*you must maintain absolute detachment*—and forced her face and her voice to quiet, concealing the resentment she felt.

"Both channels are contaminated, the left somewhat more than the right; the right only in the nerve nodes, the left all the way from the center complex. There are three focuses of resistance on the left—"

Damon sighed. "Well, Hilary," he said gently, "you know as well as I what must be done. If we wait much longer, you will go into convulsions again."

Hilary flinched inwardly with dread, but her face showed nothing, and somewhere, in a remote corner of her being, she was proud of her control.

"Go and fetch some *kirian*, Callista, there is no sense waking anyone else for this," Leonie said, and when the child returned with it, she was about to run away. But Leonie said, "This time, you must stay, Callista. There may be times when you must do this unaided, and it is not too early to learn every step of the process."

Callista met Hilary's eyes, and there was a flash of rebellion in them. She thought, *I could never hurt anyone like that . . .* but despite her terrible fear, she forced herself to stand quiet.

Will they make me go through it this time in rapport with her. . . ?

Damon held Hilary's hand, giving her the telepathic drug

which would, a little, ease the resistances to what contact they must make with her mind and body, clearing the channels. Hilary was incoherent now, slipping rapidly into delirium; her thoughts blurred, and Callista could hardly make them out.

Once again to lie still and let myself be cut into pieces and then stitched back together again, that is what it feels like . . . and they are training even little Callista to be a torturer's assistant . . . to stand by without a flicker of pity. . . .

"Gently, gently, my darling," Leonie said, and the compassion and dread would communicate itself to Hilary and add "When it is over, it will be better."

She is so cruel, and so kind, how do I know which is real? Callista could not tell whether it was her own thought or Hilary's. She knew she was tense, numb with fear, and forced herself to breathe deeply and relax, fearing that her own tension and dread would communicate itself to Hilary and add to the other girl's ordeal; and she watched with amazement and dread as Hilary's taut face relaxed, wondered at the discipline which let Hilary go limp; Callista forced herself to calm, to detachment, watching every step of the long and agonizing process of clearing the blocked nerve channels.

When they were sure she wasn't going to die, not this time anyway, they left her sleeping—Callista, feeling Hilary slip down into the heaviness of sleep under the sedative they had given her, felt almost light-headed with relief; at least she was free of pain! Damon went to find himself a delayed breakfast, and Leonie, in the hallway outside Hilary's door, said softly, "I am sorry you had to endure that, little one, but it was time for you to learn; and you needed the practice in detachment. Come, she will sleep all day and perhaps most of the night, and when she wakes, she will be well. And next month we must make sure she does not overwork herself this way at this time."

When they were in Leonie's rooms, facing one another over the small table set in the window, and Leonie was pouring for them from the heavy silver pot, Callista felt tears flooding the back of her throat. Leonie said quietly, "You can cry now, if you must, Callista. But it would be better if you could learn to master your tears, too."

Callista bent her head with a silent struggle; finally she said, "Leonie, it was worse this time, wasn't it? She's been getting worse, hasn't she?"

"I'm afraid so; ever since she began work with the energons. Last time it took her three days to build up enough energy leakage to go into crisis."

"Does she know?"

"No. She doesn't remember much of what happens when she's in pain."

"But Leonie—she wants, so terribly, not to disappoint you—" *and so do I*, thought Callista, struggling again with her tears.

"I know, Callista, but she'll die if she keeps this up. She is simply too frail to endure the stress. There may be some kind of inborn weakness in the channels—I am to blame, that I accepted her without being certain there was no such physical weakness. Yet she has such talent and skill—" Leonie shook her head sorrowfully. "You may not believe it, Callista, but I would gladly take all her pain upon myself if it would cure her. I feel I cannot bear to hurt her again like that!"

Before the vehemence in the older woman's voice Callista was shocked and amazed.

Can she still feel? I thought she had taught herself to be wholly indifferent to the sufferings of others, and she would have me.

"No," Leonie said, with a remote sadness, "I am not indifferent to suffering, Callista."

But you hurt me so, this morning.

"And I will hurt you again, as often as I must," Leonie said, "but, believe me, child, I would so much rather . . ." She could not finish, but, in shock, Callista realized that she meant what she said; Leonie would willingly suffer for *her*, too . . . suddenly, Callista knew that instead of indifference, Leonie's level voice held agonized restraint.

"My mother," Callista burst out, through the restraint, "will I suffer so, when I am become a woman?"

Could I endure it? Time and again, to be torn by that kind of pain . . . and then to be torn apart by the clearing process . . .

"I do not know, dear child. I truly hope not."

Did you? But Callista knew she would never dare to put her unspoken question into words. Leonie's restraint had gone so deep that even to herself she had probably barricaded even the memory of pain.

"Isn't there anything we can do?"

"For Hilary? Probably not. Except to care for her while we can, and when it is truly too much for her to endure, release her." It seemed now to Callista that Leonie's calm was sadder than tears or hysterical weeping. "But for you—I do not know. Perhaps. You might not wish it. If I had my way," Leonie said, "every girl coming to work here as Keeper would be neutered before she comes to womanhood!"

Callista flinched as if the Keeper had spoken an obscenity; indeed, by Comyn standards she had. But she said obediently, "If that is your will, my mother—"

Leonie shook her head. "The laws forbid it. I wonder if the Council know what they are doing to you with their concern? But there is another way. You know that we cannot begin your training until your cycles of womanhood are established—"

"The monitors have said it will be more than a year."

"That is late; which means there is still time."

Callista had eagerly awaited the first show of blood, which would mean that she was a woman grown, ready to begin her serious training as Keeper; now she had begun to think of it with dread. Leonie said, "If we were to begin your training now, it would make certain physical alterations in your body; and the cycles probably would not begin at all. This is why we are not supposed to begin this training until the Keeper-novice is come to womanhood, the training changes a body still immature. And then you would never have the problem Hilary has had . . . but I cannot do this without your consent, even to save you suffering.

To be spared what Hilary suffered? Callista wondered why Leonie should hesitate a moment.

"Because it might mean much to you, when you are older," Leonie said. "You might wish to leave, to marry."

Callista made a gesture of repugnance. She had been taught to turn her thoughts away from such things; in her innocence she felt only the most enormous contempt for the relationship between men and women. Secure in her chastity, she wondered why Leonie believed she could ever be false to the pledge she had sworn to perpetual virginity.

"I will never wish to marry. Such things are not for me," she said, and Leonie shook her head, with a little sigh.

"It would mean that you would remain much as you are now, for the cycles would not begin. . . ."

"Do you mean I wouldn't grow up?" Callista did not think she wished to remain always a child.

"Oh, yes," Leonie said, "you would grow up, but without that token of womanhood."

"But since I am sworn to be Keeper," said Callista, who

had been taught a considerable amount of anatomy and knew, at least technically, what that maturity meant, "I do not see why I should need it."

Leonie smiled faintly. "You are right, of course. I would that I had been spared it, all those many years."

Callista looked at her in surprise and wonder; never had Leonie spoken to her like this, or loosened even a little the cold barricade she kept against any kind of personal revelation. *So she is not . . . not superhuman. She is only a woman, like Hilary or Romilla or . . . or me . . . she can weep and suffer . . . I thought, when I was grown, when I had learned my lessons well and had come to the Keeper, that I would learn not to feel such things or to suffer with them. . . .* It was a terrifying thought, a new terror among the terrors she had known here, that she would not safely outgrow those feelings. She had believed that her own sufferings were only because she was a child, not yet perfected in learning. *I had believed that to be a Keeper one must outgrow these feelings, that one reason I was not yet ready was that I still had not learned to stop feeling so. . . .*

Leonie watched her, without speaking, her face remote and sad.

She is such a child, she is only now beginning to guess at the price of being Keeper. . . .

But all she said aloud was, "You are right, of course, my dearest; since you are sworn to be Keeper, you do not need that, and you will be better without it, and if we should begin your training now, you will be spared."

Again she hesitated and warned, "You know it is against custom. You will be asked if I have fully explained it to you, what it will mean, and if you are truly willing; because I could not, under the laws made by those who have never stepped inside a Tower and would not be accepted if they did, do this to you without your free consent. Do you completely understand this, Callista?"

And Callista thought, *She speaks as if it were a great price I must pay, that I might be unwilling. As if it were deprivation, something taken from me. Instead it means only that I can be Keeper, and that I need not pay the terrible price Hilary has had to pay.*

"I understand, Leonie," she said, steadily, "and I am willing. When can I begin?"

"As soon as you like, then, Callista."

But why, Callista wondered, *does Leonie look so sad?*

In the published version of *The Heritage of Hastur*, the scene between Danvan Hastur and Kennard Alton, appearing on page 46, was printed in a somewhat abridged version; the reference to Kennard Alton's first marriage passes almost unnoticed. I am here presenting the scene as I originally wrote it.

He paced the floor, his uneven step and distraught face betraying the emotion he tried to keep out of his voice.

"You are not a telepath, Hastur. It was easy for you to do what your clan required of you. The Gods know, I tried to love Caitlin. It wasn't her fault . . ."

"Was that marriage ever even consummated, Ken?"

"That question is an insult and an invasion of privacy! Do you think I didn't want a legitimate son?" he flung at Hastur, "but, knowing what I knew about myself after those years at Arilinn, I knew that if I had no sons by Elaine I would die childless. And because I chose to be fair with both the women, instead of continuing in a meaningless marriage which bound us both to a life without love, I must see my sons suffer for it! I could have kept Caitlin in my house, and forced her to foster my bastards! Elaine gave the Alton Domain two sons, and you choose to treat her as if she had never been my wife!"

Kennard's first marriage was loveless. When I wrote the paragraphs above, I did not know why. This story, perhaps, gives some hint as to the events which altered Kennard from the light-hearted youngster of *Star of Danger* to the embittered cynic of *The Bloody Sun* and *Heritage of Hastur.* ─

THE HAWK-MASTER'S SON

by Marion Zimmer Bradley

Dyan Ardais laid down his pack on the narrow cot, covered with a single rough blanket, which would be his in the cadet barracks, and started to transfer his gear into the wooden chest standing at the foot of the bed.

Third year; the final year as a cadet. He was just enough older than the others to put him out of step as a cadet; he had spent his first two cadet years here before his father's inexplicable decision—and all of his father's decisions were inexplicable to Dyan—that he should spend several years in Nevarsin Monastery. Now, an equally inexplicable whim had brought him back here.

He thought, with resignation so deep that he did not fully realize how bitter it was, that his family did not seem to care where he was—Nevarsin, the cadet corps, in one of Zandru's nine hells—so long as he was not at Ardais.

He had been glad to leave Nevarsin, however. He had learned much there, including the mastery of *laran* denied him when the Keeper of Dalereuth Tower had refused to admit him to a Tower circle; he had seriously wished to study the healing arts and medicine, and he had been given ample opportunity, at Nevarsin, to study these things normally denied to a son of the Comyn. More than this; he had been able to forget himself there, giving himself up to his first love, music and singing in the great Nevarsin choir. The Father Cantor had admired his clear treble voice and gone to some trouble to have it trained; the saddest day of Dyan's life had been the day his voice broke, and his mature singing voice turned out to be a clear, tuneful but undistinguished baritone.

But it was not really suitable, that a Comyn heir should live among *cristoforos*. He had accepted their discipline with calm, cynical obedience, as a means to an end, without the slightest intent of taking their rules of life into his personal world-view; and when the time came, he had left them without much regret. Tempting as it might be, to give his life to

140

music and healing, he had always known that his real vocation, the path laid out for every Comyn son, was here; to
serve, and later to rule, among the Comyn. There was a
Council seat awaiting him, as soon as he was old enough to
take it.

And as soon as he completed this mandatory third year in
the cadet corps there would be an officer's post in the Guard.
The Commander of the Thendara City Guard, Valdir Alton,
had only one son of an age to command; Lewis-Valentine
Lanart was nineteen. Valdir's younger son, Kennard, had
been sent to Terra, a few years ago, as an exchange student
for the young Terran, Lerrys Montray. Dyan had known Lerrys, a little, during his own second cadet year; Lerrys had
been allowed to serve a single year in the cadets, in token
that he was taking up the obligation of a Comyn son. Dyan
had heard his superiors say that the young Terran had been a
credit to his people, but Dyan felt cynical about that. They
could hardly expel or harry a political guest, so they would
find tactful praise for whatever he did right, and ignore his
blunders and it would make for excellent diplomatic rela-
tions.

Dyan wondered why the Comyn bothered. It would be better to send all of those damned Terrans yelping back to whatever godforgotten world had spawned them!

Dyan remembered Lerrys Montray as a pleasant-looking,
amiable young nonentity, but he could have been a dozen
times as capable and competent and Dyan would still have
loathed him. For Larry had taken Kennard Alton's place—
and for Dyan, no man alive, not the legendary Son of Aldones, could have done that. Dyan had fiercely resolved that
this Terran intruder get no joy of his usurped place;
he flattered himself that he had made things damned difficult
for the presumptuous Terran who thought he could stand in
Kennard Alton's boots!

As if some trace of precognition had sent the thought of
Kennard to his mind moments before the reality, a voice behind Dyan said softly "You're here before me, cousin? I had
hoped to find you here, *Janu.* . . ."

Only one person living, since Dyan's mother had died ten
years before, had ever dared to use that childish pet-name.
Dyan's breath caught in his throat, then he was swept into a
familiar kinsman's embrace.

"Kennard!"

Kennard hugged him tight, then held him off at arm's

length. "Now I really know I am home again, *bredu* . . . so you interrupted your time in the Cadets too? Third year?"

"Yes. And you?"

"I finished my third year before I left, remember? But Lewis has gone to Arilinn Tower, so Father wants me as his *seconde* this year. I'll be your officer, Dyan. How old are you now?"

"Seventeen. Just one year younger than you, Kennard—or had you forgotten, we have the same birthday?"

Kennard chuckled. "Why, so I had. But you remembered?"

"There isn't much I don't remember about you, Ken," Dyan said, with an intensity that made the older lad frown. Dyan saw the frown and quickly went back to lightness. "When did you come back?"

"Only a few days ago, just time enough to pay my respects to my foster sister and my mother. Cleindore is at Arilinn now, and of course, there is talk of marriage, or at least handfasting, for all of us. And what about you, Dyan? You're at the age when they start talking about such things."

Dyan shrugged. "There was some talk of marrying me to Maellen Castamir," he said, "but there is time enough for that; she is still playing with dolls; there might be a handfasting, but certainly not a wedding, not for ten years and more. Which suits me well enough. And you?"

"Talk," Kennard said, "There's always talk. Time enough to listen when it's something more than talk. Meanwhile I can renew my old friendships—and speaking of old friendships," he said, and broke off as two young men came into the barracks.

"Rafael!" he said, then laughed, looking at the second youth. "I mean, of course, both of you!"

Rafael Hastur, Heir to Hastur, a slight, handsome youngster, with eyes nearer to blue than the true Comyn gray, smiled merrily and held out both hands to Kennard. "It is good to see you again, cousin! And you, Dyan—do you know Rafael-Felix Syrtis, my paxman and sworn man?"

Kennard smiled at him, "We probably met as boys; before I was sent to Terra. But I know your family, of course; the Syrtis hawks are famous."

"As famous as the Armida horses," young Syrtis said, smiling. "I heard you were to be one of our officers, Captain Alton."

"Kennard will do," Kennard said genially, "There's no

need for formality here, kinsman. You know my cousin Dyan, don't you?"

Dyan frowned and gave Rafael Syrtis the most distant of nods, his frown reproving Kennard's effusive friendliness. A Syrtis, the son of the hawk-master, and a *cristoforo* too, as the Syrtis folk had been for generations, was no suitable paxman or companion for a Hastur heir, and, to look at the two of them, Dyan sensed they were not paxman and master alone, but *bredin* as well! Young Syrtis addressed his master in the familiar inflection, and he saw that the young Syrtis, though he was only a minor noble, wore in his sheath a dagger with the fine Hastur crest. Well, Rafael Hastur might have a taste for low company, but he could not force his commoner friend on other Comyn! He began talking to Rafael Hastur, pointedly ignoring young Syrtis' sycophantic efforts to be friendly. Young Hastur tried to include his friend in the conversation, but Dyan gave him only brief, frigidly courteous replies.

After a time Kennard went to attend on his father, and one of the Arms-masters sent for Dyan; Rafael Hastur and Rafael Syrtis remained in the barracks, helping each other put away their possessions.

Rafael Hastur said, in apology, "You must not mind Dyan, my friend. The Ardais are proud . . . he was disgustingly rude to you, Rafe; I regard that as an insult to myself, and I shall tell him so!"

Rafael Syrtis laughed and shrugged. "He is very young for his age," he said, "He has always been a bit like that, acting as if he thought himself far above everyone else, probably because he is self-conscious . . . his father, you know. I should not say so about a Comyn Lord, but old Lord Kyril is a disgusting old sot, the most unpleasant drunk I have ever met."

"You won't hear any arguments from me about that," Rafael said, "I have no love for my Uncle of Ardais. But Dyan used to be a nice lad."

Rafe Syrtis shrugged. "Well, I can live without his liking. But I'm sorry for the lad; he has not many friends. He would have more, no one would blame Dyan for the old man's faults, but he is prickly and over-swift to take offense and slight others before they can snub him. Dom Rafael, shall I go and look at the duty lists and see where and when we are assigned?"

"Go by all means," Rafael Hastur said, "Bring me word of where I am assigned, and forget not to take note of when we are off duty, so that we pay our respectful compliments to my sister Alisa and to her companion . . . ha, Rafael, you see, I can feel the wind when it blows from the right quarter, and need no weather vane for that!"

Rafe Syrtis made a gesture of laughing surrender. "You know me, *vai dom caryu* . . . indeed, I am eager to pay my respects to the *damisela* Caitlin . . .

"But not too respectfully, I hope," Rafael Hastur teased, then sobered. "No, I won't make fun of you, *bredu*. I am truly glad you have found someone you can love, and she is worthy of you in all ways, my foster sister Caitlin."

"But I am not worthy of her . . ." Rafe's voice trembled, "How could I look so high . . ."

Rafael Hastur laid his hand on his friend's shoulder. He said vehemently, "No, Rafe, don't speak like that. My father knows, we all know, your worth and quality. My father, too, values your father as one of his most loyal men. To me, Caitlin is only one of my cousins, all eyes and teeth, and what you want with that scrawny buck-toothed little thing—"

"Scrawny! Caitlin scrawny!" Rafe Syrtis cried in indignation, "She is divinely slender, and her eyes . . . those eyes. . . ."

"When she was a little girl, Alisa and I used to call her Pop-eyes," Rafael teased, "and I cannot see that she has grown a whit prettier. But, Rafe, don't trouble yourself. She is my father's ward, and Alisa loves her well, but she is not wealthy, so in that respect she is not too far above you; and although her family is very good, so is yours. Father will be well content to give her to you. I do not think any other has offered for her, but even if someone had done so, I will speak to Father for you, and if you will, I shall stand for you at your handfasting. Thus Caitlin will remain in our family and close to my sister as she has always been."

Rafe Syrtis' voice trembled. "I don't know how to thank you. . . ."

"Thank me?" Rafael said, "Merely by being what you have always been, my most loyal paxman and my sworn brother. I wish I thought, when the time comes for my father to find me a bride, he could find me one I was half so eager to marry. As yet I have seen no maiden in Thendara who seems better to me than any others; Father has spoken of the daughter of Lord Elhalyn, but she is still a child." He laid his hand, shyly, on his friend's arm. "Perhaps some of your good fortune will come to me, too, and I too shall be lucky in love.

But promise me, Rafe, that you will never let this new tie part our company."

"Never," Rafe Syrtis pledged, "I swear it."

For the first ten-day or so of the cadet season, the business of honor guards, of escort for Comyn lords and ladies, of assessing the training of new cadets and assigning suitable duties to older ones, kept them all too busy for the renewing of old friendships. On the morning of Festival Night, Kennard and Dyan met in a small office near the Guard Hall, where Kennard was making up duty lists before leaving for the ceremonial duties of the night's ball.

"Will you be there, Dyan? But of course you will, there is no other representative of the Ardais Domain here." He looked at the younger lad with sympathy. Dyan's father, Dom Kyril, was well known to be subject to recurring periods of derangement when he had little sense of what was fitting and proper; during one of his lucid intervals, he had arranged for Dyan to perform the ceremonial duties of the Domain, so that he might not, in a moment of vagueness or madness, bring disgrace upon them.

Kennard said, "I am fortunate in that my father and my brother Lewis are both fit to perform the public duties of the Domain; I have no liking for ceremony. I could take pride in the important business of Council, but to stand up in public and be admired like a racehorse because of my pedigree . . . no, I should find that tiresome."

Dyan said stiffly, "I hope I shall never fail any duty to Comyn, no matter how tiresome it may be."

Kennard put his arm briefly around his friend's shoulder. He said, "That's what I love about you, *bredu*. But truthfully, Dyan, it is a boring business, isn't it?"

Dyan chuckled. "I wouldn't say so in public, but it's as you say. I wonder if the prize horse gets tired of being dressed in his finest harness and paraded in the streets?"

"It's a good thing we don't know, isn't it, or we'd never have the heart to hold parades," Kennard said. "No, actually, I do know, a little. One of the things I like to do, when I have leisure, is to train our saddle horses, and I can sense, just a little, with *laran*, how they feel about the bit and the saddle. But they come to accept it, just as you and I accepted learning to stand long watches, and to write, and to do all the other things we have to do. And, speaking of tiresome duties, Lewis said that Father had chosen a wife for me, some tiresome daughter of one of the minor Hastur clans . . . have you heard any gossip?"

Dyan shook his head. "I am not particularly interested in women and I hear very little about marriages."

Kennard said with a shrug "Women, that is one thing. I discovered that, at least. But as for marriage . . . oh, I suppose it would have its merits, an established home, children for the clan . . . I bear the Alton Gift; Lewis does not. So it is more urgent for me to marry and to have sons."

"As to that," Dyan said, "I suppose, as always, I will do whatever my duty is to the Domain, but when I was so young I was so sickened at my father's women—" he did not look at Kennard, and his calm, musical voice did not change its inflection, but Kennard, who had a sizable portion of the Ridenow empath gift, sensed that Dyan was forcing the words through layers of pain and shame.

"You probably do not know . . . there were times when he brought them to Ardais, flaunting them in my mother's face, jesting about the old days when wives knew their duty, and if they did not delight in their husband's bed, choosing some woman to please their husbands . . . he forced her to foster all of Rayna Di Asturien's bastard sons and even daughters . . . even though the woman was cruelly arrogant to my mother. And he did not stop at—at making advances even to her own serving maids, and worse, before her eyes, and forcing her to witness . . . the idea that I could ever behave so dishonorably, it makes me physically ill! And yet he could not . . . could not help himself; the idea that I could ever be so enslaved to a . . . a concept of manhood, of virility . . . so that I would hurt and humiliate a good woman who had done me no harm, to whom I owed honor . . . someday, I suppose, I shall marry properly and do my duty to the Domain, but the idea that I could ever be so—so enslaved to my own lusts . . . before I could behave like that I hope I would be honorable enough to make myself *emmasca* as the whining *cristoforos* do!"

Kennard was appalled at his vehemence; he squeezed Dyan's arm with silent affection, but there was nothing he could say before the younger boy's revelation. He had had no idea. . .! At last, after a long time and diffidently, he said "Your father . . . he is not in his right senses, *bredhyu*, you must not let his wickedness deform your life."

"I will not," Dyan said, guarded again and defiant, "but I am in no hurry to have a woman's happiness and honor placed in my hands. It would be a—a terrifying responsiblity. And suppose I should find myself so enslaved to the desire for women. . . ."

Kennard said, half lightly and half seriously, "Oh, I shouldn't think there is much danger of that. Women are pleasant enough, but I have no wish to limit my attentions to only one, I would rather make them all happy, not give any one of them the right to jealousy and reproaches."

"How can you be so cynical!" Dyan said in horror.

"Dyan, I was joking! But truly, my brother, I am not particularly interested yet in marriage, I have not been home long enough even to renew all my old ties and friendships, and I would rather wait a while before forming new ones. And speaking of old ties and friendships, you and I have hardly seen anything of one another! Shall we plan a hunt? Or—Rafael Hastur spoke of spending a ten-day at Syrtis— Dom Felix knows more of hawks than anyone from Dalereuth to the Kadarin, and he has promised me one trained to my own hand. Both of them, I know, would be delighted if you joined us."

"I do not care for hawking," Dyan said stiffly. So Rafael Hastur thought he could force his friend, the hawk-master's son, on Kennard Alton by laying him under obligations with this kind of courtesy—this kind of bribe!

"Well, as you like," Kennard said. "We'll ride in the hills, then, just the two of us, if you'd prefer that. I can take three days' leave, and so can you, a few days after Festival Night."

A day or two later the invitation was actually forthcoming from Rafael Hastur to join them at Syrtis—his sister and foster sister were also to make up the party—but Dyan refused, saying that he and Kennard had made other plans. Riding at Kennard's side along the lower ridges of the Venza Hills, Dyan felt perfectly happy, as if, after all these years, they had returned to a happy boyhood. Kennard, too, seemed happy. He told Dyan something . . . not much . . . of his years on Terra, his struggle against the heavy air and the dragging gravity, the long trip from star to star, the curious offworld customs. And the loneliness, among those mostly ungifted with *laran*.

"Only once did I find real friends," he said. "On Terra, of all places, some kindred of the Montrays, who had lived on Darkover, and knew how that light hurt my eyes . . . that was the worst, the pain of the light, and even when the sun was not in the sky, I sometimes felt I should go mad under the frightful cold light of that terrible white moon . . . do you know that their word for madness is akin to their word for moonworshiper? There was a girl—her name was *Elaine,* that is Yllana in our tongue . . . but she was kin to Aldaran, too. I do not suppose I will ever see her again. But she understood, a little . . . how I feared that terrifying moon."

Dyan said, "Moon madness is easy enough to understand; we have that proverb, *What is done under four moons need never be recalled nor regretted. . . ."*

"True," Kennard laughed, "and I see there are three in the sky, and later tonight, Idriel will rise too, and then we, too, will perhaps have some adventure of madness!"

All the moons were indeed high in the sky when they made camp and cooked their meal, roasting a bird Dyan had brought down with his *courvee,* the curved throwing-stick used for hunting in the Hellers. "I have lost my skill," Kennard lamented, "it has been so long!"

They sat long beside the coals of their fire, lighted by the four moons, talking of their own childhoods, the early days in the Cadets.

"I was so wretched on Terra," Kennard said, "I wonder, often, if Larry was equally so in my place. His kindred were so kind to me, and tried so hard to be understanding. I know my father would have been kind, but what about the others, Dyan? Was he happy in the Cadets? Did any befriend him? I would have commended him to your kindness as my sworn friend."

Dyan said stiffly "Do you think anyone alive could take your place? I think we all made him realize what an interloper he was, to try that!"

Kennard shook his head in dismay. "But we were friends, Dyan, I would have had you treat him as you would have treated me, as friend and brother . . . well, it is past, I won't censure you," he said, "but I wish you could have come to know him as well as I do; believe me, he is worthy of it, *Janu.*"

But he used the old pet-name of their childhood, and Dyan knew that Kennard was not angry with him, of course not, Kennard would not quarrel with him over any *Terranan!*

The fire had burned low. Kennard yawned, and said, "We should sleep. Look, we have the four moons after all . . . what madness shall we do?"

Dyan said, with a shyness that surprised him, "Hardly

madness . . . but shall we, then, renew our old pledge, *bredhyu*, after so many years?"

For a moment Kennard was motionless, startled. Then he said, very gently, "If you will, *bredhyu*." He repeated the word with the special inflection Dyan had used, only for sworn brothers between whom there were no barriers. "It would need no renewal to be as strong as ever; I do not forget what I have sworn. And you are old enough, I would not have thought to treat you as a boy too young for women . . . but if you wish for it, my dearest brother, then, as you will."

He drew Dyan to him, their lips meeting, barriers going down in the most intimate of touches, until their minds were as exposed to one another as their young bodies . . . and in that moment, something deep within Dyan Ardais cracked asunder, never to be whole again.

Kennard had not ceased to love him. He would never cease to love him. He welcomed their reunion, and now he had given himself up completely to the warmth and tenderness of this physical reconfirmation too, he was withholding nothing. And yet . . . yet there was a profound difference, a difference heartbreaking to Dyan. What was, to Dyan, the needed, desperately longed-for wellspring of his existence, the core and renewal of his being, was nothing like that to Kennard. Kennard loved him, yes, cherished him as brother, friend, kinsman, with a thousand kindly memories. But the very center of their love, this mutual affirmation which was the whole reason for Dyan's existence, was to Kennard only a pleasant kindness, he would have been equally content if they had clasped hands and slept apart . . . and before the agony of that knowledge, Dyan Ardais felt that the whole core of his being was cracked, torn, broken into fragments.

Even while he was held tenderly in Kennard's arms, wholly absorbed in the mutual sharing, he felt the ice of death surrounding him, like the icy halls of Nevarsin, cold, alone . . . even dissolving in the mutual delight was agony, he knew he was sobbing uncontrollably, and through his own despair he sensed Kennard's bewildered grief and regret. He could not even be angry with Kennard; Kennard's thoughts were his own, *What can I do? He cannot be other than he is, nor can I. I love him, I love him dearly, but love is not enough. . . .*

"Dyan, Dyan . . . *Janu, bredhyu*, my beloved brother, don't grieve like this, you are breaking my heart," Kennard pleaded. "What can I say to you, my brother? You will always be more dear to me than any man living, that I swear

to you. I beg of you, don't grieve so . . . the world will go as
it will, and not as you or I would have it . . . there is no
one, no one I love more than you, Dyan, it is only that I am
no longer a boy . . . Dyan, I swear to you, a time will come
when this will not matter to you so terribly . . . all things
change. . . ."

Inwardly Dyan raged, *I will not change, not ever,* all of
him was crying out in anguished rebellion, but slowly he
managed to bring his weeping under control, withdrawing behind an impenetrable barricade of calm, good manners, almost light-heartedness. He reached for Kennard again, with
skillful, seductive touch, just letting Kennard sense his
thoughts, *at least there is this, and Kennard cannot pretend
he does not find pleasure in it . . .*

Kennard, still troubled, but grateful for Dyan's calm,
reached for him with gentle urgency, saying aloud . . . he
could not bear the deeper touch of minds, not now. "I will
never try to pretend that, my brother."

Summer moved on. One day, as Kennard was changing in
the small room off the Guard Hall, after giving some younger
cadets lessons in swordplay, he said to Dyan, "Well, it's happened. Father has found me a wife."

Dyan lifted an ironical eyebrow. "My congratulations. Am
I acquainted with the fortunate young woman?"

"I don't know! I don't know the girl at all. Father says she
is suitable, of a minor Hastur sept; he said that she is not
particularly beautiful, but she is not ugly either, and she is
amiable, and accomplished, and gifted with *laran*—and that
is enormously important to me. He has no doubt whatever
that we will like one another and live well together. Beauty
may be important in a man's mistresses, but good temper and
friendly disposition are more important for sharing a home
and a life, and I have no doubt we will be happy enough. She
is foster sister to Rafael and Alisa Hastur; have you met her?
Her name is Catriona, Catrine, something like that."

"Caitlin?" Dyan asked, and Kennard nodded. "I think so.
You know her?"

"No," Dyan said, "but I know who she is."

Inside he was laughing triumphant. That would teach
Rafael Syrtis to lift his eyes to a girl of Hastur kindred! Now
that they had a proper husband for the girl, Rafe Syrtis
would learn that there were limits to a commoner's ambition!

He said formally, "I wish you every happiness, kinsman," but his own happiness overflowed when Kennard smiled and said, "The girl is nothing to me, dear brother. I have never yet met the woman who can be more to me than a sworn brother, and I heartily pray that I never shall."

He was curious to know how the two Rafaels would react to this knowledge; and he was not long in finding out. Actually he was out of earshot, doing some small chore in the barracks while Rafael Hastur and Rafe Syrtis were ostensibly playing cards at the other end of the room; but he heard them mention Kennard's name and felt not the slightest ethical hesitation in extending his senses to listen in, telepathically, to what they were saying.

I could hardly believe it, Rafael Syrtis said, *I knew of course, that she was gratified and glad to see me when I sought her out, but I had never believed that she would actually send for me, would beg me . . . Rafael, I could not bear it, she had been crying so, her poor little face was swollen with tears, I think the very stones of Nevarsin Peak would have melted with pity! And of course that father of hers thinks only of what it will mean to her, to marry a Comyn heir . . . what shall I do, Rafael? I cannot lose her, not now, not when I know she cares about me as much as I. . . ."*

Dyan felt savage gratification. So this damned commoner was learning he could not force his way into Comyn circles by marrying a foster sister to Rafael Hastur, after all! Well, let him suffer, it would teach him a lesson! Then, in outrage, he heard what Rafael Hastur was saying to his friend. A Hastur, to speak like this? Disgraceful!

If you and Caitlin both have the courage . . . I will stand by you. Freemate marriage cannot be gainsaid, if it has been consummated; if you spoke to my father, he would say it was only a boyish fancy, but if you have shared a bed, a meal, a fireside . . . I do not know if the girl has the strength of mind to defy the old people's wishes, but if she does, and you, you will want witnesses, and Alisa has promised that she, too, will stand by you. . . .

And then they were discussing horses, and directions, and Dyan turned off his listening-in, as Rafe Syrtis turned and looked uneasily at him . . . had that damned commoner some scrap of *laran* after all? But he did pick up the rendezvous, *the traveler's hut on the road to Callista's Well. . . .*

You have nothing to fear from Dyan, Rafael Hastur said

calmly. *He too has suffered from the whims of an overstrict father, he would not betray us.*

Would I not! Dyan thought, enraged. Even if he had not been infuriated by Rafe Syrtis' presumption, daring to raise eyes ambitiously to the ward of a Hastur, he was angered for Kennard's sake. Who was this girl Caitlin, to prefer some impudent nobody to Kennard Alton? What a slap in the face for Kennard it would be, if it became gossip in Council that his promised bride had run away to marry someone else! And for whom? For a prince, for a nobler marriage? Not even that; for the son of her guardian's hawk-master! What an insult to Kennard! Dyan thought, in a fury, that if he had had the offending Caitlin before him, that he would have spit on her!

Kennard must know at once—that Rafael Hastur and that insolent and presumptuous favorite of his were conspiring to cheat him of his bride!

As he went in search of Kennard, he was rehearsing in his mind what to say, to make Kennard aware of how he was being insulted by the Hastur heir! Those false friends and traitors were conspiring, to cheat Kennard, to make him lose face before the Guards and the Council.

Yet his mind persisted in presenting Kennard to him, not grateful to Dyan for warning him of this humiliation they were planning, but as angry with Dyan for his meddling; it seemed he could almost hear Kennard's voice, saying, *Zandru's hells, Dyan, do you think I care about the girl? At this time of my life, one girl is very much like another to me, provided she is suitable, I've never even seen her.* And the more Dyan argued in his mind, trying to convince Kennard that he could not consent to lose his pledged bride to a commoner, the more his mind rehearsed Kennard's logical reply:

What pleasure could I possibly have in marrying a girl who is helplessly in love with another man? There are plenty of women who would as soon have me; why not let the Syrtis boy have this one, and welcome, if they want each other; who knows, perhaps some day I might be fortunate enough to find some woman who could care as much for me as this one does for Rafe!"

Confused by the voices in his mind, Dyan felt grave misgivings. Should he simply hold his peace? If Caitlin Lindir-Hastur and Rafe Syrtis cared so much, why should he rend them asunder to give Caitlin into the hands of a man who did

not care whether he had her or another? Then, in a last moment of anguished self-knowledge, still stinging with that
unintended rejection from Kennard, he knew he did not want
Kennard to marry a woman who would mean to him what
Caitlin meant to Rafe . . . *what no woman, I know it now,
will ever mean to me. . . .*

Firmly he dismissed his compunctions. Loyalty to Comyn
demanded that he prevent young Hastur from defying the
will of the Council, that Kennard Alton should have Caitlin
as a wife. Kennard should not be humiliated by being shown
that his pledged bride preferred to be the wife of a commoner, a hanger-on, the hawk-master's son!

*Kennard will know that I hold his honor as a Comyn Lord
dear to me as my own; he will be grateful to me, I will still
mean more to him than any woman . . .*

His hands were shaking. He realized that he was outside
the Hastur apartments, and as he told the grave-faced servant
to say that Dyan Gabriel, Regent of Ardais, wished to speak
to the Lord Danvan Hastur, or, failing that, to the ancient
Lord Lorill, he rehearsed, mentally, his opening words.

*Do you know, my lord, what they are planning, your son
and his shameless paxman, the son of your hawk-master?
They are planning that Kennard, Heir to Alton, shall be
cheated of the marriage designed in Council. . . .*

They were a small party; all of Comyn blood, or long-
trusted Guardsmen who could be certain not to spread scandal. Danvan Hastur himself rode with them, and Dyan
himself was the youngest of the party riding northward to
Callista's Well. Old Hastur had inquired discreetly; when he
heard that the lord Rafael and Alisa, with Rafael's paxman,
young Syrtis, and Alisa's foster sister, had ridden out before
midday, taking hawks as if it were an innocent holiday, he
had gathered the party and ridden swiftly forth. Now they
sighted the small traveler's shelter, and outside, they saw four
horses, one of them the white stallion which Rafael Hastur
rode.

Danvan Hastur's voice was low and bitter.

"Spread out; circle the house. Who knows what they will
do, these rash young ones? Disobedience, certainly; perhaps
dishonor and disgrace." With his paxman at his side, he
struck a heavy blow with his sword hilt on the door; Dyan
could see that the elderly Lord of Council was prepared for
anything, even brute defiance.

But no blow was struck. Dyan could not see, and from his post, never heard what words were exchanged inside, but after a long time, Danvan Hastur came forth. His face was cold and set; he held the weeping Caitlin by the hand. Lord Hastur signaled to two Guardsmen to ride at either side of Rafe Syrtis, who looked as white as his shirt.

"Guard him lest he do himself some hurt," Hastur said, not unkindly. "He is distraught. He has been ill-advised by those who should have known better." His eyes rested on his son Rafael, and his face was like stone.

"As for you," he said, "I know where to lay the blame for this disgraceful affair; you are fortunate that your cousin Alton does not challenge you to a duel, since Comyn immunity covers you both. No, not a word—" He raised his hand imperiously. "You have said and done quite enough, but through good fortune and fast horses it came to nothing. I shall deal with you later. Get to your horse and ride, and don't presume to speak to me tonight."

Rafael's lips moved inaudibly in protest, but his father had already turned away. He himself set Caitlin on her horse, saying "Come, my child, no harm is done, though your folly was great. I'll pawn my honor Kennard shall never hear of this, and fortunately he has nothing to forgive you. Alisa!" His voice suddenly cut like a whip. "Get to your saddle, my girl, or I shall have you lifted there! No, not a word!"

Alisa drew her green cloak around her face; it seemed to Dyan that she was weeping too. But his eyes were on the slumped back of Rafael Syrtis. Now, indeed, that detestable commoner had learned his lesson!

In the end nothing came of it; Alisa was sent away in disgrace—to Neskaya, they said; but there was surprisingly little gossip. The Guard Hall was full of it, but Dyan answered no questions; his honor had been engaged to keep silent. A few days later the handfasting was duly held, and Caitlin Hastur-Lindir was pledged to marry Kennard Alton *di catenas*. Dyan, watching the bride and groom dance together, with courteous indifference, at the ceremony, felt a curious hollow emptiness. Kennard, when he came to speak congratulations, greeted him affectionately.

"Let me present you to my promised wife, Dyan. . . . *Damisela*, this is my kinsman and sworn brother, Dyan."

For a moment the girl's dead face came alive with a flicker of wrath and resentment, and Dyan realized she must have seen him in that circle of politely averted faces, at the hut on the road to Cassilda's Well . . . then it was gone, and Dyan knew she no longer even cared about that.

"I wish you every happiness," he said formally, and Kennard replied something equally formal and meaningless; only Dyan caught his imperceptible shrug.

"Here is your foster brother to dance with you, Caitlin," Kennard said, and delivered her up to Rafael Hastur. "Come back to me soon, my lady." But he watched them move away together with an almost audible sigh of relief.

"I do not think Caitlin likes me overmuch," he said. "I suppose, soon or late, she will resign herself to the idea; I'll try to be as kind and friendly as I can, and I suppose we will agree together as well as any other married couple. She is certainly no beauty," he added candidly, looking after the girl, "but she seems to have a sweet disposition, even if she is sulking now; and she is well-spoken and gentle, and she seems to be intelligent enough! I would hate to be married to a fool. I suppose I am not really ill-content," Kennard finished, without much conviction. "My father could have done worse for me, I suppose. Well, if she gives me a son with *laran*, I won't ask much else of her." Almost visibly, he shrugged. "Oh, well, it is an excuse for a festival and a merry-making, shall we have a drink? Dyan—listen to me. Of all my acquaintances in the Guardsmen, only Rafael Syrtis has not come to congratulate me or wish me well. My brother, what can I possibly have done to injure him that he should dislike me so much?"

Dyan felt a tight constriction in his throat. It was not too late, even now . . . instead he heard himself saying, "What the devil does it matter to you what he thinks, Kennard? Who is this Rafael Syrtis anyway, that he should snub you? Nobody—the hawk-master's son!"

"We married your father to someone we thought suitable," old Hastur said, *"and they dwelt together in perfect harmony, and total indifference, for many years."*
                                                    —*The Heritage of Hastur*

As stated again and again in this introduction, women writers tend to be over-scheduled, juggling careers, babies, housework, and creative ambitions. Penny Ziegler is probably the busiest of all; for her career is one which normally demands an eighteen-hour day, and she also has three children, a daughter ten years old and sons of twelve and thirteen. At thirty-five, Penny is part way through the residency training of a psychiatrist.

She grew up in Palm Beach, Florida, went to college in Boston or nearby, lived after marriage in Colorado, then moved to the Washington, D.C. area, when she completed a B.S. in biology, did graduate work in genetics, and attended medical school, all at George Washington University.

"I have read SF and fantasy since adolescence," she wrote, when I asked her for a biographical sketch, "but never tried writing any until the *Starstone* short story contest." Penny is a beautiful, pensive, and (of necessity) harried-looking young woman, who looks as if she might have spent her first thirty years on Darkover; she is, as far as I know, the only red-haired contributor to this anthology! She also looks frail enough that she's probably going to spend much of her life answering incredulous patients who can't believe that such a delicate-looking young woman is the doctor.

A Simple Dream, her story, which won the first prize in our *Starstone* contest, is a story I have always wanted to write myself; we have had stories about Terrans who fell in love with Darkover, and I have always wanted to tell the story of a Darkovan—and there must have been many—who were beglamoured with the Terran Empire and their spaceships. I even broached this, once, to Don Wollheim; his reaction was that this story might lose something, without the atmosphere of the planet of the Bloody Sun; and so I never did anything with it. But now, without losing Darkover, Dr. Ziegler has told the story of Eduin, who wanted the starships, and of Lomie, the tavern girl (readers of the entire Darkover

156

series will recognize the episode where Jeff Kerwin berated her, from *The Bloody Sun* who befriended him.

A SIMPLE DREAM

by Penny Ziegler

The huge Empire starship stood proud on its launch pad, towering over the square where a crowd had gathered to watch the liftoff. As countdown proceeded, the area around the rocket gradually cleared of workers and machinery making last-minute preparations and adjustments. Darkover's red sun hung low in the sky, splashing the sparse clouds with brilliant hues of purple and crimson and fiery orange.

Near the gates of the spaceport stood a man dressed in the style of the mountains. Oblivious to the jostling of the other spectators, he stared up at the ship's hulk silhouetted, along with the distant peaks, against the riotous sky. Tall and strikingly thin, he looked out of place, his curly black hair too long for the fashion, his boots more suited to cliff-climbing than to city streets. And there was something about his eyes that suggested an inner steadiness and control uncommon in the city dweller.

Eduin had done many things in his thirty years. Since leaving his home in the Hellers he had worked at farming, logging, and fire-fighting, hired out as a mercenary soldier and personal guard, served as horse trainer and mountain guide. He had never before been to Thendara; in fact, he had always avoided cities, finding their pace too frantic, the close-built houses too confining. But now all that was forgotten as he found himself swept up in the excitement of the moment and the enthusiasm of the crowd, holding his breath in anticipation of the launch.

Suddenly the engines came to life with a deafening roar. The Big Ship lifted slowly toward the sky, its tail a giant fireball, trailing a broad ribbon of white smoke. As it rose higher, Eduin felt the presence of a familiar dream like the

touch of a trusted friend. All his life he had treasured the private fantasy of spaceflight—a child's wish upon the evening
star, nothing more. Now, for the first time, he almost dared
hope it would come true.

Many minutes later, when the ship had shrunk to a tiny
point of light against a darkening sky, Eduin realized that he
stood alone in the great square. The sun was setting. Quickly
he turned and walked away into the Terran Trade City,
drawing his cloak tight against the freezing wind, his head
full of plans for tomorrow.

In the third of the gaudy spaceport bars he entered that
night, Eduin overheard a snatch of conversation and recognized a familiar mountain dialect. The speaker and his companion were drinking at the bar. Hired swords, by their dress.
Eduin went to stand beside them, and order a glass of *shallan.*

". . . and I say that all the *Terranan* can bring to
Darkover is trouble," the older of the two was saying. He
brushed back a lock of graying hair, then reached for the
pitcher in front of him. "They do not keep the Compact, they
lure away the innocent daughters of good families to work in
their houses of pleasure, and. . . ."

"And there is not a decent swordsman among them," interrupted the other, a young man with a dark red scar across his
cheek. "Their ways are strange, that's sure."

"Do they hire any laborers?" asked Eduin, not bothering to
introduce himself. "The *Terranan,* I mean." Both men turned
to stare at the intruder—but his accent spoke of home, and
the older man smiled in welcome.

"Out of work, are you, lad? Aye, there are some jobs to be
had inside the spaceport. But now that the buildings are up,
they have little need for common laborers."

"True," said the other. "Now they take only those who
speak the language of the Empire, and who have the skills
and training they require."

Eduin thanked them and walked away, out into the street,
his hopes sinking. He had never laid eyes upon a Terran before coming to Thendara. He knew nothing of their ways and
customs, even less of their language. Of what use could he be
to these off-worlders?

For three days he wandered about the Trade City. It was
an alien world; its ugliness and squalor revolted him, but the
spaceport was like a magnet, holding him there. He walked
through streets which seemed always to be filled with people:

groups of Spaceforcers on shore leave, looking for excitement; Darkovan merchants and traders leading pack animals or pushing carts; knots of hollow-eyed children in ragged clothes, splashing in puddles left by the melting spring snows. The bright lights and garish colors pained his eyes. Music drifted from the doorways of Terran bars and brothels—not the familiar sound of voices in song, but a strange, discordant blending of noises, too loud for his ears.

At last he found work in a small wine shop near the old city, sweeping up and washing the glasses. The clientele was mainly working men, both Darkovan and Terran, with occasional Spaceforce men off-duty from the Big Ships. Tomaso, the shop's owner, was a black bear of a man with a thick mountain accent whose huge belly attested to the truth of his claim that he personally monitored the quality of his merchandise. When business was slow, he entertained the customers with outrageous tales of the sexual conquests and knife battles of his youth.

Drinks were served by the bar girl, Lomie, who also contributed to Tomaso's profits with a sideline business in the small back room. She was a soft, round-faced girl with thick black curls and a lazy smile. Surprisingly graceful for such a big woman, she seemed to vibrate with suppressed energy and the promise of passion as she moved about the smoke-filled room. By contrast, her eyes were cold, closed. *Haughty,* thought Eduin, puzzled by such pride in a woman who gave her body to any man able to pay the appointed price. She made him think of the marl cub he had trapped and tamed years before: warm and cuddly when it pleased her, but never quite trusting. That evening, as he watched her lead two drunken *Terran* into the back room, he felt an old longing uncurl itself like a wisp of smoke from some forgotten fire.

As the days passed Eduin spoke often with Tomaso, finally confiding some of his hopes and plans to the barkeep's well-tuned ear. At first Tomaso laughed. "What would the *Terranan* do with you in space, man? You have no skills, and it is probably too late to learn. Can an old hawk serve a new master?" They argued for hours, but in the end the older man agreed to help Eduin learn Terran Standard.

Lomie remained aloof. Eduin often stopped his work to listen to her throaty laughter from across the room as she served the patrons. When she passed near him, the smell of incense in her hair and robe was strangely enticing. But she never met his eyes, never spoke to him.

One afternoon toward sundown, there was a commotion in the far corner of the shop, and Eduin looked up to see Lomie run from the room in tears. A tall, red-haired man in Empire uniform stumbled out the door into the street, leaving his stuporous companion asleep at the table they had shared. Tomaso, busy behind the bar, signaled Eduin to go after the girl.

He found her in the back room, sobbing and clutching her loose robe over her breasts. He gripped her firmly by the shoulders, turned her around to face him, and spoke her name. Their eyes met for only an instant—then she turned away, but not before he had read the fear there, and the hurt. He questioned her in a soft, steady voice, seeking to quiet her weeping.

"Lomie, you have been insulted by these off-worlders before. What could he have said to upset you so?"

"He was no off-worlder, Eduin. He was a *Comyn* lord, I swear it!"

"*Comyn?*" whispered Eduin, stunned by the word. "How is that possible? Would proud *Comyn* wear the black leather of the hated Empire? Would they come to drink cheap wine in a spaceport bar? No, Lomie, he must have been *Terranan*, probably from the *Southern Crown* which made landfall today."

"You saw his hair, Eduin. He cursed me, and he spoke the *casta!* What *Terranan* knows the language of the *Comyn?*" She shuddered, remembering the power of his words.

"The ways of the *Comyn* are beyond my understanding, Lomie. Perhaps it would be best if we forget about this thing." His words were having their hoped-for effect. She dried her tears and looked again into his eyes, this time in gratitude.

Tomaso had come to stand in the doorway; now he entered the room and said, "I say you imagined it all, silly girl. I have always told you that imagination of yours would bring you grief." He patted her ample rump, then placed a fatherly hand around her shoulder and led her back to the bar. "Now you must get back to work, *chiva*. There are customers who want pleasing." His face hardened. "I do not want to hear you speak of this again, Lomie. Zandru's hells, I have a business to run!"

When he had finished his chores after closing time, Eduin climbed the ladder into the loft where he slept. He straightened his pallet on the straw and pulled off his boots, thinking of Lomie. Ever since his arrival he had been struggling to suppress the long-ignored need she had stirred in him with her seductive laughter and her catlike movements. Today his defenses had been badly shaken when he had gazed into her eyes and read the invitation there, along with the fear and unspoken sorrow.

As he unbuttoned his shirt he heard the ladder creak, and spun around to see her face framed by the light coming up from below, her hair falling unbound around her shoulders. She was smiling.

"Why have you come here, woman?" he demanded angrily. "I have no money to pay for your pleasures."

"The price has already been met, kind sir," she laughed, extending her hand to him. "I came to show my thanks."

Grasping her wrist in his powerful fingers, he sensed her desire rising to match his own. He pulled her up into the loft and, forcing her down onto the straw, silenced her laughter with his mouth.

Afterward, Eduin lay with his chin propped in his hands, listening to the steady rhythm of her breathing.

"Lomie?"

"Ummmm?" She rolled over and stretched in one easy, languid motion, then opened her eyes.

"How came you to this life, Lomie?" he asked, winding strands of her black hair around his fingers.

"What choice had I?" she flashed, her anger and pride striking him like a blow. "My mother was a woman of the streets. Aldones alone knows whose seed fathered me, whether Darkovan or *Terranan*. I was serving *shallan* in a wine shop before I was six winters old, and offering my body to men before my womanhood came upon me. To the brothel born!"

"You have no children?"

"Three were lost before they quickened in my womb. Each time I gave thanks to the gods, for I have no wish to bear children I cannot provide for." She looked at him questioningly. "Eduin, do you think me heartless, unnatural?"

"No, *caria*. I think you uncommon brave." He reached out to caress her face with his fingertips, then pulled her to him in a fierce embrace. "I also think you beautiful," he whispered.

Again they made love, this time without urgency, and when both were spent he held her tenderly in his arms, brushing the tears from her cheeks, and told her of his dreams. . . .

"When I was a small boy in the Hellers, I worshipped my brother Mikhail. He was much older, already a man before I was born. He left our village to seek work in the city of Caer Donn, but every year he returned home for Midsummer Festival, bringing stories of the *Terranan* and their spaceships. I would sit at his feet for hours, hearing of men from other worlds who traveled freely among the stars. I dreamed, then, of going with them. I cannot forget that child's dream, Lomie, though the gods witness I have tried!"

Her soft laughter interrupted, a stinging slap.

"You mock me like all the others! I had hoped to make you understand."

"I do not mock you, Eduin. I too have dreams, though none are likely ever to come true. But you know nothing of the world of the *Terranan*!"

"That is why I am here, Lomie, to learn of their world. I must master the language so that I may find a place for myself inside the spaceport. When I can make of myself something of value to the spacemen, then they will take me with them to the stars." His eyes were shining as he told her stories he had heard, magical names in unknown tongues whose very sound evoked mystery and adventure.

Again Lomie smiled, but there was sadness in her voice. "I am afraid for you, Eduin," she said as she got up and straightened her skirts. "I fear you will find that other worlds are not unlike your own, except that you do not belong in them."

As the months passed, Eduin indeed learned much of the Terrans and their ways. The language came easily to him, and as his fluency increased he spent more and more time conversing with the off-worlders. Tomaso had no cause for complaint, however, since his helper always finished the work, was good at breaking up fights among the customers, and even seemed to enjoy listening to the tall tales.

There were a few regulars at the bar who muttered behind Eduin's back, calling him "lover of *Terranan*" and even "traitor"; but it was hard to dislike the big mountain man who was always ready with a friendly greeting and a new story of life in the Empire. Most of the Darkovans simply smiled and shook their heads knowingly. "The crazy dreamer" grew used to their scorn; he went right on dreaming.

After closing time, he and Lomie would climb into the loft and talk for hours, Eduin teaching her the new words he had learned that day, or telling her of political events in the Empire. Sometimes they would unleash their wildest passions, clawing at each other like two *cralmacs* in rut. At other times he would hold her in a soft embrace, calling her *bredha* and stroking her musky hair.

Through the long winter nights they slept curled up together, sharing the warmth of their bodies. And when spring returned to melt some of the snows, they explored the old city, arm in arm, laughing and free. *Just like ordinary people,* Lomie thought with amazement. *He treats me like a woman, like a friend, as though he didn't know or care what I am.*

Some mornings she would wake early, before the sun, and lie watching him sleep. One part of her wanted to hold and protect him; the other hated him for awakening feelings she had thought long dead. Unable to resolve the conflict, she would bury her face in the sweet-smelling straw and weep.

One afternoon near midsummer, a warm day when the city was full of guardsmen and soldiers come to town for the opening of Comyn Council, two off-duty Cadets of the City Guard drinking in the wine shop got into an argument with a Terran Spaceforcer. Insults were traded, tempers flared hot (later no one could remember what actually started it). Finally the Earthman, who had a fair command of the city dialect when drunk, called the Darkovans every obscene name he could recall in *cahuenga*, ending with a vile suggestion regarding the sexual preferences of their mothers. Furious, both Cadets drew their swords.

Rushing out from behind the bar, Eduin pulled his own knife from his boot and shouted, "Hold! the man is unarmed!"

"Unarmed, yes, and he is about to be unsexed," said the larger of the two Darkovans, holding his sword's point inches from the Earthman's genitals. The Cadet was very young; he could not have been more than fifteen seasons. His eyes flared with indignation as he turned to look at Eduin. "Do you support the cause of this filthy *bre'suin?*"

"I support his right to a fair fight. Are we men of Darkover such weaklings that it takes two of our swords to silence one unarmed *Terranan?*"

Bellowing, the swordsman leaped at Eduin, swinging his

blade in a wide arc. Eduin dodged the sword, then brought
his knife up to slash at the other's unprotected side, drawing
first blood. As he backed away, someone put a sword in his
hand and the fight was on in earnest.

Patrons scrambled out of the way, dragging the tables back
to make room for the combatants, while at the bar men
wagered on the outcome and cheered one or the other. The
clash of metal against metal filled the shop as the two men
circled, each looking for gaps in the other's defenses: but it
was really no contest. The Cadet was only a beginner, and
Eduin's skills, though rusty, were far superior. When his
thrust produced a deep gash in the boy's thigh, the Cadet
raised his sword to signal defeat. He hobbled out of the shop
on the arm of his friend, muttering obscenities under his
breath.

"Thank you, stranger."

Eduin turned to find the Terran he had defended standing
before him, his right hand outstretched. The fight had had a
remarkably sobering effect on him. The Darkovan returned
the sword to its owner with thanks, then grasped the Terran's
hand in the manner he had observed to be customary among
Spaceforcers.

"At your service, sir?" Eduin said in Standard.

"*Z'par servu,*" replied the Terran.

They laughed together, and then all the men in the room
were laughing as they returned to their drinks and their com-
panions. Soon Eduin and the spaceman were deep in conversation.

Tomaso and Lomie stood by the bar, watching Eduin walk
out the door with his new friend. Tomaso had given him time
off as a reward for his unexpected swordsmanship and the
extra business it had brought in that afternoon.

"So, *chiya,* it seems that our boy may get his wish after all,
in spite of our efforts to convince him of its impossibility. I
shall hate to see him go, if it comes to that."

"Why, Tomaso, I believe you really care for Eduin. And I
always thought you were the perfect barkeep, the complete
cynic." Lomie's eyes sparkled with irony and concealed fear
as the man squirmed under her gaze.

"And what of you, Lomie?" he shot back viciously. "I always thought *you* the perfect *grezalis,* cold and calculating,
never one to mix business with pleasure—*your* pleasure, that
is!" He watched the color rise in her cheeks, saw her

clenched fists at her sides, but he could not restrain himself
from going on. "This time it's different, isn't it? You love
him, don't you?"

"*Gre'zu!*" she spat, fighting back hot tears as she lifted the
tray of drinks to her shoulder and walked away.

When he returned to the wine shop that evening, Eduin
was unable to contain his excitement. "I saw the whole
spaceport, Lomie, from the inside. You would never believe
it. Jim Martin took me all around. We even went on board
the Big Ship that now sits on the launch pad. It was amazing,
full of flashing lights and gleaming metal, men and women
rushing here and there." He hardly paused for breath as the
words spilled out; Lomie wondered idly if he realized he was
speaking Terran Standard. "To show his gratitude, Jim is going to help me find work on the inside. It is possible that,
with his sponsorship, I can apply for citizenship in the Empire. Then perhaps in a few months, a year. . . ."

Watching his face as he spoke, Lomie felt the dream take
hold of him, sensed the power of it, and knew that she had
lost him. *He is a child,* she thought. *Now he will have his
chance to grow, to learn. And I shall never know the man he
will become.* Tears splashed down her face as she pressed his
fingers to her lips. She wept for the child she carried, and
wondered again if it was his.

She thought about the hours they had spent together, and
realized for the first time how much this year would always
mean to her. Now he would go his way, and she would not
try to stop him, to come between this man and his consuming
dream, for she knew that that would destroy them both. She
dared not even show him her pain or remind him of her love.
He had to have his chance.

She turned from Eduin then, wiped her eyes and picked up
the pitcher of *shallan.* What had that *Comyn* called her?
Daughter of a mountain goat! Walking to one of the tables,
she bent to serve the Terran workman seated there, pressing
her soft, full body against his and purring, "You new here,
stranger? Come, let Lomie make you feel at home . . ."

Again Eduin stood in the square before the spaceport
gates, watching the *Southern Crown* soar into the skies. This
time there was no crowd, for it was night and a cold rain was
falling on the city. The roar of the Big Ship, by now a familiar sound, still caused his heart to race with excitement.

For a moment he looked away, back toward the old city. *What will become of Lomie?* he wondered. *It was cruel to leave her, but I can see no other way. If she were not what she is. . . .* He stared up at the tiny point of light that was the starship, tears coming unexpectedly to his eyes. *It doesn't matter. I cannot simply walk away, when we have been so much to each other. I must. . . .*

A hand gripped his shoulder. Eduin jumped; turned to see his friend Jim standing beside him in the deserted square, smiling in welcome.

"Come on, man, it's getting late. We have a lot of work to do, finding you a place to sleep and such." The big Spaceforcer guided him through the gates. "You're not having second thoughts, are you? Eduin, this is the opportunity of a lifetime. a chance to get off this backwater planet, see the galaxy, make something of yourself."

This is what I've wanted all my life. Remembered voices argued in his head ...

His brother Mikhail: "There are more stars than we can count, and these men of the Empire tell me that there are hundreds, thousands of worlds out there, circling those tiny lights. Think of it, *bredu!*"

Tomaso: "Only a fool would get involved with the *Terranan*. These men from the stars have no honor, they take what they want, they cannot be trusted."

Jim Martin: "Chance of a lifetime! Travel, adventure. You'll *be* somebody."

Lomie: "Other worlds are not unlike your own, except that you do not belong in them."

A light snow had replaced the rain, and the wind was stronger, colder now. With a pain in his gut like the thrust of a knife, he turned his back on the gates and followed the Earthman toward the spaceport complex. And this time he did not look back.

Patricia Mathews wrote, after the previous story ("Simple Dream," by Penny Ziegler) was published in *Starstone* as a first-prize winner, "I could hardly stand to read it; I was already working so hard to get Lomie out of there."

And so it seemed necessary to me to print these stories back to back, one as a sequel to the other. This is a story of a Terran on Darkover—and something many readers of the Darkover stories have wanted to read, a story of a woman, committed to the Empire, facing the strange world of Darkover.

UNA PALOMA BLANCA

by Patricia Mathews

So the long search ended here, in a grubby little spaceport office. The little bag containing all that was left of Caris Ridenow, xenotelepath, was a burning weight in my shoulder bag. Once, there had been four of us.

The Legate looked up from my personnel record and considered me. "McCullough, Lee C.," he said. "Survey Service pilot, almost twenty years' service. Never married."

"I never found the right one, sir," I answered, ignoring the feeble attempt at a cheap shot. The Legate was lonely and wanted to make social chit-chat; I wanted him to sign my annual leave slip and planetside permission and let me out of here.

"Five feet eight, 'lean and mean' they used to call you at the Academy—was your hair red when you were little, McCullough?"

I set the bag down and settled in for a long chat. "Yes, sir."

"I see the Rhine Institute tested you a flat negative clear across the board." The Legate's mouth slowly began to resemble a cat's with a mouthful of canary feathers. "Interesting. Very Interesting! Well, McCullough, you realize that sight-seeing around native country is at your own risk."

167

"Yes, sir." I wanted to get out of there.

"Oh, McCullough. One thing before you go. What does your middle initial stand for?"

"Cassilda," I said, and enjoyed the flabbergasted look on his face; it must be like running across a Darkovan named Venus.

Once there were four of us, I thought as I walked out into the neon-lit sky and down the crooked, blue-paved road that smelled of incense and strange woods. Dal Ambron and Caris Ridenow, Gilbert Mendoza, and Lanethea C. McCullough, yours truly. Caris died screaming in convulsions without a mark on her on the third Iceworld survey and Dal urgently recommended that we all pull out. It left a black mark on all our records.

"Cowardice . . . the Survey Service cannot take official cognizance of hunches, McCullough . . . you were in command, not Ambron, not Ridenow, not Mendoza. . . ."

Nuts to them.

A hostile murmur at the edge of hearing followed me from the spaceport gate into the native quarter. They resent the presence of the Empire, they dislike the presence on their planet of women of the Empire, and they like women in the Empire's uniform least of all. At least nobody threw stones.

Caris was my sidekick. Try explaining that concept to anyone outside the Empire! Their language wouldn't come within a light-year of it. We must have hit over a dozen planets together from the day she signed on with me at Empire Central, a bright-eyed and bushy-tailed redhead out to see the universe, until she died screaming on the glacier called Fantastic. Ambron had given it that name.

I could tell from looking that this wasn't the sort of planet where you dial City Information and ask for Ridenow. There was technology here, I could see it in the translucent blue window-walls and glowing sourceless light that kept night from ever taking over the native quarter completely, but there were also horse-apples in the streets, and the men wore swords and knives and daggers.

A handful of Service types came up behind me and one called, "McCullough, we're going for a drink. Care to join us?"

You can gain information in a bar, although right now I was just getting the feel of the planet, matching it to what Caris had told me. And, I hadn't really had my ceremonial drunk; the team had broken up in bitterness. "Coming," I said, and they all headed for a small place that spilled out into the street, and looked like a dive on the mom-and-pop scale. Either the food was exceptional, or the servers were attractive and available. Unfortunately, it was a well-stacked waitress, a big brunette with long curly hair, dressed in a flimsy half-open robe.

As we all found a table and sat down, she brushed up against me and purred, "Lomie show you good time, Spacer?"

The whole table exploded in laughter and Lomie turned bright red, poor kid. One of the boys called, "Hey, Lomie, you going for the *menhiedris* trade these days?" They laughed louder; Lomie was ready to crawl under the table, tray and all.

"Shut up, you turkeys!" I bellowed. "Miss, I'm sorry. Sit down, and I'll buy you a drink?" I could tell what she was thinking, and added, "I'm not interested in women, that way. I'm trying to find the family of a girl in my unit who died on expedition."

"Why ask me?" Lomie asked, her face and voice guarded.

"I have to start somewhere," I said bluntly, "and I think you'll play it straight with me; you're star-crazy."

She gaped at me, big gray eyes full of fear. "Comynara?" she murmured. "Comyn . . . no, not again."

"I never knew you had The Dream, kid," one of the fellows was saying sympathetically.

Another said, "Hey, Lee, I thought the Service took care of death notifications."

I downed my beer and sent Lomie for another round including hers, on me. The tables and benches were rough wood, as if in an Imperial Wilderness, but the beer came in silver mugs—I was beginning to like this crazy planet.

"The Service," I said grimly, "has decided that xenotelepaths are hysterical, unstable types that spook at a shadow, Caris died of self-induced heart failure and not in line of duty, an I should have the sense to listen to Service directives and not my teammates. Ambron's gone home to a desk in his grandfather's bank." I added. "Resigned, quit, through. Prominent family; he's not used to being patted on the head and told that his superiors *understand*. It's down to Bert Mendoza and me; I'm recruiting, if anybody's interested."

Lomie was looking at me, starry-eyed and full of hope, which changed to cynicism as she saw me watching. "Why you want family, hah?" she asked.

"To set the record straight," I explained. "Tell them the truth."

"A thing of honor," she said immediately, surprising me. "I help, you sneak me in to see Big Ship, hah?"

"Sure. Haven't you seen one before?" I asked, knowing that Spacefield Command encouraged tourism except where there was a terrorist problem. Strange, if she had the Dream.

Her face clouded over and she shoved her hair aside behind her ears. "Go 'way, whore," she growled. "No whore inside gate, inside spacefield. Look, hah. Not good enough for Big Ship. Not good enough look at Big Ship!" she screamed, and launched herself at me, shaking me. "How you woman get on Big Ship? Hah? Who you sleep with? Everybody? Captain? Hah? How you get on Big Ship?" she demanded.

The fat bear of a proprietor lumbered up, pulled her off me, and busted her one in the jaw. As close as I'd come to doing that myself just a minute before, my redheaded Scots dander was up, and I started to get up.

"*Domna,* your pardon," the man groveled while Lomie got up holding her jaw. "I'll have the slut out on the street this minute."

I pushed my chair back and got my jacket. "Fired, is she?"

"McCullough," one of the men whispered, "don't interfere."

"Shut up, Jackson. Okay, Tomaso, fire her. Immediately. Loud, clear, and legal. Lomie, get your coat."

Everybody was staring now. I didn't care. I helped her into the flimsy wrap that was all she owned and was out the door before Tomaso finished sounding off.

We had another hassle at the gate, where a Spaceforce type stopped us and informed me that prostitutes were not permitted inside the area. "You'll have to take her somewhere else, Miss," he concluded.

He was the second person that night who'd accused me of that, and I blew. "When I go whoring in the native quarter, I go with a man. Miss Paloma," I had to think of something and the name just popped out, "is my guide, my informant, my interpreter; and right now she is in urgent need of medical attention. Now, let us in or buzz Medical, I don't particularly care which." I saw him looking with narrowed eyes at her flimsy, gaudy shawl and bright robe, her totally inadequate slippers, and her hair. "The getup is from the last job; which is more important, Sergeant, suitable clothing, or medical attention for this woman?"

"Sorry, Miss," he said, robot-like.

"Jesus H. Christ and the Great Goddess Astarte!" I exploded.

One of the men who had been drinking with us had heard half the argument; I think half of Darkover must have heard my side of it, at any rate. "Captain McCullough, there's a flea market in the Quarters," he offered. "Want me to show you?"

I could tell Lomie was in pain. "Lead the way, Rodgers, and—thanks."

I found myself wondering how and why I'd gotten myself into this. Of all the guide-interpreters to pick, a bar girl who could barely speak Terran Standard and had never been outside the Quarter in her life was one of the least likely. But I do not like people busting other people in the jaw on my behalf, and if Darkover Medical's emergency room had a dress code, I was stuck with dressing her.

Caris had taught me a little Darkovan, quite as bad as Lomie's Terran Standard; I could have used an interpreter. I couldn't make any of these stall-keepers understand something as simple as a woman's winterweight trousers and top and some sort of halfway decent shoes. At last I plucked at my own clothes and pointed to Lomie and one man led me through the piles of goods for sale into the back of his house and handed me a handsome set in dark red and green, embroidered in gold, with suede ankle boots and a fine cloak. His face was full of pain as he let her try them on and handed her a pair of scissors. What for? I wondered.

She came out with her hair cut short, not only dressed for the climate, but a completely different and very impressive woman. Rodgers let out a little whistle, then took off his hat. "Miss Paloma," he said respectfully. The proprietor was holding her old clothes and the rest of her hair. He called something after her that sounded like, *"Adelandaya, com'hi-letzii."* He began to cry. *"Adelandaya, mestra."*

The same guard stopped us again and said respectfully, "Your pardon, *mestra*, but I need a gate pass or some form of identification."

"Mestra Paloma is with me," I said firmly, and walked on by. I checked into Medical and leaned on the buzzer until somebody came. Her jaw was broken; they gave her an anesthetic and injected it with bone-set and kept her in the clamp for half an hour while the medic bawled me out for not getting her in there earlier.

The dope wore off on the way back to my quarters, and Lomie moved her jaw a little. Then, experimentally, she said, "Paloma. Means bird." She demonstrated with her hands.

"I know. Beautiful white bird. Una Paloma Blanca."

She caught a look at herself in a mirror and said wonderingly "Paloma. *Mestra* Paloma. *Not* grezalis, daughter mountain goat."

I thought of something then. "What was eating the man who sold you the suit, Lomie?"

Her face grew sober. "Holiday suit. His child. Live? Dead?"

I felt like a crumb.

That night Lomie tried to get in bed with me, so I had to set the record straight. "Look, kid, I don't give a damn about you personally. I picked you because I think you'll play it straight with me—and I'll play it straight with you unless you pull something I can't live with—but no more. Understand?"

There was a picture of Caris on the dresser. "Your *bredha*, she dead," Lomie said knowingly.

I took a deep breath. "Yeah. My best friend. I liked her a lot. Look, don't be mad."

"No. *Mestra* Macullah, why you people live in cages?" she asked then, looking around the narrow little room. So we rapped till midnight—Terran/Darkovan differences, my story, her story, why I was here—she said, "I think you *Comynara*, telepath, read minds. No *Comynara* ever come to Quarter, come to Tomaso place. Stay warm behind walls, proud, sacred."

Dull.

We rented horses and bought provisions from a place on the outskirts of the city, at the end of the main street. I hoped Lomie had ridden horseback before or we were in for a hard time. The other people on the path that called itself a road were mostly men, in clothes as heavy and bright and attractive as Lomie's, armed to the teeth. I don't carry a knife, not being a back-alley thug, but Caris had brought a couple from home, and once she had given me one and insisted I take it. I fished it out of my saddlebag and tucked it into my belt where everyone could see it. Lomie, who might well *be* a back-alley thug, had already done the same.

The sky was purple and the air smelled pungent, as pine woods do. I liked it. For one thing, I like mountains; I'm from New Mexico, where mountains alternate with endless plains. For another, it was wide open, as parts of New Mexico still are. I've seen fifteen worlds if you count this one and Earth, all different, all much alike; this was one of the better ones.

I always had the Dream, and faithfully read every issue of *Imperial Astrographic*—and every space adventure magazine—I could get my hands on. I collected maps and pictures, and used to watch *Survey Team Alpha*. I kept my grades up, and refused half a dozen dirtside jobs and two offers of marriage; I sold my hotrod triphib and dropped the soccer team the day before Regionals, all to get into Survey, and on the day before my eighteenth birthday, I made it. I have never regretted it till now.

We were a team. Caris and I came in together, and Ambron the year after. His homeworld is as urban as Darkover is rural, but he and Caris took to each other immediately. We picked up Bert on Dia, where his father is Legate. Juan Alvárez Mendoza is the only desk man I have a positive respect for; he heard about the hearing and promptly sent Bert a letter by space mail—expensive as all hell, and time-consuming—that was probably all that kept him on the team.

Darkovan roads all have these travel shelters spotted along the way like an Earthside rest stop, with hay for the horses and fireplaces and wood. We stopped at one the first day that was full of men; they made room for us and one party offered to share their wine. My sixth sense told me to refuse, and we kept to ourselves that night. Lomie was sore and stiff. "You told me you could ride a horse," I said.

"Never all day," she said as I rubbed her with muscle-ease. We were practicing each other's languages; any conversation was conducted in broken Standard and worse Darkovan. Then she said "Your *bredha*, she tell you right road?"

I explained a map to her and we looked over ours; she puzzled over it and asked how I knew one mark from another. I hadn't thought to ask if she could read; I don't think it had occurred to her that I could.

She laughed at me once. "You say, her mother Lord Damon Ridenow," she explained.

Now how do you get across the concept of biomother, nurturing parent, and all the rest, in a language that might not even have the concept? Damon Ridenow was the person I was trying to see; who had borne her or contributed to her genetic heritage might or might not be relevant; Ridenow had brought her up.

"Lord Damon not at Ridenow Forst," Lomie said then. "Is family Alton Domain."

Huh?

It was a long story, as most improbable things are, but Lomie's source was irreproachable; some of Valdir Alton's men were regulars at Tomaso's, and Lomie's mind was as thirsty as a sponge. I thought of the time she'd wasted just trying to survive on the streets and got mad again. What a waste!

"Cassilda," Lomie said on the third day out. "Maybe mama Darkovan, hah?"

I shook my head. "Lya-beth Kroginold; her people have been around the northern New Mexico-Arizona border for years. Nobody knows quite where they came from, although there's a legend about a crashed spaceship and a nova sun, but they're even more psychic than Caris is. I'm a good old-fashioned hard-headed Highland Scot, the kind they always cast as the engineer on a starship."

"Understand machine, that stranger *laran* than any," Lomie said.

Five days out, a party of men joined us. The one in the lead, a lean chestnut-haired man in his middle thirties, with an air of competence and quiet authority, rode up beside us. "Mestra, may we ride together?" he asked—in perfect Terran Standard. His hair was longer than any Earthman ever wore it, and he had a jewel around his neck very much like one Caris wore, and I would have bet half a month's pay he was native. High ranking native.

Lomie answered. "We would be honored to share the road, *vai dom*."

"Loris Ridenow," he said. "My *com'ii*. I've been expecting you, Lanethea McCullough. Your companion. . . ."

"Paloma n'ha Martina," she answered, and trembled as if telling a dreadful lie although it was the truth. She told me later that two of Ridenow's *com'ii* were regulars at Tomaso's and either didn't know her or took her new appearance at face value, I think the latter. She was turning into quite an outdoorswoman and I was beginning to wonder about recruiting her for Survey, illiterate or no.

"Caris was my sister," Ridenow said, his eyes, as gray as hers, sober. They didn't look particularly alike, but I could feel the similarity and believed him right away. "She was a Renunciate—"

I'd heard her say that once. I couldn't see her as renouncing the world; she enjoyed it too much.

He smiled. "She chose to live the life you lead," he ampli-
fied. It was two or more day's ride to our destination, especially since I'd gotten us off on the wrong road at first; we
spent the night at one of the shelters, with the men at one
fire; they left us the other. I saw Ridenow light the fire by
concentrating on his blue jewel; Caris has used hers that way,
and for a lot of other things. It was deactivated now; as far
as I could tell, that had happened automatically when she
died. If I watched him with my eyes narrowed a certain cock-
eyed way, I could almost tell how it was done. It made me
dizzy. Watching Caris use her starstone—she called it that—
always made me dizzy, too.

Ridenow saw me watching and said without surprise "You
have *laran*."

"Flat negative all the way."

"I know. That's a very good quality mind-shield." He invited us to share food and fire with his men; this time I accepted.

"On Orado, you can buy commercial mind-shields," I said,
digging into the fruit-bean-meat mixture—chili con manzano?
"Pesky little verses you can't get out of your head, or whatever fantasy occupies your mind the longest; that costs
more." I didn't want to look at Loris; I was starting to feel
attracted, and that's the one thing you don't want to mess
with in a strange culture. You can't tell what you'll end up
committed to. I generally hit dirt with fellows from the Service; we all go by the same rules, by and large, and there is a
basic fellow-feeling.

It suddenly occurred to me there were two of us and five
of them, armed, and total strangers, camping together in a
cold stone building, and stupidity was the kindest word for
that. *McCullough, the Service cannot take official cognizance
of hunches.* It was on the same order as picking up Lomie to
show me around Darkover; rationally, nothing could justify
it. Of course, all Survey people have to be a little bit psychic
or they'd never survive.

If they're too psychic, I thought bleakly, remembering
Caris, they don't survive either.

The room exploded around me; and suddenly my head was
inside-out.

Loris Ridenow was holding my head. "Don't fight it," he
advised. "Delayed awakening. The older you are, the worse it
gets. Empire Central isn't stupid; if you're of The People on

one side and Highland Scot on the other, with a psi test that shouts of well-developed block, and they let you loose on Darkover, they must have expected this. Your problem is the biological boundary coming up; nobody's seen that particularly lethal combination before, but it will probably be painful. . . .

I was a fly on the ceiling, looking down on a little red-headed bug run on about biological boundaries, and I was spacesick with all the worst symptoms of a trainee run directly from free-fall into hyperspace. They do that to knock out the weak stomachs before wasting millions on their training.

I felt something cool on my head and Lomie crying; my God, the kid had attached herself to me like a puppy dog, poor kid. I heard her protest "*comh'ii-letzii* swear by Great Goddess, not God or Jeez H." She sounded like my mother, who to her dying day had tried to break me of the Krogonold habit of tough talk. Not that she stood a chance against my uncles and Aunt Clemency.

"Loris," I asked suddenly, my mind as clear as February sunlight and as painfully sharp. "How do you know about my background or have the slightest idea what it implies?"

Loris laughed and it hurt my ears. It sounded like, "My part-father is an Arizona horse rancher from the same part of the country as your uncles. Caris occasionally wrote letters, and we're in deep-link."

My head was splitting wide open and I suddenly understood that woman in first-grade Basic who was always screaming that the kids were driving her mad: everybody was screaming at me at once, all in different voices and accents, all different messages, all totally urgent emergencies and peremptory demands to Do Something Or Else. I felt like screaming.

"That is one hell of a block," Loris said soberly. "Overcrowded worlds like Mother Earth must be hell on telepaths." I could see his imagery of endless undeserved torture; he wasn't swearing, he was using a technically precise term; it was hell. The average kid on Earth has fifteen different people pulling on him fifteen different ways, none of them taking any excuses for not making his particular thing Number One Priority. Coach, science teacher, manners-and-customs, nutritionist, health counselor, career counselor, you name it, before he's six he's learned to juggle it or he is absolutely round the bend. Or she is. That's why The People settled in New Mexico, up around Navajo country, back when the Navajo Nation was still rural.

(I imagined my father and Senator Yazzie in one of their endless shouting matches over power plants versus human values; suburban Socorro, where I grew up, is not at all like industrial Shiprock. I pictured Darkover now and laid the pictures alongside each other, and then the room started to go round again.)

Loris wiped my face. "That's why we want no part of the Empire," he said, and at long last it made perfect sense. Then the world exploded in a daze of unseen colors. I heard him say something about Father Damon and Mothers Callista/Ellemir and the next thing I knew I was sitting in their front room watching a real wood fire burn and drinking a hot tangy something.

Some cold worlds don't go much for comfort—Karhide is a freezing example—Darkover does. The four older folks who were sitting with me needed no introduction; I knew them, with total certainty. "Thank you, Damon," I said.

I was wrapped up in a series of long plaid skirts and a thick woolly turtleneck and a robe on top of that, with sheepskin slippers on my feet; it suddenly seemed too warm. Lomie was in the room; she had refused to wear skirts because she was terrified of slipping back into her old life, and her current costume was a total armor against it.

"You'll have to go to the Guildhouse, Paloma," Ellemir told her; it was apparently an ongoing argument. How long had it been?

"Three days," Callista told me.

And Andrew Carr was saying, "Is Old Man Yazzie still pushing for industrial development at all costs? I have a score to settle with him for what he did to my father."

"He had a heart attack six years ago," I said, and took another bowl of chili con manzano. This time they served it with a nut bread, sweet, but good. "Lomie, do you want the Big Ships, or don't you?"

"How does a girl like me stand a chance of getting on the Big Ships?" she asked reasonably; either her Terran Standard had taken a quantum jump, or my Darkovan had.

"They took Caris Ridenow. Telepathy doesn't really qualify as an irreplaceable skill: too many of the data-pushers don't believe in it, although Survey lists it as an official position."

"Caris was a Ridenow, an aristocrat, Comynara," Lomie argued.

I whistled. "You do not know your Terran Empire mentality at all, sweetheart. If anything, that'd count against her."

"They take Renunciates—Free Amazons—for Space Service," Callista said suddenly. "Lady Ardais' fosterling is one of them. They know the Amazon is there as a worker; I would not offend you, Lomie, but they dare not hire a woman whose basic living comes through men, or the galaxy would be littered with discarded mistresses living on Imperial charity. The Amazon is sworn by oath, you know—"

Lomie interrupted, her face angry, her dialect back. "*Comh'ii letzii* say, filthy *grezalis*, look at filthy *grezalis* like piece of turd, say go 'way, filth, no speak to you."

My dander was getting up again. "Oh, they did, did they?"

"They are sworn not to turn away any woman who comes to them for help," Callista exclaimed, and then said "Oh, I see. You did not ask. You only assumed they would say this."

Lomie sniffed. "They despise my kind."

I was obligated to her. "Try it, kid, and I'll be right beside you. If they give you a hard time, I'll give them a few choice words. If you don't try it, I'll dump you where you sit; moral courage may get you a court martial, but if you don't have it you can get your whole damn team killed."

I did the right thing, I realized suddenly, and it felt like a great relief. I had never doubted that I'd done the right thing by pulling out, hearing or no hearing, black mark or no black mark, but now I *knew* it beyond question, and it was like being relieved of guilt.

"Yes," said Loris, and then I knew something else.

I liked him. I liked him enough to want to team up with him, to want him for a friend, and as a man, but not enough to leave Survey for him. I liked him, but I was not sure how much was for himself and how much was because he was so much like Caris.

I said I liked Caris. The word was love.

I would never quit the Service. My whole life was the team and the new worlds and the dangers and the entire lifestyle. The biological boundary was in sight, and it would be nice to have a child, but I was no more cut out to be a mother—a nurturing parent—than a cow is to fly.

Back when we picked up Mendoza, I got to know some friends of his father's, free-lance mercenary captains, a man and a woman operating as a team—rare for these sword-and-sorcery worlds—and I could have a place on their team any time I want one. Even at the worst of it, the hearing, the breakup of the team, I never once thought of it.

I had tried to recruit them for Survey, but they rejected the man as overage, and he laughed, saying he'd chosen his life and lived it forty years, as I had mine; we each must be the thing we are. It was his wife who added that, and she wore a broadsword over her skirts.

"Yes," Loris said at last. "You could have a place on our team, too, if you wanted one; and I thank you, but I would not want one on yours. My life is here." Then he added, "You have your recruit already; if Ambron is a true telepath, and bonded to you, try asking him back."

I heard an echo of my own words to Lomie, and shook hands with him then. "If I had time, I'd biomother a child for your team," I said. It was as far as I could go. Then I added. "I think I'd like that. Loris."

We saw Lomie checked in at the Guildhouse shortly afterward, and contrary to her fears, nobody said a word but "Welcome." They greeted me as one of them and offered to let me stay, but you have to cut the silver cord sometime.

"I'll be back, kid," I promised her. "Whenever you're ready to sign up, let me know." I stopped at the spaceport and sent a message first-ship-out to Ambron on his world. "New recruit found Darkover, get your tail down here to meet her before the debits and credits unbalance your brain, Your Captain." I added, "That's an order, D'Alembert." He hates his pompous first name.

Then I headed back for Loris'—and Caris' home. I'd have just enough time if I hurried the job a little.

If I had a girl I'd call her Caris. If it was a boy, I'd call him for his father.

"No," Loris said. "Damon Andrew."

It was Damon Andrew, and I found myself crying a little as Lomie and Gilbert Mendoza and Dal Ambron and I lifted ship again. He'd be in good hands; Caris' brother would be a good father. Cute little fellow; I never knew they came so tiny, especially those fingernails.

Bert put his arm around my shoulders and Dal squeezed my hand. "Come on, Captain, he'll be in good hands," Dal repeated my thoughts.

Then liftoff began, and Lomie and Bert and Dal and I were on our way again. *Goodbye, Caris,* I thought, and we were out of gravity and going.

People are often asking me which of the Darkover novels I personally prefer, and with which character I personally identify. That is a very hard question to answer, and I normally try and dodge it. Of the early books, *The Bloody Sun* is my favorite, because, in writing it, I first took the measure of my powers as an adult writer; of the later books, I personally identify greatly with the struggles of Magda Lorne among the Free Amazons, and I find Damon Ridenow the most likable of my own characters. But whatever the value of the later characters, my own personal "voice" in the Darkover novels has always been the very first character I created for them; Lew Alton.

Lew Alton was the hero of the very first pre-Darkover fantasy sketch I wrote as a young girl. It is very difficult to detach my own viewpoint from Lew's; this is why I reinvented, for *Heritage of Hastur*, the technique Charles Dickens had used in his great novel *Bleak House*, with alternate characters told in first person by the protagonist, and in third person describing the great external events of that time. In a later novel, *World Wreckers*, I said, "Within every man there is a hidden woman, and within every woman, a hidden man." It takes no great insight into psychology to deduce that in all likelihood, Lew Alton represents my own *animus*, the "hidden man" from whose viewpoint I still sometimes write fiction. Feminists don't like this theory, and feel that women should not write from a male viewpoint, nor men from a female viewpoint; to which my answer is, in the words of Dion Fortune, that it is a free country and they are entitled to their opinion.

But I admit I have been curious from time to time to know how Lew, who is not, at least on the surface, a very attractive character, would appear from the outside. It is rather difficult for me to see him except from inside his own skin, and I have backed away, before this, from trying to see him through other eyes.

On two or three occasions in these prefaces I

have mentioned the *Starstone* short story contest, to which all stories were submitted anonymously. After reading some of the entries (I later commented that the commonest fault was trying to write a novel in thirteen pages) I wondered if I could write a story submitting to the limits I had put on the contestants; and so "Blood Will Tell" was born. I also intended to play a deadpan joke on my fellow judges; to send my anonymous story out to them with the other entries and see how they rated it on "authenticity"; I thought it might be fun if people who thought I was a good writer, were able to see my faults without a "name" to blind them. After all, the opera singer Caruso, whose appearances were greeted with screams and hysteria later limited to such people as Elvis and the Beatles, once, on a whim, chose to sing from behind the curtain the little "Siciliana" which opens the opera *Cavalleria Rusticana*. His effort was greeted with only mild polite applause; without the Caruso mystique, his voice was not considered outstanding.

But in the end I didn't; which Jacqueline Lichtenberg later explained as follows. "MZB decided it would be unfair and embarrassing if she won—but even more so if she lost."

And so the story has never appeared before. Here is Lew Alton, from *Sword of Aldones,* and his first meeting with Dio Ridenow.

BLOOD WILL TELL

by Marion Zimmer Bradley

Dio Ridenow saw them first in the lobby of the luxury hotel serving humans, and humanoids, on the pleasure world of Vainwal. They were tall, sturdy men, but it was the blaze of red hair on the elder of them that drew her eyes. Comyn red. He was past fifty and walked with a limp, stiff-kneed; his back was bent. Behind him walked a young man in non-descript clothing, tall, dark-haired and black-browed, sullen with steel-gray eyes. Somehow he had the look of deformity, of suffering, which she associated with lifetime cripples, hunchbacks; yet he had no visible defect except a few half-healed scars along one cheek. The scars drew up one corner of his mouth into a permanent sneer, and Dio turned her eyes away with a faint sense of revulsion. Why would a Comyn lord have such a person in his entourage? Some hanger-on, poor relation?

For it was obvious that the man was a Comyn lord. There were redheads in the galaxy, on other worlds, but the facial stamp, the features of the Comyn, were unmistakable, combined with that hair; flame-red, dusted with gray now, but still—Comyn. And what was he doing here? For that matter, who was he, anyhow? It was rare to find Darkovans any-where except on their home world. The girl smiled and thought to herself that she, too, might have been asked that question, for she was Darkovan and far from home. Her brothers came here because, basically, neither was interested in political intrigue; but they had had to defend and justify their absence often enough.

The Comyn lord moved slowly across the hall; limping, but with a kind of arrogance that drew all eyes, though he did nothing unusual. Dio framed it to herself, in an unfocused way: he moved as if he should have been preceded by his own drone-pipers and wearing high boots and a swirling cape—not the drab featureless Terran clothing he actually wore.

And having identified his Terran dress she suddenly knew who he was. One Comyn lord, and only one as far as anyone knew, had actually married, legally and with full ceremony, a Terran woman. He had managed to outface the scandal, which in any case had been before Dio was born; Dio had not seen him more than twice in her life, but now she knew who he was; Kennard Lanart-Alton, Lord Armida, self-exiled lord of the Alton Domain. And now she knew who the young man with the sullen eyes must be; this was his half-caste son, Lewis, who had been horribly injured during a rebellion back in the Hellers—Dio took no particular interest in such things and didn't know the details, she had still been playing with dolls when it all happened. But she knew Lew's foster sister, Linnell Aillard, who had a sister who was Keeper in Arilinn; and Linnell had told her of Lord Kennard's son Lewis and

that her foster father had taken Lew to Terra in the hope
that they could help him.

The two Comyn were standing beside the central computer
of the main hotel desk; Kennard was giving some quietly
definite order about their luggage to the human servants who
were one of the luxury touches of the hotel, of the pleasure
world. Dio herself had been brought up on a world where human servants were commonplace and could accept it without
embarrassment, but many people could not overcome their
shyness or dismay at being waited on by people rather than
servomechs or robots. Dio's poise about such things had given
her status among the other young women of Vainwal, many
of them new-rich people who flocked to the pleasure worlds,
knowing nothing of the refinements or niceties of good living,
unable to accept luxury as if they had been brought up to it.
Blood, Dio thought, watching the exactly right way Kennard
spoke to the servants, would always tell.

The younger man turned; Dio could see now that one hand
was kept concealed in a fold of his coat, and that he moved
awkwardly, struggling to handle some piece of their equip-
ment which he did not want touched by anyone else. Kennard spoke to him in a low voice, but Dio could hear the
impatient tone of the words, and the young man scowled, a
black and angry scowl which made Dio shudder. Suddenly
she realized she did not want to see any more of that young
man. But from where she stood she could not cross the lobby
without crossing their path.

She felt like lowering her head and pretending they were
not there at all. After all, one of the delights of pleasure
worlds such as Vainwal was to be anonymous, free of the restrictions of class or caste on one's home world. She would
not recognize them, give them the privacy she wanted for
herself. But as she crossed their path the young man made a
clumsy movement; he did not see Dio, and banged full into
her. Whatever piece of luggage he was carrying slid out of his
awkward one-handed grip and slid to the floor with a metallic
clatter. He flung an angry word at her and stooped to retrieve
it. It was long, narrow, closely wrapped; it might have held a
pair of dueling swords, prized possessions never trusted to
anyone else to handle. Dio automatically stepped back, but
the young man could not get his hand on it, it slithered away,
and she bent to reach for it and hand it to him.

"Don't touch that!" he said angrily. His voice was harsh,
raw, and grating; he actually reached out and shoved her

away from it and she saw the folded empty sleeve at the end of his arm. She stared, open-mouthed with indignation; she had only been trying to help!

"Lew!" Kennard Alton's voice was sharp with reproof; the young man scowled and muttered something like an apology, turning away and scrambling the wrapped dueling swords, or whatever they were, awkwardly into his arms, turning ungraciously to conceal the folded sleeve. Suddenly Dio felt herself shudder, a deep shudder that went all the way to the bone. But why should it affect her so? She had seen wounded men before; surely a missing hand was hardly reason to go about as this one did, with a continual outraged, defensive scowl, a black refusal to meet the eyes of another human being!

With a small shrug she turned away from him. There was no reason to waste thought or courtesy on this graceless fellow whose manners were as ugly as his face! Kennard was asking. "But you are a countrywoman, *vai domna?* I did not know there were Darkovans on Vainwal."

She dropped him a curtsy. "I am Diotima Ridenow of Serrais, my lord, and I am here with my brothers Lerrys and Geremy, by leave of my brother and my lord."

"I had believed you were destined for the Tower, mistress Dio."

She shook her head and knew the swift color was rising in her face. "It was so ordained when I was a child; I—I was invited to do so. But in the end I chose otherwise."

"Well, well, it is not a vocation for everyone," Kennard said genially, and she contrasted the charm of the father with the sneering scowl of the son, who stood frowning, without the most elementary formal phrases of courtesy! Was it his Terran blood which had robbed him of any vestige of his father's charm: In the name of the Blessed Cassilda, couldn't he even *look* at her? It was the scar tissue at the corner of his mouth which had drawn his face into a sneer; but he had taken it into his very soul, it seemed.

"So Lerrys and Geremy are here? Are they in the hotel?"

"We have a suite here, on the ninetieth floor." Dio said, "but they are in the amphitheater, watching a competition in null-gravity dancing. Lerrys is an amateur of the sport, but he was eliminated early in the competition. when he twisted a muscle in his knee and the medics would not allow him to continue."

Kennard bowed. "Convey them both my compliments," he

said, "and my invitation, lady, for the three of you to be my guests tomorrow night, when the finalists perform in the amphitheater here."

"I am sure they will be charmed," Dio said, and took her leave.

She heard the rest of the story that evening from her brothers.

"Lew? That was the traitor," Geremy said. "Went to Aldaran as his father's envoy and sold Kennard out, to join up with those pirates and bandits at Aldaran. His mother's people, after all, and believe me, Aldaran blood isn't to be trusted. They had some kind of super-matrix back there, and young Aldaran was experimenting with it. Burned down half of Caer Donn when the thing got out of hand. I heard Lew switched sides again, joining up with one of those hill-woman bitches, one of Aldaran's bastard daughters, I heard, and sold out Aldaran like he sold out the rest of us; and got his hand burned off. Serves him right, too. But I guess Kennard couldn't admit what a mistake he'd made, after all he went through to get Lew declared his heir. Did they manage to regenerate his hands?" Geremy wriggled the three fingers lost in a duel, years ago, and regenerated, regrown good as new by Empire medics. "No? Maybe old Kennard thought he ought to have something to remember his treachery by."

"No," Lerrys said, "you have it wrong way round, Geremy. Lew's not a bad chap. He did his damnedest, so I heard, to control the fire-image when it got out of hand; and the girl died. I heard he'd married her. One of the monitors of Arilinn told me how hard they worked to save her, and to save Lew's hand; but the girl was too far gone, and Lew—" He shrugged. "Zandru's hells, what a thing to face! Lew was one of the most powerful telepaths they ever had at Arilinn, I heard; but I knew him best in the cadets. Quiet fellow, standoffish if anything; but he had to put up with a lot of trouble from people who felt he had no right to be there, and I think it warped him. Good enough in his own way, though. I liked him, though he was touchy as the devil, and like a monk in some ways." He grinned. "He had so little to do with women that I made the mistake of thinking he was one of my kind, and made him a certain proposal. Oh, he didn't *say* much. But I never asked him *that* again!" Lerrys chuckled. "I'll wager he didn't give you a kind word, either? That's a new thing for you, isn't it, little sister, to meet a man who's not at your feet within a few minutes?" Teasing, he chucked her under the chin.

Dio said pettishly, "I didn't like him. I hope he stays far away from me!"

"Oh, you could do worse," Geremy mused. "After all, he *is* Heir to Alton; and Kennard's old and lame and probably not long for this life. How would you like to be Lady of Alton, sister?"

"No." Lerrys put a protective arm around her. "We can do better than that for Dio. Council will never accept him, after that Sharra business. Ken forced them to accept Lew, but they never accepted his other son, though young Marius is worth two of Lew; and once Kennard's gone, they'll look elsewhere for someone to inherit the Domain of Alton. No, Dio—" Gently, he turned her around to look at him. "I know there aren't many young men of your caste here, and Lew's Darkovan, and, I suppose, handsome as women think of these things. But stay away from him. Be polite, but keep your distance. I like him, in a way, but he's trouble."

"You needn't worry about that," Dio said. "I can't stand the sight of him."

Yet, inside where it hurt, she felt a pained wonder. She thought of the unknown girl Lew had married, who had died to save them all from the unknown menace of the fire-Goddess. So it had been Lew who raised the fires, then, and suffered in order to quench them again? She felt herself shiver in dread and terror. What must his memories be like, what nightmares he must live, night and day! Perhaps it was no wonder that he walked apart, scowling, and could give no one a kind word or a smile!

Around the ring of the null-gravity field, small crystalline tables were suspended in midair, their seats apparently hanging from jeweled chains of stars. Actually, they were all surrounded by energy-nets, so that even if a diner fell out of his chair (and where the wine and spirits flowed so freely, some of them did) he would not fall; but the illusion was breathtaking, bringing a momentary look of wonder and interest even to Lew's closed face.

Kennard Alton was a generous and gracious host; he had commanded seats at the very edge of the gravity ring, and sent for the finest of wines and delicacies; they sat suspended over the starry gulf, watching the gravity-free dancers whirling and spinning across the void below them, soaring like birds in free flight. Dio sat at Kennard's right hand, across from Lew, who, after that first flash of reaction to the illusion of far space, sat silent, motionless, his scarred and frowning face oblivious; past them galaxies flamed and flowed and the dancers, half-naked in spangles and loose veils, flew like exotic birds, soaring on the star-streams. His right hand—evidently artificial and motionless—lay on the table, unstirring, encased in a black glove. That unmoving hand made Dio uncomfortable; the empty sleeve had seemed somehow more honest.

Only Lerrys was really at east, greeting Lew with a touch of real cordiality; but Lew replied only in monosyllables, and even Lerrys finally tired of trying to force conversation, and bent over the gulf of dancers, studying the finalists with unfeigned envy, commenting on the skills, or lack of them, of the performers. Dio knew he wished he was among them.

When the winners had been chosen and the prizes awarded, the gravity was turned on, and the tables drifted, in gentle spiral orbits, down to the floor. Music began to play, and dancers moved onto the ballroom surface, glittering and transparent, as if they danced on the same gulf where the gravity-dancers had whirled in free-soaring flight. Lew murmured something about leaving, but Kennard called for more drinks, and under the confusion Dio heard him sharply reprimanding Lew; all she heard was, "Damn it, you can't hide forever!"

Lerrys rose and slipped away; a little later they saw him moving onto the dance floor with an exquisite woman whom they recognized as one of the dance performers, in starry blue now covered with drifts of silvery gauze.

"How well he dances," Kennard said genially. "A pity he had to withdraw from the competition, though it hardly seems fitting to a Comyn lord—"

"Comyn means nothing here," Geremy laughed, "and that is why we come here, to do things unbefitting Comyn dignity on our own world! Come, wasn't that why *you* came here, kinsman, for adventures which might be unseemly or worse in the Domains?"

Dio was watching the dancers, envious. Perhaps Lerrys would come back and dance with her. But she saw that the woman dancer, perhaps recognizing him as the finalist who had had to withdraw, perhaps simply impressed by his dancing, had carried him off to talk to the other finalists, and now Lerrys was talking intimately with a young, handsome lad, his red head bent close to the boy's. The dancer was clad only in nets of gilt thread and the barest possible gilt patches for decency; his hair was dyed a striking blue. It was doubtful, now, that he remembered that there were such creatures as women in existence, far less sisters.

Kennard, watching the direction of her glance, said, "I have not been able to dance for many years, Lady Dio, or I would give myself the pleasure; I can see you are longing to be with the dancers. And it is small pleasure to a young maiden to dance with her brothers, as I have heard my foster sisters and now my foster daughters complain. But you are too young to dance in such a public place as this, except with kinsmen—"

Dio tossed her head, setting her fair curls flying. She said, "I do as I please, Lord Alton, here on Vainwal!" Then, seized by some imp of boredom or mischief, she turned to the scowling Lew. "Will you dance with me, cousin?"

He raised his head and glared at her; Dio quailed, wishing she had not started this. This was no one to flirt with, to exchange light pleasantries! He gave her a glance of pure hate; but even so, he was shoving back his chair.

"As you wish, cousin. If you will do me the kindness." His harsh voice was amiable, even friendly—if you did not see the look deep in his eyes. It hardened Dio's resolve. Damn him, this was arrogance! He was not the only crippled man in the universe, nor on this planet, nor even in the room—his own father could hardly put one foot before the other, and made no bones about saying so!

He held out his good arm to her. "You will have to forgive me if I step on your feet. I have not danced in many years. It is not a skill much valued on Terra, and my years there were spent mostly in different hospitals."

He did not step on her feet, though. He moved as lightly as a drift of wind, and after a very little time, Dio gave herself up to the music and the pure enjoyment of the dance. They were well-matched, and after a few minutes of moving together in the perfect matching of the rhythm—she knew she was dancing with a Darkovan, nowhere else in the civilized Empire did any people place so much emphasis on dancing as did the Darkovan culture—she raised her eyes and smiled at him, lowering mental barrier in a way any Comyn would have known to be an invitation for the telepathic touch of their caste.

For the barest instant, his eyes met hers, and she sensed

him reach out to her, as if by instinct, attuned to the sympathy between their moving bodies; then the barriers slammed down between them, hard, leaving her breathless with the shock of the rebuff. It took all her self-control not to cry out with the pain of that rebuff, but she would not give him the satisfaction of knowing he had hurt her; she simply smiled and went on dancing at the ordinary level, enjoying the movement, the sense of being perfectly in tune with his steps.

But, inside, she was dazed and bewildered. What had she done to merit such a rebuff? Nothing, certainly; her gesture had been bold, indeed, but not indecently so. He was, after all, a man of her own caste, a telepath and a kinsman. So, since she had done nothing to deserve it, it must have been made in response to his own inner turmoil, and had nothing to do with her at all.

So she went on smiling, and when the dance slowed to a softer, more romantic movement, and the dancers around them were moving closer, cheek against cheek, almost embracing, she moved instinctively toward him. For an instant he went stiff and she wondered if he would violently reject the physical touch, too; but she moved instinctively toward him, and after a moment his arm tightened around her. Through the very touch, though his mental defenses were locked tight, she sensed the starved hunger in him. How long had it been, she wondered, since he had touched a woman? Far too long, she was sure of that. The telepath Comyn, particularly the Alton and Ridenow, were well-known for their fastidiousness in such matters; they were hypersensitive, much too aware of the random or casual touch. Not many of the Comyn were capable of tolerating casual love affairs.

The dance slowed, the lights dimming, and she sensed that all around them couples were moving into one another's arms. A miasma of sensuality seemed to lie over the whole room, almost visible. Lew held her tight against him, bending his head, and she raised her face to him, again inviting the touch he had rebuffed. He did not lower his mental barriers, but their lips touched, and Dio felt a slow, drowsy excitement climbing in her and they kissed. When they drew apart his lips smiled, but there was still a great sadness behind his eyes.

He looked around the great room filled with dancing couples, many now entwined in close embrace. "This—this is decadent," he said.

She smiled, snuggling closer to him. "Surely no more than

midsummer-festival in the streets of Thendara. I am not too young to know what goes on when the moons have set."

His harsh voice sounded gentler than casual. "Your brothers would call me out and challenge me to a duel."

She lifted her chin angrily. "We are not in the Kilghard Hills! Lew Alton, I do not allow any other person, even a brother, to tell me what I may or may not do! If my brothers disapprove of my conduct, they may come to me for an accounting of it, not to you!"

He laughed, and with his good hand touched the feathery edges of her short fair hair. It was, she thought, a beautiful hand, sensitive and strong without being over-delicate. "So you have cut your hair and taken on the independence of a Free Amazon? Have you taken their oath too, cousin?"

"No," she said, snuggling close to him again. "I am too fond of men ever to do that." When he smiled, she thought he was very handsome; even the scar that drew his lip tight only gave his smile a little more irony and warmth.

They danced together much of the evening, and before they parted, agreed to meet the next day for a hunt in the great hunting preserves of Vainwal. When they said goodnight, Kennard was smiling benevolently, but Geremy was sullen and brooding, and when the three of them were alone in their luxurious suite, he demanded wrathfully, "Why did you do that? I told you, stay away from Lew! We don't really want an entanglement with that branch of the Altons!"

"How dare you try and tell me who I can dance with? Or, if I choose, who I can make love with? I don't censure your choice of entertainers and singing-women and whores, do I?"

"You are a lady of the Comyn. When you behave so blatantly—"

"Hold your tongue!" Dio flared at him, "You are insulting! I dance one evening with a man of my own caste, because my brothers left me no one else to dance with, and you already have me bedded down with him! Geremy, I will tell you once again, I do what I wish, and neither you nor any other man can stop me!"

"Lerrys," Geremy appealed, "can you reason with her?"

But Lerrys stood regarding his sister with admiration. "That's the spirit, Dio. What is the good of being in an alien world in a civilized Empire if you keep the provincial spirit and customs of your backwater? Do what you wish, Dio. Geremy, let her alone!"

Geremy shook his head, laughing. "You two! Always one in mind, as if you had been born twins!"

"Certainly," Lerrys said. "Why, do you think, am I a lover of men? Because, to my ill-fortune, the only woman I have ever known with a man's spirit and a man's strength is my own sister." He kissed her, laughing. "Enjoy yourself, *breda*, but don't get hurt. He may have been in a romantic mood tonight, but he could be savage, I suspect."

"No." Suddenly Geremy was sober. "This is no joke. I don't want you to see him again, Diotima. One evening, perhaps, to do courtesy to our kinsman; I grant you that, and I am sorry if I implied there was more than courtesy. But no more, Dio, not again. There are enough men on this world, to dance with, flirt with, hunt with—yes, damn it, and bed down with if that should be your will! But let Kennard Alton's damned half-caste bastard alone—do you hear? I tell you, if you disobey me, I shall make you both regret it."

"Now," said Lerrys, still laughing, as Dio tossed her head in defiance, "You have made it sure that she will see him again, Geremy; you have all but spread the bridal bed for them! Don't you know that no man can forbid Dio to do anything?"

In the hunting preserve the next day, they chose horses, and the great hawks not unlike the *verrin* hawks of the Kilghard Hills. Lew was smiling and good-natured, but she sensed that he was just a little shocked, too, at her riding breeches and boots. "So you are the Amazon you said you were not, after all?" he teased, and she smiled back into his eyes and said, "No; I told you why I could never be an Amazon, and the more I see of you, the more certain I am of that."

He was a good rider, although the lifeless artificial hand seemed to be very much in his way, and she wondered if he could not, after all, have managed better one-handed. She would have thought that even a metal hook would have been better, if they could not, for some reason, regrow the hand. But perhaps he was too proud for that, or feared she would think it ugly. He carried the hawk on a special saddle-block, as women did, rather than holding it on his wrist as most Darkovan men chose to do, and when she looked at it he colored and turned angrily away, swearing under his breath. Again Dio thought, with that sudden anger which he seemed able to rouse in her so swiftly, *Why is he so sensitive and self-indulgent about it? What arrogance! Does he think I really care whether he has two hands, or one, or three?*

The hunting preserve had been carefully landscaped and terraformed to beautiful and varied scenery, low hills which did not strain the horses, smooth plains, a variety of wildlife, colorful vegetation from a dozen worlds. But as they rode she heard him sigh a little. He said, just loud enough for her to hear, "It is beautiful here. But I wish I were in the Domains. The sun here is—is wrong, somehow."

"Are you homesick, Lew?" she asked.

He tightened his mouth. "Yes. Sometimes," he said, but he had slammed down his defenses again, and Dio turned back to attend to the hawk on her saddle.

The preserve was stocked with a variety of game, large and small; after a time they let their hawks loose: Dio watched in delight as hers soared high, wheeled in midair and set off on long strong wings after a flight of small white birds, directly overhead. Lew's hawk came after, swiftly stooping, striking at one of the small birds, seizing it in midair. The white bird struggled pitifully, with a long eerie scream. Dio had hunted with hawks all her life, and watched with interest, but as drops of blood fell from the dying bird, spattering them, she realized that Lew's face was drawn with horror; he looked paralyzed.

"Lew, what is the matter?"

He said, his voice strained and hoarse, "That sound—I cannot bear it—" and flung up his two arms over his eyes, the black-gloved artificial hand striking his forehead hard and awkwardly; swearing, he wrenched it off his wrist and flung it to the ground under his horse's hooves.

"No, it's not pretty," he mocked, in a rage, "like blood, and death, and the screams of dying things! If you take pleasure in them, so much the worse for you, lady! Take pleasure, then, in this!" He held up the hideously scarred bare stump, shaking it in fury at her; then he wheeled his horse, jerking at the reins with his good hand, and riding off as if all the devils in all the hells were chasing him.

Dio stared in dismay; then, forgetting the hawks, set after him at a breakneck gallop. After a time they came abreast; he was fighting the reins with his one hand, struggling to rein in the mount; but as she watched in horror, he lost control and was tossed out of his saddle, coming heavily to the ground to lie there senseless and stunned.

Dio slid from her horse and knelt at his side. He had been

knocked unconscious, but while she was trying to decide if she should go bring help, he opened his eyes and looked at her without recognition.

"It's all right," she said, "the horse threw you. Can you sit up?"

"Yes, of course." He sat up awkwardly, as if the stump pained him, wincing; then saw it, colored and tried to thrust it quickly into a fold of his riding cloak, out of sight.

"It's all right, Lew, you don't have to hide. . . ."

He turned his face away from her, and the taut scar tissue drew up his mouth as if he were ready to cry. "Oh, God, I'm sorry, I didn't mean. . . ."

"What was it, Lew? Why did you lose your temper like that?"

Dazed, he shook his head. "I—I cannot bear the sight of blood, now, or the thought of some small helpless thing dying for my pleasure," he said, and his voice sounded exhausted. "I heard the little white bird crying, and I saw the blood, and I remembered—oh God, I remembered—Dio, go away, don't, don't, in the name of the merciful Evanda, Dio, don't—" His face twisted again and he was weeping, his face ugly and crumpled, turning away so that she would not see, trying to choke back the hoarse painful sobs. "I have seen . . . too much pain . . . Dio, don't. . . ."

She put out her arms, folded him in them, drawing him against her breast. He resisted, for a moment, frantically, then let the woman draw him close. She was crying, too.

"I never thought," she whispered. "Death in hunting, I am so used to it, it never seemed quite real to me. Lew, what was it, who died, what happened, what did it make you remember?"

"She was my wife," he said hoarsely, "my wife, bearing our child. And she died, died horribly in Sharra's fires—Dio, don't touch me, somehow I hurt everyone I touch, go away before I hurt you too—I don't want you to be hurt."

She said, "It's too late for that," and he raised his one hand to her face, touching her eyes. She felt him slam down his defenses again, but this time she knew it was not the rebuff she feared, only the defense of a man unimaginably hurt, a man who could endure no more.

"Were you hurt?" he said, his hand lingering on her wet eyes, on her cheeks. "There is blood on your face."

"It's the bird's blood. It's on you too," she said, and wiped it away. He took her hand in his and pressed the fingertips to his lips. Somehow the gesture made her want to cry again, and she asked, "Were you hurt when you fell?"

"Not much." He sat up, testing his muscles. "They taught me, in the Empire hospital on Terra, how to fall without hurting myself, when I was . . . before this healed." Uneasily, he moved the stump. "I can't get used to the damned hand, though. I can do better one-handed."

"Why do you wear it, then? Do you think I would care?"

His face was bleak. "Father would care. He thinks when I wear the empty sleeve I am making a show of my lameness. He hates his own so much. I would rather not—not flaunt mine at him."

Dio thought swiftly, then decided what she could say. "It seems to me that you are a grown man, and need not consult your father about your own arm and hand."

He sighed, nodded. "But he has been so good to me, never reproached me for these years of exile, and the way in which his own plans had been brought to nothing. I do not want to distress him." He rose, went to collect the grotesque, lifeless thing in its black glove. He put it away in the saddlebag, and fumbled one-handed to pin the sleeve other the stump. She started, matter-of-factly, to offer help, then decided it was too soon for that. He looked into the sky and said, "I suppose the hawks are gone beyond recall and we will be charged for losing them."

"No." She blew the silver whistle around her neck. "They are birds with brains modified, so they cannot choose but come to the whistle . . . see?" She pointed as they spiraled down and landed, standing patiently on the saddle blocks, awaiting their hoods. "Their instinct for freedom has been burnt out."

"They are like some men I know," said Lew, slipping the hood on his hawk. But neither of them moved to mount. Dio hesitated, then decided he had probably had enough of politely averted eyes and pretenses of courteous unawareness. "Do you need help to mount? Can I help you, or shall I fetch someone who can?"

"Thank you, but I can manage, though it looks awkward." Again, suddenly he smiled, and his ugly scarred face seemed handsome again to her. "How did you know it would do me good to hear that said?"

"I have always been very strong. But I think if I were hurt I would not want people to pretend everything was exactly the same and perfectly normal. Please don't ever pretend with me, Lew." And then she asked, "I have wanted to know. Don't tell me if you don't want to, I'm not trying to pry. But—Geremy lost three fingers in a duel. The Terran medics re-grew them, just as they were before. Why did they not do that with your hand?"

"They—tried," he said. "Twice. Then I could—could bear no more. Somehow, the pattern of the cells—you are not a matrix technician, are you? I wonder if you can understand . . . the pattern of the cells, the—the knowledge in the cells, which makes a hand a hand, and not a finger or an eye or a bird's wing, had been damaged beyond renewing, and what grew on my wrist was—was a horror. I—when I woke from the drugs, just once, and saw, I—I screamed my throat raw; my voice will never be right again, either; for half a year I could only whisper. I was not myself for—for years. I can live with it, now, because I must. I can face the knowledge that I am—am maimed. What I cannot face," he said with sudden violence, "is my father's pretense that I am—am whole!"

Dio felt sudden violent anger. So even the father could not face the reality of what had happened to his son! Could not even face the son's need to face what had happened to him. She said, voice low, "Don't ever think you have to pretend to me, Lew Alton."

He seized her in a rough grip, dragged her close. It was hardly an embrace. He said, in that hoarse voice, "Girl, do you know what you are saying? You can't know!"

She said, shaking, "If you can endure what you have endured, I can bear to know what it is that you have had to suffer. Lew, let me prove that to you!"

In the back of her mind she wondered, *why am I doing this?* But she knew that when they had come into each other's arms on the dancing floor, last night, even behind the barriers of Lew's locked defenses, their bodies had somehow made a pact. Barricade themselves from one another as they would, something in each of them had reached out to the other and accepted what the other was, wholly and forever.

She raised her face to him. His arms went around her in grateful surprise, and he murmured, still holding back, "But you are so young, *chiya*, you can't know . . . I should be horsewhipped for this, but it has been so long, so long . . ." and she knew he was not speaking of the obvious. She felt herself dissolve in total awareness of him, the receding barriers, the memory of pain and horror, the starved sexuality, the ordeals which had gone on beyond human endurance; the black and encompassing horror of guilt, of a loved one dead, self-knowledge, blame, mutilation, guilt at living on when the beloved was dead. . . .

In a desperate, hungering endurance, she clasped him closer, knowing it was this for which he had longed most, someone who could touch him without pretense, accept his suffering, love him nevertheless. For an instant she saw herself reflected in his mind, not recognizing, glowing with tenderness, warm, woman, and for a moment loved herself for what she had become to him; then the contact broke and receded like a tide, leaving her awed, shaken, leaving tears and tenderness that could never grow less. Only then did he kiss her; and as she laughed and accepted the kiss she said in a whisper, "Geremy was right."

"What, Dio?"

"Nothing," she said, light-hearted with relief. "Come, love, the hawks are restless and we must get them back to their mews. We will have our fee refunded because we have claimed no kill, but I for one have had full value for my hunt. I have captured what I most wanted."

"And what is that?" he asked, teasing, but she knew he did not need an answer. He was not touching her now, as they mounted, but she knew that somehow they were still touching, still embraced.

He flung up his empty sleeve in a laughing gesture. "Come on," he called, "we may as well have a ride, at least! Which of us will be first at the stables?"

And he was off, Dio after him, laughing. She knew as well as he how this day would end. And it was only the beginning of a long season on Vainwal.

It would be a beautiful summer.

Linda Frankel describes herself as "a twenty-three-year-old B.A. in history who preferred to devote myself to writing, rather than go to graduate school." She has appeared in various *Star Trek* fanzines, and her story "Betrayer and Betrayed," in *Starstone*, was her first appearance in print.

"Otherwise," she says, "rejections have been the bane of my life."

"Ambassador to Corresanti," written for the Friends of Darkover short story contest, received an honorable mention; and I considered it the best attempt to write from an alien viewpoint which the Friends of Darkover had yet seen. Many readers have been intrigued by the catmen, introduced in *Spell Sword*, but Linda is the first to try to see what their purposes and psychology might have been. "Readers may be surprised to learn that I've been only briefly acquainted with two of the feline species. The last of these beings so impressed me that I have incorporated his attitude toward humanity into this story. . . ." An intriguing statement which makes us wonder if Linda, also, might not possess a measure of ESP through which she can establish communication with an alien species! "Why was it written? I felt that the cat-folk in *Spell Sword* had received a raw deal! Their redemption was imperative, since I've alwasy favored the underdog (which is definitely a cross-species metaphor!)"

Linda adds that she is a committed feminist, but doesn't believe that her writing must always reflect this. "Limitations of that kind could only harm my development."

Many writers for this anthology chose to place their story in the Ages of Chaos, an unknown period of Darkovan history. Linda Frankel has chosen, instead, the period after *World Wreckers*, of which I have, as yet, written nothing.

AMBASSADOR TO CORRESANTI

by Linda Frankel

I sense the presence of the humans as they approach our hills. The Regent of the Domains has sent a small party—a sign of trust. I am not certain who is the greater fool—the Hastur lord or my brother.

The cave floor reverberates with their clumsy footsteps. Is there any grace to be found among them? No, humans are born to stumble where cats may glide freely.

My sibling's obsession to communicate with these ungainly creatures developed slowly over the ten years that he has held the office of Great Cat. (There has always been some intercourse with the humans of the Dry Towns, but it was kept at a minimum; contact seemed as distasteful to them as it was to us.)

Disagreement on this matter divided both clan and council. Never before has a Great Cat acted with so many voices raised against him. But Nyal has always walked alone—that was always so, from the days when we were cubs together. Not for him the usual games of tail-lash and catchclaw!

Despite my discomfort, I could not shirk my duty to receive these guests. Mind-speech gives their names as Regis Hastur and Lerrys Ridenow (ah, *there* is a flavor that is nearly feline. His thoughts form patterns that seem . . . yet he cannot be one of us!). Those who accompany them are guardsmen of Thendara city.

City! My reason balks at the very concept. Its odor is as fetid as a stagnant pool. Why must humans crowd themselves into a series of artificial dwellings? Why can't they be content with what the Goddess has made? Humans have so little respect for what is theirs without effort, that satisfaction is forever beyond their grasp.

They speak to one another in their ungainly and incomprehensible tongue. I detect . . . surprise. Yes, they are astonished that I am not chained! They had thought us to be like the men of Shainsa who chain all their females. Only humans

198

would find virtue in such consistency. The custom of chaining is meant to preserve the peace from the whims of the irresponsible, and to protect the violently insane among us. No one who has demonstrated rationality and control need wear them. The female heritage is such that violent throwbacks appear almost exclusively among our sex—yet if a male were found whose ferocity passed the normal bounds, he too would be required to walk fettered by the laws of every clan.

It seems I cannot probe beneath the surface emotions. These Comyn representatives are closely barricaded; they conceal vast capabilities held under tight control. The legends of this clan did not grow from nothing. That is certain. My own grandfather, Myor, suffered defeat from some Comyn adept when he attempted to wrest some portion of power from them. His blasted corpse failed to reveal the identity of his murderer.

Why have they come? Have they not shown us how unwilling they are to share their vaunted matrix technology? It is rumoured that the Comyn have weakened. Let us strike at them now! Let us take possession of proud Arilinn and mighty Neskaya! My brother will not listen to such counsel. Oh, he is far wiser. Let us hope that Nyal's wisdom is not our downfall.

I show them into the Great Cavern where my brother will confer with them—alone! He has dismissed all those attending him. This is truly madness. I am reluctant to depart.

"You must be forceful, Nyal."

"The cat who pounces upon living prey may end at best with empty paws."

"It is also said that no one need guard against foes who has undermined them at their weakest points."

"Now is not the time to bandy old familiar sayings, sister. Go and inform the Mothers that there will be no sacrifice to the Goddess so long as these humans remain among us."

"You would dictate to the Mothers? You risk their wrath, Nyal."

"I will take that risk. Now go!"

There is no arguing with him when he snarls in such a voice. I feared the consequences of such a decree. Would the humans be somehow offended by our sacrifices? Why should their good opinion be of so much importance to one who is Great Cat? He will exhaust his accumulated *gyar* (the Dry Townsmen refer to it as *kihar*; they garble everything beyond recognition) with such kowtowing—unless he can persuade the Council that *gyar* redounds to the cat who can establish a Comyn alliance.

Yet they would not be allies, but masters! Is it not told that in ancient days cats wore the collars of enslavement and lapped the milk of humility? Those cats were similar to us, as the occasional wild simian creature of the forests resembles the trailfolk. Our ancestors were content with a show of human benevolence. It was then that the Goddess intervened, and transformed us with the knowledge of what is true. The humans came to fear us, and sought our destruction (which was only to be expected, for they then feared and destroyed one another). We took refuge in the caves, and thus we have remained . . .

No, we will not bow to the Domains! Today it is the suspension of sacrifices; tomorrow it may be a demand to worship their Aldones! I know what must be done. My decision is clear.

I gather the Mothers in the Hall of the Clans. They question me about the Comyn guests. I can supply few answers. One cannot grasp a Comyn mind. It flows away with the inherent treachery of water.

"Mothers," I began, drawing all eyes to me, "the Goddess requires that we pay special honor to Her. . . ."

There is little resistance to my plan, and carrying it out is a simple matter. There is only one place where guests might stay. When the first Dry Town traders arrived with their goods to charm the unwary, they built a hut not far from the entrance to the cave system. They refused to pass their nights roofed in stone—though I doubt that any clan would willingly have endured their presence. It is in that same human-built edifice (many times patched, repaired, and renewed) that the Comyn pair would lie this night.

The human guardsmen are a barrier which is not so easily surmounted. There is one who fights with the fury of the chained; perhaps he has risen from one of their nine hells. When it is done a few lie dead, some are severely injured, and others merely unconscious. The Hastur does not defend himself, but accompanies me quiescently toward the fate that he must surely foresee.

His companion, he of the disturbingly keen sensitivity, feigns sleep. I am relieved that I need not face that unsettling mirror reflection; so catlike an image in an alien brain cannot be natural.

Taken to the place of preparation, Regis Hastur actively assists the Mothers as they bathe and perfume him for the sacrifice. It is as if he were eager to give himself to the Goddess. I don't understand . . . he seems as willing as any one of us who might have been chosen for this duty. Every cat lives with the awareness that the balance must be maintained; the birth of cubs signals the wish of the Goddess to replace members of that clan with the newly born. So it has always been—but the Hastur could not be expected to know this! The humans are not closely bound to the central core of existence, as we are.

I check the blade of the ritual knife to ascertain . . . *images of warmth and compassion suddenly appear before me. A catmother suckles her young. Words of affection float to the surface of my consciousness—words that I myself have never uttered. I sense a oneness of all beings and the great love that could be shared if only . . . we must reach out beyond ourselves and submerge the distractions between . . .* my fur prickles with the suspicion of what I—what we are *all* experiencing. A vicious blow! A Comyn trick! I want to shout this discovery aloud.

A soothing, caressing entity enters to vanquish vengeance and melt the masses of curdled hatred in my blood. *Not a trick,* the entity explains in low, purring rhythms. *I am Lerrys Ridenow. The Ridenow are empathic. My emotions are yours. My thoughts are yours. Flow with me. Learn how close a merging is possible between our species.*

Yes . . . it is truth. It is the truth of the Goddess! *Oh wise one, why did you not reveal your nature when first you came among us?*

We thought you unprepared for such knowledge. We had planned to seek gradual acceptance from you. When you placed Lord Regis in jeopardy, I had to take swift action.

It is well that you did, kinsman, the Hastur interjects with some amusement. *To end up with my throat slit upon an altar of the catfolk isn't exactly the death I would have preferred.* . .

Yet you showed no fear. Your demeanor has won you much gyar. I do not attempt to conceal my admiration from the human. It would have been useless in any case.

Sister, comes a well-known thought-pattern, *you see now the reality of the dream for which I fought. The humans need not be feared. They know that they will never again be our masters. The gift of the Goddess has made that impossible. Yet we can be equals. We can coexist in friendship.*

In a dream-like state, without knowing the significance of my action, I offer the Hastur the hilt of the sacrificial knife I still hold. He takes it solemnly. I don't consider it strange that I understand the words he speaks.

"This is a pledge that the blood of Hastur will never be shed by you or your kindred." He retrieves a knife from the piled garments on the floor of the sacred cave. "And this seals the bond. Hastur swears friendship to you and your kind, so long as there are Hasturs on the face of Darkover."

This ritual of the Domains is repeated formally by Nyal before all the Council in the Great Cavern. The bond of what these new allies call *bredin* now lives forever between us.

There is a tower a-building in these hills. It is the collective effort of cat strength and cat will. It will rise tall above the caves—the symbol of a future that I never thought would be. And when the minds of the first feline circle leap into the overworld, there will be human minds to reach out to them across the gap. Hand in paw. The world will be one.

Paula Crunk said of herself, when she sent this story to *Starstone,* "unrehabilitated" Free Amazon, illegal matrix worker, catperson-lover, mean mad *chieri,* and a few other vocations not to be mentioned in polite society."

When we decided to use this story—as we mentioned elsewhere, humor is rare in apocryphal Darkover fiction—we elicited the following: "I do not believe the story of my life will thrill anyone to the heart's core, but . . . I'm a thirty-six-year-old, single psychiatric caseworker, living and working in semirural suburbs of Alton, Illinois; I was the typical frumpy unpopular kid who quickly becomes a bookaholic. and got hooked on s-f/fantasy at about age ten. My dreams of becoming an English teacher were shattered by the realities of the job market; I wasted a few years trying to make it in the hippie scene, finally realized I was too old and too straight to be acceptable as counterculture. . . . I am also owned by seven snooty cats of various types. I'll never be more than a marginal fan, being rather reclusive. . . ."

All this proves to me, despite Paula's self-deprecating tone, is that Paula was born out of her time; when *I* was in fandom, we were *all* rather reclusive, and made friends in science fiction fandom via letter-hacking, writing to friends and to the magazines, rather than going to conventions. The rise of fandom showed most of us, myself included, that most fans were sociable enough, provided (and it's a BIG if) that they could get the kind of society they wanted; but many of us were so damaged by the enforced isolation of a society where conformity was valued above all other teenage virtues, and book-lovers were ridiculed or worse by peers, parents and teachers, that we preferred our own company and that of books.

And so we stayed home; and when fan activity wore thin, we took up writing. I went that way; and it just might be that Paula will follow.

About her story, I prefer to introduce it in her own words. It is "The last word about which

weapons are permissible under the Compact; or
happy modern times in post-World-wreckers
Darkover."

A VIEW FROM THE RECONSTRUCTION: OR, HAPPY TIMES ON MODERN DARKOVER

by Paula Crunk

"Pardon me, *vai dom*," said Piedro the shepherd,* looking
fairly bewildered, "but how am I to defend my flock against
bandits, without my crossbow? Lord Alton always permitted
this, or at least he said nothing against it—"

"Please just address me as Raphael. You know the old
titles have been abolished," the new acting head of the Alton
Regional District said crisply. "The Compact expressly for-
bids any weapon that strikes beyond the hand's reach. You
were caught with such a weapon in your possession. I believe
the evidence is clear, but if you were to appeal for mercy—"

"Mercy, sir?" Piedro grimaced oddly. "Aye, I will ask for
that, else you lock me up in one of your new-fangled *Terranan* cages and my sick wife and bairns starve."

"There is no need for such breast-beating. Since your
record is otherwise clean, a small fine will suffice. And may I
advise you, my man, if you are having difficulties with that
Des Trailles bunch, to report it to the local guardspost."

"But sir, the chief guard requires one to submit a report in
writing, and with four copies made, or he can do nothing. I
am told that is the proper efficient modern way of doing
things. Unfortunately I can neither read nor write; and the
village scribe cannot help me, being tied up until Midwinter
with your honor's paperwork."

* We are quite aware that the animals Piedro herds may not be
correctly termed *sheep;* but imagine whatever creatures you will,
up to and including banshee-birds, if you have a boggle-proof
mind. We are ever anxious to avoid the charge of "incon-
sistency!"

"You should go the adult classes being offered at village hall."

"I havna the time!"

"Well, make time then. Perhaps if your ignorance were corrected, you would know what is legal and what is not. Half my mornings are spent trying to explain to simpletons what should be common knowledge," the young man grumbled. "Now, about this fine. . . ."

"I havna the sum of money." Piedro said, restraining a gasp as an amount was named. "But if the *vai dom* would accept a fine young ewe and her two lambs, all healthy—" *It's less than I would have lost to Des Trailles,* he thought darkly.

The administrator rolled his eyes skyward. Aldones alone knew what his superiors would make of this very primitive way of dispensing justice! However, in certain instances, he had been instructed to go slowly; one could not expect a Catman to change his yellow eyes to blue overnight, or a backward people suddenly to achieve enlightenment.

"Have the court clerk price the value of the animals. That should conclude our business. But I must warn you, if ever you are caught again with a crossbow, it will go hard for you."

"Yes, sir, I understand." Piedro respectfully doffed his cap again, as he took his leave. Raphael affected not to notice.

"Now about this matter of the *chieri* protest against the new lumber mill in the Yellow Forest—isn't it out of our jurisdiction?" he was asking his assistant as the shepherd closed the door behind him.

Once outside, Piedro took a few gulps of cold, crisp air, doubly refreshing after several dismal minutes spent in smoke-filled chambers. Why, that young man did not even bother to hide his pernicious addiction! "I'll bet he's a sandal wearer as well," Piedro muttered.

He went promptly to collect the sheep he would give over in lieu of the monetary fine, and also a small sack of *sekals*, kept against such calamities as this. A judicious bit of haggling, and he was sure he could meet the arresting guardsman's "fee" for releasing his confiscated crossbow back to him.

As soon as he was able, he would move his family and herd onto the old di Asturien lands, where, he'd been informed, things were done in a most satisfyingly old-fashioned manner. The world might be changing indeed; but surely a man had the right not to change along with it, whatever the consequences.

But the incident with his High-and-Mightiness rankled; so much so, that he laid certain plans, which should flower just after his departure. The old *leronis* living down the hill, who had fled the noise and pollution of the small Trade City going up around Arilinn, was only too happy to assist Piedro. She even discounted her usual fee.

A few tendays later, it became common gossip around Armida that its latest tenant had been taken away to the psychiatric wing of Thendara General, in a pitiful state. Some even said he had been bespelled, although this kind of language was now frowned on as superstitous by the Terran-trained teachers.

The unfortunate administrator had fallen into a kind of waking trance, from which he could not be roused. It was reported he kept whispering, "The banshee-bird is almost upon me—Aldones, help me! Oh, where is my crossbow?" And then he would say, in a very different tone, "But that is not allowed." He would make frantic motions as if reaching out for something, then stop himself with a stern effort. It was indeed a sorrowful thing to watch, particularly when it appeared that the dream-bird was nuzzling at his neck. . . .

The good folk of the village shook their heads, and said cannily this was to be expected, when the New Council chose an overlord from a cadet branch of the notoriously unstable Ardais. The villagers were informed, of course, that this post had been, and would be filled again, "by examination," as was proper. Considering this, some decided to follow Piedro's lead. Armida saw them no more.

As for Piedro, the last this chronicler heard was that he was living in the Hellers, prospering no more poorly than most men do who refuse the help of our generous *Terranan* friends. He has supplemented his low income by now and then turning in for reward a wounded bandit, supposedly caught trying to thieve from the worthy shepherd. Of the delirious babblings of these rogues concerning Piedro's alleged violations of their rights, as well as the Compact, no sane man takes heed.

A note from the publisher concerning:

THE FRIENDS OF DARKOVER

So popular have been the novels of the planet Darkover that an organization of readers and fans has come into being, virtually spontaneously. Several meetings have been held at major science fiction conventions, and more recently specially organized around the various "councils" of the Friends of Darkover, as the organization is now known.

The Friends of Darkover is purely an amateur and voluntary group. It has no paid officers and has not established any formal membership dues. Although the members of the Thendara Council of the Friends no longer publish a newsletter or any other publications themselves, they serve as a central point for information on Darkover-oriented newsletters, fanzines, and councils and maintain a chronological list of Marion Zimmer Bradley's books.

Contact may be made by writing to the Friends of Darkover, Thendara Council, Box 72, Berkeley, CA 94701, and enclosing a SASE (Self-Addressed Stamped Envelope) for information.

(This notice is inserted gratis as a service to readers. DAW Books is in no way connected with this organization professinally or commercially.)